Killer

REUNION

Books by G.A. McKevett

Just Desserts
Bitter Sweets
Killer Calories
Cooked Goose
Sugar and Spite
Sour Grapes
Peaches and Screams
Death By Chocolate
Cereal Killer
Murder a' la Mode
Corpse Suzette
Fat Free and Fatal
Poisoned Tarts
A Body to Die For
Wicked Craving
A Decadent Way to Die
Buried in Buttercream
Killer Honeymoon
Killer Physique
Killer Gourmet
Killer Reunion

Published by Kensington Publishing Corporation

G.A. McKevett

Killer REUNION

A SAVANNAH REID MYSTERY

KENSINGTON BOOKS
www.kensingtonbooks.com

KENSINGTON BOOKS are published by

Kensington Publishing Corp.
119 West 40th Street
New York, NY 10018

All Kensington titles, imprints and distributed lines are available at special quantity discounts for bulk purchases for sales promotion, premiums, fund-raising, educational or institutional use. Special book excerpts or customized printings can also be created to fit specific needs. For details, write or phone the office of the Kensington Special Sales Manager: Kensington Publishing Corp., 119 West 40th Street, New York, NY, 10018. Attn. Special Sales Department. Phone: 1-800-221-2647.

Library of Congress Card Catalogue Number: 2015958937

Kensington and the K logo Reg. U.S. Pat. & TM Off.

ISBN-13: 978-1-4967-0078-0
ISBN-10: 1-4967-0078-3
First Kensington Hardcover Edition: April 2016

eISBN-13: 978-1-4967-0079-7
eISBN-10: 1-4967-0079-1
First Kensington Electronic Edition: April 2016

10 9 8 7 6 5 4 3 2 1

Printed in the United States of America

This book is dedicated to librarians everywhere,
who daily instill and nurture the love of reading in others.
Bless you.

A special thank-you to Leslie Connell for her many years of service to Moonlight Magnolia Enterprises. Her work, her loyalty, and her friendship are greatly appreciated. What a lovely lady.

I also wish to thank all the fans who write to me, sharing their thoughts and offering endless encouragement. Your stories touch my heart, and I enjoy your letters more than you know. I can be reached at:

sonja@sonjamassie.com
and
facebook.com/gwendolynnarden.mckevett

Killer
REUNION

Chapter 1

Staring across the table at her dearly beloved, relatively new husband, Savannah Reid wondered if any man in the history of the world had been bludgeoned to death at the kitchen breakfast table because he read his newspaper too loudly.

If not, Dirk was in danger of becoming the first.

Would they list him in *The Guinness Book of World Records*?

Would Madame Tussaud build a special display in the Chamber of Horrors at her wax museum, dedicated to the unfortunate victim and his dastardly wife?

Savannah could just envision it now: the wax version of Dirk slumped forward onto the table, his face buried in his oversized bowl of cornflakes, the *San Carmelita Star* spread in front of him, taking up far more than his reasonable half of the table. Standing slightly behind and looming over him would be the figure of Savannah herself—her flannel Minnie Mouse pajamas spattered with blood, a broken coffee mug in her hand—wearing the maniacal grin of a woman who had finally, utterly, irrevocably snapped.

"Whatcha thinkin' about?"

"What?" Jerked from her morbid and far too pleasant reverie, Savannah realized that he was speaking to her.

"I asked you what you were thinking about just now." He reached down, grabbed the right lower corner of the newspaper page, and with the amount of energy commonly expended to hurl a discus seventy meters or more, he heaved it to the left. The deafening racket, created by what should have been such a simple movement, set Savannah's teeth on edge and caused her to grip her *Beauty and the Beast* mug so tightly that the Beast grimaced. She braced herself for what would inevitably come next.

No sooner had the leaf settled into place than Stage Two of Page Turning commenced—the dreaded Smoothing of the Paper.

The love of her life and current source of great torment began to slap the recently turned sheet with his open palm. Moving from corner to corner in a clockwise motion, he pounded each area repeatedly and thoroughly. That accomplished, he attacked the center of the page, smacking, smoothing, and flattening with all the vim and vigor of an arachnophobe who feared his morning paper was infested with a horde of black widow spiders.

"So, what *were* you thinking about?" he asked again, leaving the paper for a moment and assaulting his cereal.

"Why do you ask?" She watched him raise an impossibly large spoonful of flakes to his mouth and shovel it in.

He gave her a sweet, loving smile, enhanced by the flakes dangling from his lower lip and the milk oozing from the right corner of his mouth. "I was just wondering, because you look so happy, so contented."

She shrugged and batted her eyelashes in her most demure Southern belle fashion. "Why, just a little daydream," she drawled.

"About?"

"Madame Tussaud."

He looked puzzled for a moment, then dropped his spoon into his bowl. The clang of metal hitting metal sounded like Quasimodo and the bells of Notre Dame announcing the top of the hour. But it was a necessary evil. After he had broken two of her favorite china bowls, Savannah had restricted him to using an indestructible graniteware bowl—the dark blue, white-speckled kind that cowboys used around their campfires. Or so she'd assured him. She had given the bowl to him for his birthday and had told him it was a vintage collectible that had actually been used on the set of *Bonanza*.

Yes, she was learning that successful matrimony required a certain degree of ingenuity, bolstered by an occasional whopper of a soul-blackening lie.

"Madame Tooth-So?" He quirked one eyebrow as he searched his memory banks for the reference, then nodded knowingly. "Oh, yeah. I remember her. She was that gal we busted who was running the cathouse on Lester Street. The mayor was playin' footsie with a couple of her gals when we rousted the place."

Savannah laughed, wax museum horrors momentarily forgotten, as the memory took her back to the "good old days" when she and Dirk had both been cops, partners even. Dirk was still with the San Carmelita Police Department, but she and they had long since parted ways.

But that didn't stop her from wallowing in the memories.

"Yes," she said. "As I recall, he was tickling more than their feet when we charged through the door of that bedroom."

"And remember the look on the captain's face when he saw you hauling his mayorship in . . . cuffed and wearing nothing but his boxers?"

Savannah groaned. "That had to be one of the bigger nails in my law-enforcement coffin."

Sharing a companionable laugh, they were, once again, on common ground. Domestic tranquility had been restored.

Dirk stood, picked up his bowl and spoon, and carried them to the sink. As he rinsed them and placed them into the dishwasher, Savannah congratulated herself on the minor improvement in his behavior. Who said a wife couldn't change her husband if she only nagged loudly and frequently enough?

"Wanna ride along and keep me company today?" he asked as he pitched the abused but gloriously spider-free newspaper into the recycle bin.

Another uptick on the Civility Meter.

She eyed him suspiciously. "Won't this be your fifth day staking out that strip-joint dive there in Twin Oaks?"

He shot her a guilty look. "Yeah. So?"

How typical of him to invite her along when his assignment was as exciting as watching a snail marathon. "I'd best stick around here and pack for the trip." She sighed, thinking about her upcoming journey back in time. Back home to the tiny rural town of McGill, Georgia, where she had been born and reared, not to mention teased and tormented.

A chance to reconnect with her past at a joyous event called a high school class reunion. Woo-hoo. She could hardly wait.

But then, she would also be celebrating Granny Reid's birthday. And that would make the effort all worthwhile.

Or mostly worthwhile.

Dirk donned a self-satisfied smirk and said, "Rather than leave it to the last minute, *I* packed last night."

"Big whoop-de-do. Underdrawers and your spare toothbrush. You fellas have it easy."

"And you gals take way too much junk and expect us guys to lug it for you."

She thought of all the clothes spread across her bed upstairs, next to her still empty suitcase. Yes, he had her there. In an attempt to wear something that showed off her overly generous bustline without accenting her overly abundant butt line, she would be dragging half of her closet to McGill and back.

Okay . . . *he* would be.

Bless his little pea-pickin' heart.

She stood and carried her own bowl to the sink. Once she'd rinsed it and placed it into the dishwasher, she turned and slipped her arms around his waist. Hugging him tightly against her, she closed her eyes and breathed in the delicious smell of him: freshly applied deodorant, shave lotion, and the faint unique scent of his skin. He smelled like protection, companionship, and strength. But mostly, he smelled like love.

Reluctantly, she released him, and as he walked away to gather up his essentials—cell phone, notebook, badge, and weapon—she did a quick mental tally of how long it would reasonably be until she laid eyes on him again.

If the stakeout was a bust, eight and a half hours. If he actually nailed some dude or dudette dealing meth out of the so-called "gentlemen's" club, it would be ten or twelve, at least, by the time he had them snuggly situated behind bars and had completed all the paperwork.

"Be careful, darlin'," she said as he headed for the back door.

"I always am."

She thought of what a usual shift entailed in the world of Detective Sergeant Dirk Coulter. The safest thing he did all day was merge into rush-hour traffic on the 101 freeway with an apple fritter in one hand and a mucho grande coffee in the other. "Yeah, well, be more careful than that."

He gave her a grin that warmed every part of her body, and said, "Love ya." Then he sailed out the door and slammed it, rattling the dishes in the cupboards and sending her cats running for cover.

"You better love me, boy," she replied as she turned back to the sink and the half-washed coffeepot. "After all I put up with offa you, you'd better be plumb nuts about me."

"You okay, babe?"

Dirk reached over and placed his hand on top of Savannah's. She was hanging on to the armrest of the airline seat as tightly as she usually gripped the lap bar of a triple-loop roller coaster.

True, she wasn't crazy about landings, but she usually didn't mind them this much. She seldom broke out in a cold sweat and felt the overwhelming need to shriek, "We're all going to die! We're all going to die!" as the plane banked, then straightened and descended, lining up with the runway.

Below she could see Atlanta, Georgia, spread before her, remarkably greener than the beige desert landscape she had left behind in Southern California.

She liked green. She loved the smell of the Georgia pines and the peach orchards. Hearing the soft, sweet drawls, so like her own, did her heart good.

Then there was the less health-conscious regional cuisine. It probably did her heart far less good, but it certainly nourished her spirit, and that alone was worth the trip.

She was looking forward to fewer kale chips and bean sprout wraps and more pecan pie à la mode and peach cobbler.

There was a lot she loved about Georgia and Georgians. So, ordinarily, she didn't mind a homecoming.

She had been back a few times in the past twenty years and didn't recall experiencing quite so much dread at the prospect of being returned to the bosom of her native soil.

"It ain't the soil's bosom I'm worried about," she muttered. "It's the natives."

"What?" Dirk gave her a quizzical look, the one he wore when she spoke her thoughts aloud without any explanatory preamble.

"Nothing. I'll be okay," she told him with a sigh as the wheels hit the tarmac and the plane bounced along, as though happy to be on land once more. "Everything will be fine and dandy . . . just as soon as I see Granny."

Indeed, all was right with Savannah's world the moment Dirk drove the rented car off the two-lane rural highway and down the narrow dirt road leading to her grandmother's house. The mere sight of that tiny shotgun shack lifted her mood and brought peace to her soul in a way that no luxury estate on earth could have done.

It wasn't so much the run-down structure, with its peeling paint, sagging front porch, and missing tar-paper roof tiles, that warmed Savannah's heart. It was what this humble piece of property represented. Or, more importantly, *whom*.

As children, Savannah and her eight siblings had been removed from their mother's custody and placed in the care of Granny Reid. Savannah would never forget the night when superheroes dressed in dark blue uniforms, with shining badges pinned to their chests, had scooped her and her brothers and sisters into their strong arms and had delivered them from their dark world of chaos, squalor, neglect, and abuse.

They have been driven away from their furious, shrieking mother in big, powerful black-and-white cars with magical red and blue flashing lights on their tops. And from the moment those heaven-sent warriors had transported them to this little house at the end of the dirt road, their childhoods—their lives—had changed forever.

Humble but tasty meals appeared three times a day, with the punctuality of a Marine Corps mess hall. Fresh, clean clothes were available every morning, and a bath with plenty of soap and vigorous scrubbing was required every evening.

Good manners and bedtime prayers were mandatory. Discipline was consistent and fairly administered, tempered with copious amounts of love in the form of hugs, kisses, encouragement, and sage advice.

Now, all these years later, although Savannah wasn't exactly giddy at the prospect of reuniting with her school chums, she considered it worthwhile just to see Granny in her own natural habitat.

"It'll be nice to visit with Granny here, in her own house, for a change instead of at our place," Dirk said.

Savannah was often taken aback by how frequently and how precisely his thoughts echoed hers. It had been bad enough when they were partners on the force and friends, but now that they were married, it certainly appeared that "two had become one."

A little scary, she thought, *considering it's Dirko.*

"I'll bet that's what you were thinking, too," he said. "You ever noticed how often me and you are thinking the same thing?"

"Knock it off. You're creeping me out."

"What?"

"Nothing. Pay no attention to me. I'm just out of sorts, you know, what with the reunion and all."

"What are you talking about? It'll be great! A chance to rub elbows, drink punchless punch, and eat dried-out cake with a bunch of knuckleheads you never wanted to see again for the rest of your life."

"Yeah, well, that's the least of it," she replied as, once again, she felt tiny drops of sweat appear on her forehead. Perspiration that had nothing to do with the humidity of a Georgia summer.

Dirk pulled the car up to the front of the house and killed the engine. He reached over and took her hand in his. Giving her fingers a squeeze, he said, "Okay, so that's the *least* of it. What's the *most* of it?"

She gulped. "Let's just say I wasn't exactly socialite material back then. The clothes I wore, my hairstyle and makeup, or lack thereof, were all hot topics of lunchroom gossip. That and the fact that I never showed up for school functions."

"Not even football games?" he asked with a look of shock and horror. "Why the hell not?"

Savannah gave him a sweet smile; that was her guy, all right. Always the jock. Missing a sporting event, anytime and for any reason, was simply unthinkable.

But her expression soon turned solemn again as she recalled the long hours spent on Gran's back porch with the wringer washer. She could still hear the hypnotic rhythm of the machine's agitator as it sloshed the load back and forth in its tub of hot, soapy water. She could still smell the acrid scent of bleach and strong detergent in the humid summer air.

She would never forget the anxiety provoked by feeding washed, wet clothes through the powerful wringer as she tried to keep her hand from slipping between the hard rollers, which would have surely crushed her fingers.

Then there were the endless afternoons and weekends spent in the backyard, where baskets overflowed with cold, wet laundry, and miles of heavy-laden clotheslines sagged with clothes flapping in the breeze.

"I didn't have time to hang out with the other kids," she said, "because I was too busy hanging their clothes out to dry. And then for extra fun, on weekends we scrubbed their houses." She chuckled wryly and shrugged. "Gran and I had a lot of mouths to feed, and, Lord, how those younguns could eat."

Dirk lifted her hand and pressed a kiss to her fingers. A look of sadness and a hint of repressed anger crossed his face as he said, "I'm sorry, sweetheart, that you had to work so hard, and you were just a kid."

"Oh, I didn't mind the work," she replied. " 'Hard work never killed nobody,' as Gran frequently told us. What I minded was the other kids—a certain group of girls in particular—never letting me forget that I was beneath them."

Dirk pulled her close and nuzzled her hair. "*You* ain't beneath *nobody*, darlin'. And tomorrow night the two of us are gonna walk hand in hand into that gymnasium, with all its tacky crepe paper and balloon decorations. And my head's gonna be held high. The lady I'll be escorting will be not only my wife and the prettiest woman ever to come out of Georgia, but also the best person I've known in my life."

Savannah looked into her husband's eyes and knew with every cell of her being that he meant it. He told her that often, and she usually delivered a smart-aleck response, like "If I'm the best person you've ever known, boy, you need to get out more."

But at that moment, sarcasm was the farthest thing from her mind. "And I love you, too. Plumb to pieces."

"I know you do. But we better get in that house right now, 'cause your granny's at the window, watching us make out. And from the scowl on her face, I'd say she disapproves."

Savannah sighed and laughed. "Reckon some things never change."

Chapter 2

"It's not that I minded the two of you swappin' slobber in front of my house," Granny told Savannah and Dirk once she had hugged them hard enough to make their ribs ache. "Seein's how y'all are married now, it's allowed and even encouraged. But not when I'm in here, itchin' to get my hands on you."

Savannah gave her grandmother an extra hug and marveled at the essence of pure feistiness that radiated from this eighty-plus Southern belle, wrapped in a pink and purple floral caftan. Her thick silver hair was neatly arranged, every curl in place, and from her ears dangled fuchsia chandelier earrings.

Every birthday since Gran had turned eighty, she had challenged herself to do something "new and daring." Wearing shoulder-sweeping chandelier earrings was last year's bold fashion foray. Savannah couldn't wait to see what this upcoming birthday would bring. Granny had already warned everybody to beware; it was going to be a doozy.

"So, where is everyone?" Savannah asked, looking around the strangely empty house. She had expected to be mobbed by a gaggle of Reids and Reid younguns. Even half of her siblings, along with their rambunctious offspring, could fill the average living room.

"I told 'em not to descend on you like a pack of hyenas the minute you got here this evenin'," Gran replied. "They'll all be swoopin' in like a flock o' pigeons first thing tomorrow mornin', bright-eyed and bushy-tailed, lookin' for breakfast."

Savannah grinned at the imagery of bushy-tailed pigeons, but mixing her metaphors was just part of Gran's charm, so Savannah wouldn't dream of correcting her.

"They'll be lookin' for you to cook for 'em, you mean," Savannah said.

Gran chuckled. "I don't mind. Vidalia's biscuits are heavy enough to sink a battleship, and Marietta fries her eggs so hot, they have them tough ruffle things around the edges. I don't mind cookin', especially for you, sugar."

With eyes the same striking sapphire blue as Savannah's, Gran gazed lovingly up at her granddaughter. But the affection quickly turned to concern. "What's the matter with you, girl?" she snapped.

"What? Oh, nothing, Gran."

"Yes there is. Somethin's amiss for sure."

She grabbed Savannah's hand and pushed her across the tiny living room to an ancient plaid sofa covered with a large afghan—just one of Granny's many creations that decorated the otherwise plain but cozy house.

"Sit yourself down right there," she said, "and tell me all about what's ailin' you."

Gran gave Dirk a shove toward the overstuffed armchair in the corner, its threadbare areas covered with snowy crocheted doilies . . . also products of Gran's skilled fingers. "And since you're my grandson-in-law now, I'll let you sit in my comfy chair."

"Why, thank you, Granny. I'm deeply honored," Dirk said. He settled into the chair, but after placing his hands briefly on the doily-covered armrests, he seemed to think better of it and folded them demurely on his lap. He looked anything *but* comfy.

Savannah grinned, watching her husband squirm. Dirk had never been at ease among "girlie" stuff. Discarded beer cans, empty pizza boxes, and rusty TV trays were what he considered to be perfectly acceptable items of home décor. But ruffles and floral prints sent him into a dither. So an overtly feminine home like Granny's was the stuff of nightmares for a manly man like him. He lived in mortal terror that he would break a delicate ceramic angel or snag a lacy something or spill iced tea on an heirloom quilt.

Savannah had tried in vain to convince him that a woman who had raised nine children in a tiny house was quite adept at gluing broken items and removing even the most stubborn stains.

Savannah couldn't count the times over the years when she had heard Gran say to her or one of her siblings, "Accidents happen, sugar dumplin'. Don't fret. There ain't nothin' in this house that means half as much to me as *you* do."

Whatever Gran did or said, it came from a heart filled with love. Even interrogations like the one that was about to begin.

But no sooner had Gran settled herself next to Savannah on the couch than they heard the back door open, then slam closed. No doubt, it was one of the Reid offspring. Neighbors and friends would have been polite enough to knock.

Savannah was grateful for a possible reprieve from the pending "What's wrong with you?" Gran cross-examination.

"Yoo-hoo! Granny? You here?" yelled a less than melodious female voice from the kitchen.

"In the front room, Marietta," Gran called back.

"I brought your casserole dish back, like you told me to. I didn't get a chance to wash it. I'm pokin' it here in the sink."

Savannah braced herself as the approaching *click-click* of high heels announced the arrival of Marietta. She was sister number two, right behind Savannah in the long line of siblings. Miss Mari was Savannah's least favorite of the batch.

She actually qualified as one of the other reasons why Savannah wasn't thrilled to be "home."

"I thought I'd fetch it over here before that ornery, nasty, mule-headed sister of mine and her old man come sailin' in," Marietta babbled as she made her way from the kitchen, through the bedrooms, and toward the living room. "I'm gonna try my best to avoid crossin' paths with—" Marietta stopped so abruptly in the living room doorway that she nearly fell off her four-inch zebra-striped mules. "Oh. You done got here."

Savannah flashed her sister her best fake smile, which looked more like a grimace worn by wolves fighting over the carcass of a dead elk. "Sorry for the inconvenience," she said. "If I'd known, I would've asked the captain to circle over Atlanta a few times before landing."

Propping her hands on her ample hips, Marietta lifted her chin and stuck out her chest, which, in typical Reid gal fashion, was more than voluptuous. So voluptuous, in fact, that if she took one deep breath too many, she might "volupt" right out the front of her low-cut leopard-print blouse.

As Savannah took in the tiger-striped purse, it occurred to her that Miss Marietta wanted to make sure every male in the county knew that she would be a virtual tear-cat between the sheets, if only they were fortunate enough to get the chance to bed her.

A shockingly large percentage of them had lucked out at one time or the other. Much to Granny's consternation.

But Savannah just thought her sister looked like a billboard advertisement for a zoo. Also, she had seen enough of Marietta's heavy-duty body-shaping foundation garments hanging on the shower curtain rod to know that it was mostly false advertisement.

Granny cleared her throat and said, "I'll thank you girls to be civil to one another when you're under my roof. And if you reckon you can muster it, a smidgen of sisterly love would be a fine thing, too."

Marietta tossed her head, wriggled her hips, and delicately patted her oversized bouffant as she flashed a sideways look at Dirk that could definitely be classified as come-hither.

Dirk looked down, suddenly fascinated by the design of the doily on the armrest.

"It's a lot to ask there, Granny, expecting the two of us to pretend we even *like* each other, let alone *love* one another," Marietta said. "This here precious sister of mine pert near took my head clean off the last time I saw her. Whopped the holy tar outta me right there in the middle of her living room. And me, a guest in her house. It was plumb shameful."

Savannah opened her mouth to retort, but Granny placed a warning hand on her knee and gave it a squeeze.

"I remember that squabble all too well," Gran said. "If you'll recollect, I was in the house when it happened and heard you squawkin', Marietta, all the way upstairs to the guest bedroom, where I was tryin' to get a nap. I also remember 'tweren't nothin' but a pillow fight and your big sister didn't give you one lick amiss that day. What you got, you had comin'."

Savannah could be quiet no longer. "That's for sure, missy. You go flaunting your womanly wiles—which may or may not be all that wily—in front of another woman's husband, you're going to get trounced. Especially when that woman's your big sister."

Marietta gave Savannah a catty smirk. "Well, now, you always was a sight bigger than me, 'specially in the hip area, but I figure I better watch what I say on that topic, or I might get beat to death for that, too."

Savannah smiled, recalling the Catfight of the Century with the sort of delicious satisfaction reserved for those whose portion of well-deserved revenge had been a long time coming.

So what if the battle had done more damage to her sofa accent pillow than it had to her overly flirtatious, highly immodest sister? Having to restuff a cushion was a small price to pay for getting to knock the stuffing out of a sister who so thoroughly deserved it.

Secretly, Savannah half hoped that Marietta would flash Dirk another unsolicited view of her scant knickers. Probably also leopard print. Savannah had no doubt that given the chance, she would score a knockout in round two, as well. But, of course, that sort of sporting event could never occur on such hallowed ground as Granny Reid's living room.

Maybe before the visit was over, she'd have the opportunity to lure Miss Hussy Pants into a dark alley or a peach orchard and rearrange her hairdo once again.

One could always dream.

But as Savannah was fantasizing about the gory details such a rematch might offer, the front door opened, and Alma Reid entered the house. Like a sudden and unexpected parting of the clouds, Alma's sunny presence immediately dispelled the darkness.

At least for Savannah.

If Marietta was her least favorite sibling, Alma was dearest to her heart. Shy and sweet, ever thinking of others, Alma seemed the exact opposite in every way to Marietta—to the point where Savannah couldn't help wondering if they were truly from the same gene pool.

Savannah jumped up from the sofa, ran to Alma, and folded her into a hearty Reid embrace. When Savannah finally released her, Alma gazed up at her older sister with adoring eyes and said, "Shoot f'ar. I wanted to be here when y'all got in. I've been dyin' to see you. It's been so long."

Casting a quick glance at Marietta, Savannah saw her roll her eyes. Yes, Marietta and Alma were as different as a soft pink rosebud and an out-of-bloom prickly pear cactus.

As Alma hurried over to Dirk and he rose to greet her, Savannah felt the gentle nudge of Granny's elbow in her ribs. "You doin' all right, dumplin'?"

Savannah managed a chuckle and said, "Right as rain after a long dry summer."

"Bull pucky."

Okay. So much for fooling Gran, Savannah thought. When would she learn that it was nearly impossible to hide your inner being from someone who knew you better than you knew yourself?

"It's just that . . . well . . . coming home . . . It's a mite hard," Savannah confessed.

She was surprised and annoyed to hear the shakiness in her own voice. Savannah liked to think of herself as a pretty darned tough cookie. Getting choked up about a simple thing like coming home to your birthplace and the loving arms of your family didn't exactly fit Savannah's carefully constructed self-image.

She preferred to think of herself as a gal who ate nasty criminals over easy for breakfast, along with a side order of sharp nails—all spiced with a drizzle of rattlesnake venom.

And while she didn't fully believe her own illusion, she certainly didn't see herself as a weepy female, prone to getting the vapors over nothing.

"It ain't easy, Savannah girl, comin' home. You got a lot of history here, and not all of it's good."

"That's for sure," Marietta piped up. "I wouldn't want to be in your shoes, coming back to town, seeing people you haven't seen in ages, looking twenty-five years older and a heap wider through the backside. And speaking of shoes, I hope you brought some good ones, not those old lady loafers you usually wear."

Granny shot Marietta a reproving look. "Miss Mari, I will thank you to keep your words soft and kind while you're under my roof. Your sister here is facing what you might call 'the dark night of the soul,' and we should strive to be supportive in her time o' need and sorrow."

Savannah stifled a chuckle; Granny had a tendency to wax dramatic and poetic at times like this. "I wouldn't say it's a particularly 'dark night,'" she said. "I'm just a bit nervous about runnin' into people I was glad to be rid of when I left here."

Breaking his uncharacteristically long silence, Dirk added, "Don't worry about Savannah, Granny. She's fine. Since she started goin' through this change of life business, she'll start bawlin' over an inspiring margarine commercial."

Silence reigned in the room.

The level of estrogen-charged indignation rose by the moment.

Finally, it was Marietta who came to Dirk's rescue. "I don't know what all the fuss is about. Tell me the truth, Savannah.

These people you're so in a tizzy about seeing . . . Do you like 'em?"

"Do I *like* them?" Savannah didn't even have to think about it. "No, I can't stand them. They're a bunch of conceited, snotty bit—" She gave Granny a quick look. "Um, disagreeable females who made my life miserable. I wouldn't give you two cents for the whole batch of 'em, not if they were dunked in chocolate and rolled in pecans."

A sly grin crossed Marietta's face as she reached up and fingered her rhinestone earring thoughtfully.

As Savannah locked eyes with her sister, she seemed to sense that she was about to hear something important. Something life changing. Something profound.

From *Marietta*.

Go figure.

"Well, now, dear sister of mine," Marietta said, her Georgia drawl as thick as sorghum syrup. "Here I figured you were a whole lot smarter than that. If you don't give a hoot about them, got no use for 'em, and think they're just a pack of disagreeable, worthless females . . . why the heck would you care what *they* think of *you*?"

Later that night, as Savannah snuggled close to Dirk in Granny's bed, beneath Gran's handmade tulip quilt, she whispered, "I feel guilty, taking the best bed in the house. But Granny wouldn't accept no for an answer. That's Southern hospitality for you."

"Yeah. Thank goodness for Southern hospitality. After being scrunched up in that airline seat for hours, it feels good to stretch out. I'm dead tired. Good night, darlin'."

"Thanks for coming with me," she whispered. "I know

traveling long distances—you know, like out of town—is not really your thing."

He chuckled and pulled her closer. "No problem. But I'll let you make it up to me. Sometime when I'm not too tired to breathe."

Laying her head on his shoulder, she ran her hand lightly over his chest and felt the warmth of his skin, the masculine bristling of hair against her palm.

"That was something else, what Marietta said, huh?" she whispered. "Imagine Miss Prissy Leopard Pants coming up with something all enlightened like that."

Dirk replied with a snore.

It was another hour or so before Savannah drifted off to sleep, still pondering the simple logic of her sister's statement.

Why *would* she care what these people thought of her? As long as she had the affection and respect of those she loved, wasn't that all that truly mattered?

Yes, ole Marietta had nailed it.

Finally, as sleep overtook her, Savannah's last thought was, *True wisdom has come . . . out of the mouths of babes. Or, in this case, a nitwit, dingbat floozy. Wonders never cease!*

Breakfast at Gran's house was an event. A *major* event.

Not exactly Christmas Eve or Thanksgiving dinner, but close.

In the Reid household every meal was an extravaganza. If not for the sophistication of the cuisine, then for the sheer volume of it.

Savannah had always been astonished at the amount of food it took to feed her clan and the space required to seat even her next of kin.

The cheap aluminum dining table with its gray, pearlescent surface, which had borne the burden of thousands of such feasts, had been stretched with extra leaves made of plywood until it practically filled the old country kitchen.

Less fortunate city folks who seldom consumed more than a bagel, donut, or fiber bar with their morning coffee might have been astonished at the glorious, if somewhat gluttonous repast spread upon that humble table. But the Reid family considered it perfectly normal to begin the day with a hearty, calorie-dense, and cholesterol-laden breakfast.

Granny Reid appeared to live in mortal terror that some member of her family might faint dead away in the street late some morning from lack of nourishment. And the townsfolk would gossip about it for the next fifty years. Long after Gran was resting peacefully in the cemetery on the hill, McGillians would be shaking their heads, tsk-tsking oh, so sadly, and whispering about how "Granny Reid always was a mite stingy with her sausages and overly tight with her buttered biscuits, and a body had to practically pry the jam jar out of her hand."

Rather than have her legacy tarnished, her character disparaged in such a brutal fashion, Gran made sure that everyone who pushed away from her table had to readjust their belt, loosening it at least two notches just to be able to breathe.

Savannah had never once questioned where she might have inherited the tendency to overfeed her guests. And she would bet dollars to donuts that not one person around Gran's table that morning would suffer a hunger pang again. At least not until lunchtime.

Gran presided at the head of the table, as was her honor as the octogenarian matriarch. Though she did little sitting. She was constantly jumping up to add a bit more cream gravy to the bowl, a few more biscuits to the basket, and peach preserves to the crystal candy dish that had been pressed into service for Savannah's sake.

On either side of her sat Savannah and Dirk. The chair next to Gran's had always been Savannah's by firstborn birthright. And although her siblings had complained about it from time to time, Gran had always defended Savannah's position by pointing out the added responsibilities shouldered by the oldest child in a family of nine kids.

"Them who works the hardest gets the seats of honor," she had proclaimed time and again to quell a row.

That also explained why the grandchildren were lined up, sans chairs or any other form of creature comfort, at the kitchen counter, their plates in front of them and dour expressions on their faces. In Granny's home it was still the 1950s, and although she was fine with them being seen and heard, they were definitely *not* in charge.

"How come when Aunt Savannah comes to call, us kids have to eat standin' up instead of sittin' at the table?" whined one of sister Vidalia's adorable eight-year-old twins.

"Oh, hush your bellyachin'," Vidalia snapped, turning around and swatting Jack's backside. "It ain't because Aunt Savannah's here. Not this time, anyways. It's 'cause you and your sister were jumpin' like a pair of wild jackrabbits on the table last Sunday a week ago and broke the other leaf. So you're standin' at the counter, and it's your own blamed fault."

She turned her wrath on her daughter. "Jillian, stop playing with that bowl of oatmeal, or I swear, I'm gonna make you wear it for a hat, oats and all."

She crumbled some biscuits onto the high chair trays of her second set of twins, who were seated behind her and next to Savannah.

A moment later, Savannah felt a half-chewed, soggy bit of

something hit the side of her neck. *Apparently, the kid doesn't like Gran's biscuits*, Savannah thought as she wiped away the slimy blob with a paper napkin. Thankfully, it hadn't been buttered.

She thought of Tammy, her health-conscious assistant and best friend back in San Carmelita, who was five months pregnant. Savannah made a mental note never to sit downwind of that child, either, in the coming months. The kid would probably smack her with a half-gnawed-upon celery stick.

Farther down the table sat the rest of Savannah's family. At least the ones who were still living in town.

Next to Vidalia was Butch, Vi's long-suffering husband. Between his hard work as an auto mechanic in McGill's only garage, Vidalia's frequent hissy fits, and two sets of twins, poor old Butch did well to retain his sanity. More than once he had threatened to "cut my strings and go straight up." And while Savannah wasn't sure quite what that meant, she wouldn't have blamed him if he had.

Next to him, wearing her usual baggy black pencil skirt and equally saggy plain white shirt, sister Cordele looked like a twenty-seven-year-old going on seventy-seven.

Her dark hair was slicked back, held with an extreme amount of gel, and fastened with a black barrette. Though, in typical Reid fashion, the tiny ringlets at her neckline were managing to escape and curl down onto her tightly buttoned collar. As always, the look on her pretty but unadorned face was as severe as her fashion choices.

Beside Cordele sat Jesup, Cordele's exact opposite. Jesup had allowed her thick, dark hair to go on its own flights of fantasy, and it pointed in every direction, in a wild array. Except for where she had shaved off a wide strip just above her right ear and had had her initials tattooed on her scalp. She had gotten the name of a boyfriend, now five guys ago, over the left.

Granny had not been thrilled.

Though Gran had been slightly less irate than when Jesup had come home sporting a Celtic ink chain around her neck. And far less unhappy than when she had gleefully displayed a new skull and crossbones on her left buttock.

More than once, Savannah had heard Gran praying under her breath for strength while dealing with Jesup. The phrases "cross to bear" and "thorn in the flesh" had been uttered, along with the words "beat the tar outta."

The rest of the gang was absent from the breakfast table for a variety of reasons.

Much to Savannah's delight, Waycross had moved to San Carmelita and would soon be marrying Tammy.

Atlanta had relocated to Nashville, where she was fulfilling her life dream, singing backup at a recording studio.

Macon, the family rare-do-well, was serving the last two weeks of a three-month hitch in the county jail for yet another DWI. Like their mother, he had yet to learn that cheap whiskey and curvy country roads weren't a complimentary mix.

"Marietta told me to send you her regrets," Vidalia said, nabbing another biscuit for herself. "She had something important she had to do, or else she'd have joined us this morning."

"Like watch her toenail polish dry?" Dirk muttered into his coffee mug.

Savannah noted his scowl with a minor sense of alarm. Her husband wasn't particularly jovial this morning. Far from it, in fact.

If nothing else, Dirk was a creature of habit. But he was trying desperately to eat his breakfast—while having to share a table occupied with Reids galore—without a newspaper to smack and abuse, and without his *Bonanza* bowl.

Not for the first time, she realized this solitary, routine-enslaved curmudgeon had sacrificed a great deal to become her mate.

No wonder she loved him.

Snatching the biscuit basket from Vidalia, she said, "As far as Marietta, I'll just bet she was plumb overcome with contrition at missing the chance to see me again."

Vidalia looked slightly puzzled. "If that means she was all broke up about it, I'd have to say she looked like she'd survive. Maybe even thrive. I wouldn't feel too sorry for her, if I was you."

Savannah grabbed the platter with the bacon and sausages as it made a second round about the table, and helped herself. "I saw her last night. That was enough to hold me for a while."

"She said you were frettin' about having to see the old gang at the reunion tonight," Butch offered, making a rare contribution to the conversation. "But if it's that uppity snit Jeanette Parker you're worried about seeing, you can rest easy. She's got a lot more on her mind right now than tormenting you."

"That's for sure," Alma said, jumping up from the table and hurrying to the refrigerator to fetch more butter. "She's a widow, fresh made."

"And your ole beau, Tommy Stafford," Cordele added, "he's the sheriff now. And he's been doing his best to prove that her bereavement was intentional. On her part, that is."

Savannah perked up and nearly choked on her bacon. "Really? Jeanette Parker married Mr. Barnsworth, and now he's dead?"

"Dead as a roadkill skunk," Butch supplied.

Granny nodded. "And the whole sorry affair smells even worse. Jacob Barnsworth has gone on to his eternal reward, and that Jeanette gal has her sticky fingers on all his money."

"And on a lot of other women's husbands," Vidalia added with a giggle. "You know she's always been a slut."

Gran cleared her throat. "Now, Vidalia, you know we don't use language like that in this household. I much prefer 'maiden of ill repute.'"

"Or two-bit hussy," Savannah suggested.

Nodding thoughtfully, Gran said, "Considering the female in question, that would work, too."

Dirk gave Savannah a mischievous grin over the rim of his coffee mug. "I wasn't impressed with that old boyfriend of yours the last time we were here," he said. "Maybe I can offer Sheriff Tom Stafford the benefit of my extensive expertise. Maybe you and me could nail this Jeanette gal for murder, Van. Now, wouldn't that be fun?"

A thrill coursed through Savannah's body and soul, and it had little to do with the caffeine content of Granny's potent coffee or the sugar in her preserves. It had a lot to do with the fantasy of settling old scores and maybe even reaping a long-delayed harvest of pure ole vengeance.

Of course, such reveries weren't noble, virtuous, or particularly worthy of a fine Southern lady. But the more Savannah thought about it, mulling over the possibilities, the more she imagined how delicious such a scenario might be.

Sweet, indeed. Maybe even sweeter than Granny Reid's best apple butter.

Chapter 3

"Oh, wow!" Savannah whispered to Dirk as they entered the gymnasium. Grotesquely overdecorated, the room was a virtual jungle of balloons, crepe-paper drapes, and tinsel streamers.

"Oh, *yuck*, is more like it." He grimaced, as though he had just popped a sour candy into his mouth right after brushing his teeth. "Purple? Your school colors were purple and purple?"

"No. Green and gold. But Jeanette's favorite color has always been purple. Even when she was in kindergarten. And something tells me she was head of the decorating committee."

Dirk nodded toward the buffet table, which was spread with a suspiciously high percentage of purple edibles, including periwinkle deviled eggs and strawberries dipped in lavender-tinted white chocolate. "Looks like ole Jeanette gets around."

"Let's just say that Miss Jeanette has her way with everybody and everything. Always did and, apparently, still does."

As Dirk searched the rows of name badges on a nearby table, looking for theirs, Savannah scanned the room, checking out the assembled alumni. Here and there in the crowd she spotted vaguely familiar faces, but she could name only a few. Apparently, she wasn't the only one who had changed a bit in the past twenty-five years.

The attendees' attire rivaled the room's for pure gaudiness, with sequins and glitter galore. Glancing down at her simple wraparound dress, Savannah realized she was severely underblinged. But the sapphire silk complimented the blue of her eyes, the V neckline showed a hint of ample cleavage, and the sash set off her hourglass figure to its best advantage. And Marietta had sent a pair of risqué sandals with four-inch heels to Granny's house, along with a note strongly suggesting that she not embarrass the family by wearing loafers. At the last second, Savannah had relented and strapped them on.

Her feet were already complaining, but she had to admit she felt pretty sexy in them, in an expensive call girl sort of way.

"You're hot as a pistol tonight, darlin'," Dirk whispered as he handed her their name badges. "Best-lookin' gal in the room, hands down."

She took the badges, peeled the back off his, and pressed it onto his lapel. She ended the ritual with an extra little pat. "You're just saying that to make me feel better."

"Is it working?"

She grinned up at him. "Oh, yeah. Keep it comin'. All night long."

He rolled his eyes and sighed. "How many times have I heard *that*?"

"Get me through tonight, big boy, and you'll hear it even more."

"Don't worry about nothin'. I'm not going anywhere." He slipped his arm around her waist and pulled her closer. "I have to guard my interests, you know, from what's-his-name."

"His name is Thomas. Prefers Tom. Call him Tommy. He hates it."

"I'll have to remember that."

"And while you're remembering, remember that none of your interests need to be guarded. Certainly not from the likes of him. He had his chance, and he blew it big-time."

"Messed around on you, right?"

"Yes. He traded in three years of sweet high school romance for some one-time romps up at Lookout Point with the likes of Miss Prissy Pants Jeanette and her right-hand lackey, Lisa Mooney."

Dirk snorted. "He's lucky to still be alive—"

"And male."

"Ouch."

Savannah shrugged. "I briefly considered homicide or gender reassignment. But in the end I just dropped his sorry butt and moved on . . . as far as I could get without falling into the Pacific Ocean."

"I'm sorry you went through that, babe. But I'm not the least bit sorry you relocated to California. His loss is my gain."

She gave him her best dimpled smile. "I'm certainly not frettin' about it anymore. All's well that ends well, and all that good stuff."

Leaning his head down to hers, he said in her ear, "But just the same, if you want me to catch him in the parking lot or in a dark alley somewhere, I could settle the score in your favor, if you know what I mean."

"I know exactly what you mean, and don't even think about it."

"Aw, come on. Just a couple of good solid whacks. It would make me so happy to do that one little thing for you."

"No. This is supposed to be a vacation. Once this shindig's

over, and we escape hell's purple waiting room here, I want to have some fun. I intend to spend my free time baking Gran a birthday cake, not making you a banana-nut loaf with a file filling."

Dirk craned his neck and perused the room's inhabitants, from the dancers gyrating under the oversized disco ball to the long line at the buffet table, to the guests gathered in small, tight knots, whispering to each other. From the furtive glances they were casting at other attendees, it appeared they were the purveyors of the juiciest gossip. "Where is the ole boy, anyway?"

"Haven't seen him. But then, I haven't especially been looking."

The moment Savannah uttered the words, she could practically feel her nose start to grow. Of course she had been looking. Even before entering the "city" limits of tiny, "blink 'n' you'll miss it" McGill, she'd had her eyes peeled, anticipating the first Sheriff Tommy Stafford sighting.

It wasn't that she was still in love with him. Far from it, in fact. All it took for her to conjure up a major case of loathing was to think of him with Jeanette Parker in the peach orchard or with Lisa Mooney up at Lookout Point, while he was supposedly still her steady boyfriend.

To say that her first love had proven untrue was a vast understatement.

Tommy had always been a pretty boy with no shortage of horny females throwing their bloomers in his direction. Usually while they were still wearing them. Exceptionally tall, with thick blond hair, bright green eyes, and muscles galore, he would have garnered far more than his fair share of female attention just based on looks alone. But he also had a slow, sexy grin and a charming way with women that made them feel oh, so special. At least for five minutes.

And Tom Stafford had made Savannah feel extremely special for more than five minutes.

Over the years, as other boyfriends had come and gone, Savannah had never had a problem letting go. Except with Tom.

Maybe because he was her first. Maybe because he was drop-dead gorgeous. But she suspected it had more to do with the fact that he was in law enforcement. And she had been in love with cops since that dark night, years ago, when the boys in blue had carried her in their strong arms to a safer, healthier place.

However, Savannah had a cop of her own now. Big, strong, brave, and true. Even if he was a bit loud when it came to newspaper reading and cornflake eating. And he was standing right beside her, her Knight in a Dark Blue Suit—his one and only suit—willing to do battle on her behalf.

Eager, in fact.

Far more than she wanted him to be.

"Savannah."

She caught her breath as her heart started to pound. Even before she turned around to face the person behind her who had spoken her name, Savannah knew who it was. There was no mistaking that deep, sexy voice. Heaven knows, she had heard it often enough, whispering sweet nothings into her ear in moonlit peach orchards.

As she slowly turned toward him, she heard Dirk mutter, "Speak of the devil, and he'll appear."

No kidding, she thought, wondering how much of their previous conversation Tom had heard.

Donning her very best poker face, she looked up at her old love, the source of seemingly endless angst and tears aplenty. She searched her repertoire for the perfect response—neutral, civil, but slightly frosty, articulate, and poised, with just a touch of "withering" thrown in for good measure.

"Hey." She gulped. Choked on her own spit. "Whuzup?"

Wow, she thought. *That's tellin' 'im. He'll never recover from such a tongue-lashing.*

He flashed her *the* smile, and it occurred to Savannah that he'd had his teeth whitened since she'd last seen him.

Tommy had always been a bit vain. She wondered if he still made his mom iron creases into his jeans and polish his sneakers white. But she would just have to wonder, because he wasn't wearing jeans and sneakers tonight. Sheriff Thomas Stafford was in uniform and was looking dadgum good in it, too.

Not that she'd noticed, of course.

And yes, she silently observed, *he wears that uniform even to his high school reunion.*

Tommy had always been darned proud to be a cop. She suspected he was tickled pink to be sheriff.

Probably sleeps in his uniform and takes a shower in it, too, she thought. *There. That's more like it, Savannah girl. Find a way to work* that *into the conversation.*

"I wasn't going to come to this thing," Tom was saying, "until I heard that you'd be here."

Savannah cringed.

She heard Dirk clear his throat.

She reached back, grabbed her husband's arm, and pulled him forward to stand beside her.

"If you heard that I was coming," she said, her voice silky, "then you must've heard my other big news, too." She patted Dirk's forearm. "Since you and I last laid eyes on one another, Deputy Tommy, I've gone and acquired myself a husband."

No, Stafford hadn't heard. She could tell by the look on his face. Surprise, hurt, and anger were all mixed into a tasty, satisfying cocktail, which she mentally sipped slowly, savoring every intoxicating drop.

His jaw was tight and his words were clipped when he said, "I'm *sheriff* now, and I prefer *Tom*."

"Oh, really? I hadn't heard."

She stifled a snicker, but Dirk didn't bother. A quick sideways glance at her husband's ear-to-ear grin told her that she had just scored some major "wife" points.

She made quite a show of examining the empty spaces to the right and left of the now haughty and highly miffed sheriff. "Where's your date tonight, Tommy? In the little girls' room, freshening her makeup?"

The sheriff lifted his dimpled, shaving-commercial-perfect chin and replied, "I ain't here in a social capacity. I'm on duty."

"Ooooh! I'm impressed." Savannah turned to Dirk. "Aren't you impressed, too?"

Dirk nodded. "Impressed. Impressed as hell. Sheriff Tommy Stafford sacrifices his evening of gaiety to protect and serve mankind."

Savannah's eyes went icy. "Oh, Sheriff Stafford services *wom-en*kind, too," she said smoothly. "But either way, with the likes of him on patrol, the world's a safer place. No doubt about it."

"I'll have you know that I'm in the middle of a possible homicide investigation," Tom shot back. Savannah could practically see his bristles lifting beneath his slightly too tight khaki shirt.

"Then you're here to keep an eye on your number one suspect, Miss Jeanette Barnsworth herself?" Savannah asked.

Dirk cleared his throat. "Hmm. I figured you'd just take her up to Lookout Point and give her a thorough investigation."

Stafford caught his breath and glanced back and forth between Savannah and Dirk. To her delight, she watched the color rise in his cheeks, along with his mortification.

Not only was Tom's former girlfriend now married to someone else, but she had apparently told her new hubby all their secrets, too.

Well, almost all, Savannah reminded herself. She was pretty sure that Dirk would not have appreciated hearing what a great kisser Tommy Stafford had been among those moonlit peach trees on sultry Georgia summer nights.

But as much as she was enjoying seeing her old boyfriend squirm, Savannah the investigator came to fore, along with the little girl who needed some measure of comeuppance for past injuries suffered.

"Do you think she did it?" she asked far too eagerly for her own liking. "I mean, we all know that Jeanette's a witch on a tattered broomstick, but do you really think she'd kill her old man?"

Tom seemed to relax slightly, as though happy to be on a less personal and far less embarrassing topic. "She might've. He may have just kicked the bucket from natural causes. Haven't ruled out nobody or nothin' for sure just yet."

Savannah was moderately ashamed of how disappointed she felt to hear that he was looking at others, along with Jeanette.

First thing upon awakening that morning, Savannah had literally prayed that the killer would turn out to be Jeanette. Of course, she had immediately felt guilty about it, but not enough to take the prayer back. Although Granny Reid was considered the Bible scholar in the family, Savannah was pretty darned sure that a prayer like that wasn't going to make it all the way to heaven. And if it did, it might not be welcomed or answered by the Almighty.

"I've never met the lady personally," Dirk said, "but I'd lay money that she just walked through the door." He nodded in that direction, and Savannah and Tom turned to look.

Sure enough, a vision in purple had just glided into the room and was floating across the floor in their direction.

Years ago, even in elementary school, Savannah could recall Jeanette expounding, frequently and with great authority, about the importance of females walking with queenly grace. She would instigate impromptu contests in which the girls would attempt to walk from one side of the classroom to the other with books on their heads without dropping them.

Of course, Jeanette had been quite accomplished at the feat, while her competitors had usually lost their copies of Nancy Drew's *The Hidden Staircase* or Judy Blume's *Tales of a Fourth Grade Nothing* after only a step or two. Further proof that Jeanette was, indeed, a superior, more highly evolved human being than almost anybody else on the planet.

As the queen of the reunion slithered across the highly polished gym floor, heading in their direction, Savannah took the opportunity to survey her former competition.

While Savannah hated the way some women evaluated every other female they met, employing a slow scornful scan of the other's appearance, taking in every detail of the hair, makeup, jewelry, clothing, and shoes, she found herself doing the same thing.

From the too-high jet-black updo to the thick Cleopatra eyeliner, the gaudy jewelry, the rhinestone tiara, and the overly sequined, two sizes too small purple dress, Savannah could tally at least a dozen major fashion faux pas. Obviously, she hadn't gotten the memo about avoiding the "matchy-matchy" trap. Her dress, purse, and high heels were all of the same satin and were all equally bespangled with sparklies galore.

Of course, Savannah knew that if she liked Jeanette Barnsworth, nothing so trivial would matter one iota to her. Never before in her life had Savannah judged another woman by her fashion sense or lack thereof, and she wasn't proud of doing so now.

But then, she also wanted to grab ole Jeanette by her lofty beehive, rip that ridiculous crown off her head, and wrestle her for a half an hour or so in a muddy pigpen. So, as far as Savannah was concerned, it was all too obvious that Miss Prissy Pants Jeanette just brought out the worst in people.

What could she do?

It wasn't until Jeanette was only a few feet away from them that Savannah realized she wasn't alone. Trailing along in her wake, like a hooked trout behind a fishing boat, was the town mortician, Herb Jameson.

Was Mr. Jameson her date? Savannah wondered. If so, she couldn't imagine why.

As nice as he was, and as nice looking as he had once been many years ago, Savannah couldn't understand how Jeanette could be attracted to this man, whose daughter, Amy, had been in their graduating class.

But then, it was commonly believed that Jeanette had married her recently departed husband, Jacob Barnsworth, for money—not love or lust—and he was even older than the mortician she now had in tow.

Jameson might be the only undertaker in town and fairly well off by McGill standards, but Savannah couldn't imagine that his wealth was significant enough to entice Jeanette. She had inherited her parents' substantial estates, and now that she had her mitts on Jacob Barnsworth's money, as well, she was surely rolling in the dough.

As Jeanette walked up to them and stood between Dirk and Tom, leaving her date to stand meekly behind her, Savannah searched her mind for an appropriate greeting. But none came to mind that didn't contain at least two or three curse words that Granny Reid would deplore. So Savannah said nothing. And for what seemed like about ten long, awkward years, neither did anyone else.

Finally, it was Dirk who broke the silence. "Lemme guess. You're Jeanette. The gal who likes purple and figures all the rest of us do, too." When she didn't reply, he added, "I mean, why else would you decorate this place so's it looks like some giant barfed grape punch all over everything?"

Jeanette raised one darkly penciled eyebrow, lifted her chin a notch, and turned to Savannah. Nodding toward Dirk, she said, "Yours, I presume?"

Savannah laced her arm through Dirk's and pulled him closer. "Absolutely. This is my husband, Detective Sergeant Dirk Coulter." Glancing over Jeanette's shoulder, she said, "And I do believe that's Mr. Herb Jameson you've got there. Good evening, Mr. Jameson. How nice to see you again."

"You, too, Miss Savannah," the mortician replied with a courteous nod. "It's a pleasure." Though the strained look on his face belied his words. His eyes wouldn't meet Savannah's when he spoke. He shifted his weight from one foot to the other as he adjusted and readjusted his tie, as though it was choking him.

Savannah had known the undertaker her entire life, and he had never been anything but kind and open with her. Only a few years ago he had assisted her and her family, helping to prove her youngest brother innocent of murder.

So why was he hiding, quite literally, behind his date's skirts and acting like a kid who had just been caught pilfering a dollar from his grandma's purse?

One quick glance at Dirk and Tom told Savannah that she

wasn't the only one in the room who had noticed the mortician's unusual behavior. Both men were staring at him with the predatory eyes of professional investigators, evaluating, questioning.

Tom took a step closer to the older man, quite obviously invading his personal space. "You're hard to get ahold of these days, my friend," Tom said without the slightest note of friendliness in his tone. "I've been by your funeral parlor four times in the past two days, lookin' to have a little chat with you. And even though that big black hearse of yours has been parked there in the back, I can't seem to rouse nobody to come to the door."

Jameson gulped and shifted the knot in his tie for the third time. "Well, Sheriff, that's a bit of a stumper. Did you knock hard? Sometimes if I'm in the back, in my office, I might not hear you if you don't knock hard enough to—"

"For heaven's sake, Tom," Jeanette interrupted. "Herb doesn't drive that hearse around all the time, you know. He's got a regular car."

Tom nodded thoughtfully. "Yup. I know. I heard he's got a brand-new Cadillac. Bought it Monday off Arthur Johnson's lot. Paid cash for it, too, I hear."

Savannah couldn't help being impressed. "Seems there's not a lot you don't hear," she said.

Tom grinned. "There are a few advantages to policing a small town."

Dirk gave a snort and added, "Yeah. In a place this size, you'd know what everybody had for dinner last night and who burned the bologna."

"Supper," Savannah whispered.

Dirk looked confused.

"Around here, if you eat it at night, it's *supper*," she explained. *Dinner* is what we call lunch."

"And here I thought I was fluent in Southern."

Jeanette sighed and patted her updo, obviously bored with the conversation, which was not centered around her, and anxious to get on with her evening. She reached back and grabbed Herb Jameson's hand. "If you are finished interrogating my date, Tom Stafford, we've got us some serious dancing to do."

Tom gave her a curt nod. Then, to Jameson, he said, "Y'all have a good time tonight, but the next time I come knocking at your funeral parlor, you better hightail it to answer that door before I take my boot to it. You hear?"

Jeanette pulled Herb away before he could answer, but the frightened look in his eyes showed that he had received the message quite clearly.

Savannah had never been good at containing her curiosity. "What do you want to talk to him about, Tom?" Of course she hoped to score at least half a point for using his preferred name.

She did.

"Not that it's any of your business," he said, "but I got a few questions to ask him about a recent autopsy that he performed."

Dirk cleared his throat. "Wouldn't happen to be a postmortem on old man Barnsworth, would it?"

When Tom didn't reply, Savannah pressed ahead. "I heard that you're not convinced he died of natural causes. That you are thinking maybe the self-coronated queen of the ball might have personally introduced him to his Maker. And I'm guessing you might be questioning Mr. Jameson's autopsy findings. Am I right? I mean, he's got himself a new, cash-bought Cadillac, and it appears he's got a girlfriend for the first time in years. Maybe she made it worth his while to come to that conclusion."

Tom gave her an annoyed look, but Savannah could also

read a smidgen of grudging respect in those green eyes. "Sounds like *you* hear a lot yourself, gal. But then, your ears always have been on the stretch, listenin' to what ain't none of your business. And your imagination's always worked overtime."

Dirk slipped his arm around Savannah's shoulder and hugged her to his side. "And *those*, Sheriff Stafford, are just two of a thousand qualities that make her an amazing woman and a helluva detective. I can't tell you how glad I am that she's on my team now. Not yours."

Savannah didn't have enough time to savor fully the ugly mixture of anger, humiliation, and frustration that distorted her ex-boyfriend's perfectly handsome face before her husband whisked her away and onto the dance floor.

But as he pulled her into his arms and, chuckling all the while, pressed a kiss to her earlobe, it occurred to her that she had never in her life been so in love with a man.

Chapter 4

By the time the reunion party festivities started to wind down, Savannah was in a much better mood than when they had begun. Between getting to dance a dozen slow songs with her husband—who, for all his size and his reputation for moving like Godzilla tromping through Tokyo, was fairly light on his feet—and enjoying a generous portion of chocolate-dipped strawberries, she had decided that this event, which she'd been dreading for so long, didn't stink. At least not as badly as she'd feared.

Several of the attendees had greeted her warmly, showing genuine affection and pleasure at seeing her again. A few of the girls who had performed the duties of ladies in waiting for Queen Jeanette during their school years appeared to have matured and moved on to more worthwhile occupations, like getting lives of their own.

To Savannah's surprise and deep soul satisfaction, she detected a bit of regret and a sense of apology in their manner when they approached her and initiated conversations about the "good old days."

So when all the good-byes had been said, the last straw-berry pilfered, and the class song sung, Savannah was happy she had come. But thanks to Marietta's ridiculously high and tight sandals, she was even happier to be leaving.

As she and Dirk strolled arm in arm down a hallway that led to a rear door, they passed a glass case filled with sports trophies and memorabilia.

"You must've won more than your share of those when you were in high school," she said, "you being a jock and all."

"What makes you think I was a jock?" he said softly.

"I don't know. You're a big, strong guy. You love sports. I just figured . . ."

"Naw. The school there at the orphanage didn't have much of a sports program. Duking it out on the playground when the bigger boys picked on us, running after guys who stole our stuff—that's pretty much what passed for phys ed."

Savannah gulped, mentally kicking herself for momentarily forgetting his own unfortunate childhood.

She squeezed his arm and leaned her head on his shoulder. "I'm sorry, sugar," she said. "I am an idiot. Sometimes I just get wrapped up in myself and forget that you had a tough time growing up, too."

He kissed the top of her head. "No big deal. We've both seen plenty of little kids who had it a lot worse."

"That's for sure."

Her soul shuddered as she remembered the pathetic circumstances of so many children she had tried to protect and serve while on the police force. Though it caused her pain to recall those memories, the exercise of doing so certainly put things into perspective. While being ridiculed and humiliated by others had blighted her childhood, those indignities paled in comparison to the atrocities she had seen visited upon other innocents.

As they continued on down the hallway and passed through the back entrance, Dirk noticed that she was limping.

"It's those stupid shoes that Marietta loaned you, right?" he asked.

"Yeah. I should've known better than to borrow any sort of fashion accessories from Mari."

"I don't know. You'd probably look cute in those neon blue leopard-print tights of hers. A lot better than she does, anyway."

She grinned up at him. "Bless you for that."

"Why don't you just wait here while I go get the car?" he said. "I'll pull right up, like a proper chauffeur, and open the door for you. You can even sit in the backseat if you want to."

She snickered. "That's a sweet offer, and I'll let you go get the car since you suggested it. But sitting in the backseat all by my lonesome wouldn't be much fun. Not without you to keep me company."

He raised one eyebrow and gave her a sexy smile, which Tom Stafford could only aspired to. "Maybe we'll take the long way home to Granny's. Stop by Lookout Point perhaps?"

"Now you're talking. We can play 'Studly Chauffeur Gives His Rich Mistress a Tune-up.' "

"I'll be back as quick as I can."

"I'm sure you will."

She watched him hurry away, fleet of foot and light of step. But then, he could afford to; he wasn't wearing Marietta's sexy strappy sandals.

With the promise of adventurous hanky-panky looming on his horizon, she was sure he would make the trip in record time.

Although she was equally certain that his ETA would be

delayed somewhat by the fact that he would spend at least five minutes wandering around the large, dark parking area, trying to remember what their rental car looked like. It was a white, midsized four-door sedan. Not exactly a standout vehicle in a crowded lot.

Yes, Dirk was big, he was cute, he was brave, and he was obnoxiously masculine. And he was intelligent, in a street-smart sort of way. Unfortunately, he didn't always think things through. Especially when he had sex on the brain.

True to her expectations, it took him forever to return. But she wasn't alone for long. As she waited, Savannah saw a couple of women exit the door and walk in her direction. Before they reached her, they paused near a garbage can. One of them reached into her purse, pulled out a pack of cigarettes, and tore off the top.

As she tossed the litter into the can, Savannah heard her say, "I tried to stop. And I did for a while. But I packed on ten pounds in no time flat, so I had to start again."

Her companion nodded. "I understand completely. That's the worst part about quitting. You pork right out. Your good clothes don't fit you anymore. It's just not worth it."

As the women continued to chat about the downfalls of giving up nicotine, they turned their faces slightly toward Savannah, and she could see them more clearly owing to the dim halogen lights that lit the entrance.

She recognized Amy Jameson immediately. She looked a lot like her father, Herb. Although his hair was now silver and thin, it had once been auburn, thick, and curly like Amy's. And they both had soft, sweet faces and easy smiles, readily offered to everyone they met.

Until tonight, anyway, Savannah reminded herself. Once again, she found herself wondering at the change in the undertaker's personality. People seemed to change around Jeanette, and not for the better.

The person who had always been closest to Jeanette was the smoker who was speaking with Amy at the moment. Lisa Mooney—now Lisa Riggs, since she had married the middle Riggs boy, Frank—had been Savannah's second least favorite female at McGill High. She had always emulated Jeanette in every way possible. For as long as Savannah had known her, Lisa had dressed like Jeanette, had walked with the same prissiness as Jeanette, had talked like her, and had tormented other girls in fine form, under Jeanette's rigorous tutelage.

Savannah had assumed that one day Lisa would outgrow Jeanette and become her own person. But apparently, she hadn't, judging from her attire. She was wearing an outfit that was almost identical to Jeanette's, except for the color. Lisa's dress, purse, and high heels were all hot pink, and though a bit less rhinestone encrusted than Jeanette's, her attire definitely qualified her as second runner-up in the "gaudy" category at the reunion.

But Lisa's mood seemed far less festive than her overstated costume. She looked perfectly miserable as the two women conversed in hushed tones.

"I don't understand how you can still be friends with the likes of her," Amy was saying to Lisa in a voice far more harsh than Savannah had ever heard her use. "How can you still talk to her? How can you be nice to her, knowing what she's done?"

"I don't know for a fact that she did it, and neither do you," was Lisa's quick retort. "I like to think of myself as a loyal person. I don't turn my back on my best friend just because of some mean-spirited gossip."

Amy dropped her voice even lower, and Savannah had to strain to hear her say, "You know it's true, Lisa. You, of all people. You know her better than anybody, and you know in your heart what she did. It's time she was held accountable for all the lives she's destroyed."

To Savannah's surprise, Lisa threw her cigarette onto the sidewalk, covered her face with her hands, and began to cry. She wept so bitterly that Savannah couldn't help feeling sorry for her.

Did it really matter that twenty-five years ago a teenage girl had made love to her boyfriend? A relatively worthless boyfriend at that, as it had turned out. Who hadn't committed a few youthful indiscretions in their day? Tonight the woman Lisa had become was hurting badly, apparently paying a heavy price for being loyal to the wrong person.

Savannah thought back over the years, recalling how Lisa had been Jeanette's ever-present sidekick, fighting her battles for her, doing the more aggressive girl's bidding, all without question.

It must be hard, Savannah thought, *to pass the age of forty and only then realize that the person you've spent your life idolizing may have committed murder.*

"I can't believe it. I just can't believe she would stoop that low." Lisa fished around in her purse but brought out nothing but her cigarettes, a hairbrush, and a lipstick.

Amy produced a tissue from her pocket and handed it to Lisa. "I know what you mean," she said, her tone softer and less accusatory than before. "I have a hard time believing that he'd go along with it, too. I sure thought better of him than that. But Jeanette's always had a way with men. She knows just how to get whatever she wants from them. He's not the first to give in to her, and he sure won't be the last."

Savannah could hear the pain and disappointment in Amy's voice, as well. She tried to imagine how difficult it would be to realize that your own father had aided and abetted a murderess—all for the price of a new Cadillac and a roll in the hay.

Amy's mother had died when she and her two sisters were very young, and Herb Jameson had raised his girls with loving devotion. Savannah had never heard a cross word pass between Herb and his daughters or seen any sign of dissension in their relationships.

Leave it to Jeanette to cause problems where there had never been any before.

As though materializing from their conversation, Jeanette sauntered out the back door with Herb at her heels.

Savannah took a step backward, deeper into the shadows.

Amy and Lisa froze, looking like a pair of rabbits whose hutch had just been invaded by a fox.

But as Jeanette headed in their direction, Lisa suddenly sprang to life and said in a far too loud and animated voice, "I've gotta skedaddle. Frank had to work tonight, but he's probably home by now. Promised to make it up to me with a nice romantic dinner. So I'd better git goin'."

Her unconvincing speech delivered, she scurried away and disappeared into the darkness among the parked cars.

Jeanette walked up to Amy, her backbone even stiffer and her chin even higher than usual. "Well, well. That one took off like somebody'd lit a bonfire on her skirt tail."

After a long, tense moment, Amy said, "I reckon she had somewhere to be."

Jeanette sniffed. "Oh, yeah. Like that tightwad Frank would treat her to a romantic dinner. She'd do well to weasel a cheeseburger and the small fry out of that cheapskate."

"As it turns out," Amy said with a quick hurt look at her dad, "I've got someplace to be myself."

"Really?" Jeanette said as Herb stared down at the sidewalk. "And where's that?"

"Anywhere but here," was Amy's curt reply before she turned and strode away into the darkness without another word to Jeanette or any further acknowledgment of her father.

Herb looked perfectly miserable as he watched his daughter leave. It occurred to Savannah that he, too, would prefer to be anywhere other than in his present situation.

But it was Jeanette's response that fascinated Savannah. As Jeanette stood, glaring at the departing Amy, her face darkened with anger so intense and ugly that, even knowing her history, Savannah was taken aback.

Apparently, the years had not improved Jeanette's temperament. Quite the contrary, it seemed.

But Savannah wasn't surprised. Having dealt with people during some of their worst moments, she had formulated a theory about mankind. She'd decided that with age, good people tended to become better, bad people got worse, and sometimes good folks went wrong. But she had yet to see a bad person become a good one.

So it was no shock that a spoiled and temperamental child had become an angry and potentially dangerous woman.

As Savannah watched the humiliated woman huff and puff, fists clenched, she could feel Jeanette's rage building. Having not one, but two former friends disrespect her so blatantly wasn't something that McGill's closest thing to a socialite was accustomed to.

Savannah wasn't surprised when Jeanette turned her wrath on her date.

"Well, thank you very much, Herb," she said, her voice thick with sarcasm. "I sure appreciate how you rushed to my defense there."

Herb shrugged. "Sorry, sugar, but I don't know what you expected me to say or do."

"You could have at least told that smart-mouthed daughter of yours to show me a bit of respect. I've been nothing but good to her over the years, introducing her and her sisters to important people, inviting them to all the best parties. Parties they never would've been able to attend, them being nothing but run-of-the-mill undertaker's daughters."

Savannah watched as the mortician squared his thin shoulders. "I suppose, if that's the way you feel, you won't mind if this run-of-the-mill undertaker finds himself another way home."

"What other way?" Jeanette's rage burned several degrees hotter. Even in the semidarkness, Savannah could see that she was trembling with fury as she reached out and poked Herb's chest hard with her long acrylic fingernail. Purple, of course. "*What* other way?" she repeated. "Are you going to embarrass yourself and me, too, by hitchhiking your way home, when everybody here knows you're my date?"

Herb grabbed her hand in mid-poke and squeezed it hard. "I might hitchhike," he said. "If that's what it takes. I don't care, as long as I'm not with you. This date's over, Jeanette. In fact, the whole thing's over. I'm done with you. And frankly, I've got to tell you, you weren't worth it. Not even close."

As yet a third person walked away from Jeanette in less than five minutes, she shouted at his retreating back, "I don't suppose that new Cadillac was worth it, either, huh?"

Glancing briefly over his shoulder, he said, "I'm returning it to Arthur tomorrow. I'm sure he'll give you some sort of refund."

"Too bad there ain't some sorta refund for dating an impotent old man!"

Herb paused in mid-step for half a second, then continued on, his stride even faster and more purposeful than before.

Ouch, Savannah thought. *Low, low blow.*

Even in the course of a heated argument, some topics needed to be off-limits. Apparently, Jeanette hadn't heard that rule or, more likely, had given herself permission to violate it.

As Savannah stood still and silent in the shadows, watching her enemy's humiliation, it occurred to her that she should be enjoying this moment more. At least she would have expected to.

How many times in her imagination had she told this person off, given her a piece of her mind, set her straight? How many times had she fancied a hundred different ways that Jeanette might get her comeuppance in the most humiliating ways possible?

But while the fantasies had given Savannah a great deal of pleasure at the time, the reality seemed far less sweet. More than anything else, she felt sad.

So much drama, so much pain, for so many people . . . and for what?

Nothing.

It was all completely pointless.

Such a waste of time, of energy . . . of life.

For years she had hated Jeanette and had wished her ill, and now, seeing her nemesis in the flesh, in the act of living out her own miserable existence, it occurred to Savannah that the worst punishment Jeanette could receive was simply being Jeanette.

"What are *you* lookin' at?"

It took a second for Savannah to realize that Jeanette had spotted her and was speaking to her.

The rudeness of the question and how it was asked dispelled any momentary sense of pity Savannah was feeling. Anger, the cold kind, hit her bloodstream like an instant four-liter transfusion of frosty iced tea.

"I beg your pardon?" she said in a flat, sinister tone, one that might have concerned a somewhat more timid soul.

But Jeanette Barnsworth had no link labeled TIMID on her DNA chain.

"I asked you what you're lookin' at. Hiding there in the shadows, eavesdropping, listening to stuff that's none of your business."

Slowly, Savannah stepped out of the darkness and into the dim yellow light.

As anemic as the halogen glow was, Jeanette appeared to see something in Savannah's eyes that registered at least a bit of caution. She took one step backward, putting a little more distance between them.

"I wasn't eavesdropping," Savannah said. "I was just standing there with my teeth in my mouth, waiting for my husband to bring the car up, when you started screaming nasty things at your date. If they were secrets, maybe you shouldn't have been shouting them out for God and everybody to hear."

"Yeah, well, I reckon since they kicked you off the police force for being so fat, you're one of those private detectives who go around spying on people for money. 'Pears you're good at somethin', after all."

Savannah swallowed a gasp as the sharp blade of the woman's words drove deep into her heart. What was it about catty, cruel women that they always knew your soul's deepest wound and how to pierce it, at whim, with breathtaking accuracy?

She forced her voice to be even, her breathing slow and calm, as she said, "Your investigation skills are sadly lacking there,

Miss Jeanette. Part of being a good detective is making sure you've got all the facts in hand before you go accusing people. And not just the facts that suit your purpose."

"And what purpose do you reckon I've got?"

"Putting other people down so you can feel good about yourself and the rotten things you do."

"I feel just fine about myself."

Savannah nodded thoughtfully. "You shouldn't. But I suspect you do. I used to think that, just maybe, what appeared to be arrogance on your part was some sort of cover-up for a deep-rooted insecurity. But there are plenty of people who actually think they're better than everybody else. They're not insecure or troubled or tormented. They're just plain ole conceited."

Jeanette absorbed the insult without even flinching and took a couple of steps closer to Savannah. "And then," she said, "there are people like me who know what's what and who's who. Like that my family's always had a pot to piss in, and yours had a stinkin' outhouse. Like that my grandpa was mayor of McGill, and yours dug graves in the cemetery. Like that my mom was president of the garden club, and yours is a worthless drunk who spends all day and night holding down a bar stool and swiggin'—"

"You need to shut up, Jeanette. And you need to do that now," Savannah said softly, calmly.

Jeanette smirked. "Woo-hoo! Look at you gettin' your dander all up. Hurts to hear the truth, doesn't it? And while you're out there in sunny California, pretending to be some highfalutin private detective, you probably don't want to remember how you used to spend every Saturday doing our laundry."

Again, Jeanette stepped closer, until the two women were less than a yard apart. "Did you know," she said, her eyes bright with perverse pleasure, "that I used to leave little . . . um . . . treats on my underwear just for you?" When Savannah didn't reply, she continued, "But you always got them clean. Yes, if there's anything you and your grandma was good at, it was gettin' stains out of other folks' underdrawers."

Time slowed for Savannah as she stood there, watching, listening, evaluating. Often, when seeing cruelty up close and in sharp detail, she had wondered how society could embrace the idea that no person was actually bad, only troubled, in pain, or misinformed. While Savannah had seen many criminals whose misdeeds were merely echoes of abuses perpetrated on them, she had also seen too many sadistic narcissists in the world to believe that was always the case.

Some people truly enjoyed inflicting pain on others. And some of them, like Jeanette, had not been mistreated in their early lives. Some had been coddled, pampered, and told that the world revolved around them. And as a result, they believed that others existed only to serve them, to make their lives easier and more pleasant, to raise them up simply by being under their feet.

"The only thing you ever had going for you," Jeanette continued, "was Tom Stafford. But you lost him, too, didn't you? All I had to do was crook my finger, and, boy, he came running."

Savannah was vaguely aware that some people had come out of the building and were standing nearby, close enough to overhear this exchange. She could feel other eyes watching from the darkness of the parking lot, eavesdroppers listening to every word they were saying. But she didn't care. She felt nothing except that strange icy coldness coursing through her veins as Jeanette's words flowed over her.

Over, but not through.

"Of course, I didn't *want* him," Jeanette was saying. "He was cute and all, but frankly, he wasn't all that good in the sack. Didn't rise to the occasion, if you know what I mean. Besides, he always said he was gonna be a cop. And who'd wanna marry a cop?"

A hundred images flooded Savannah's mind. Those big, handsome men in blue uniforms carrying the Reid kids out of their mother's house in their strong arms. Their deep, comforting voices telling them not to cry, that everything was going to be fine.

Countless memories of the men and women who had stood beside her on the police force, risking their lives, placing their vulnerable bodies between strangers and harm's way. All because it was their duty, even to die, if need be. To protect and serve.

And even more pictures of Dirk, her husband, interjecting himself over and over again into the most horrific circumstances, trying to make a difference. She had seen him bruised, bleeding, spit upon, with filth hurled at him, along with words that seared the soul. Any soul. Even that of a street-hardened cop.

She had seen tears fill his eyes as he held the ones he couldn't save in his arms and watched them, felt them, slip away.

"I mean, really," Jeanette rattled on, "who'd want a lousy cop for a husband? Not me, that's for sure. They don't make beans, you know. I could never settle for a crap lifestyle like—"

Crack!

At first Savannah thought it was a gunshot. The sharp report echoed throughout the parking lot. Those standing nearby were struck silent.

The only sound was that of Jeanette Barnsworth hitting the sidewalk.

Slowly, Savannah became aware of the burning sensation in

her right hand. Then she felt Dirk beside her, his arm around her waist, his breath against the side of her face.

She heard him whisper, "Holy shit, babe. What did you . . . what did she . . . what the hell? She's out cold!"

And she was.

Queen bee Jeanette was sprawled on her back across the sidewalk, her arms out flung. The skirt of her rhinestone-studded dress fluttered up to her waist, revealing a less than attractive tummy-tucking foundation garment.

For a moment Savannah thought Jeanette was dead.

And judging from the burning sensation in her hand, she just might be the one who'd killed her.

But in her left hand Savannah could feel her purse and the weight of the Beretta that she was carrying inside it. So at least she hadn't shot her.

A moment later someone left the bystanders and walked up to stand on the other side of her. "Whoa. Howdy," she heard Tom Stafford say. "You got one helluva right cross there, gal. She's out for the count."

It occurred to Savannah that perhaps someone should be checking Jeanette for vital signs. Out of curiosity, if for no other reason, just to make sure she still had some.

But no one was rushing forward to administer CPR or scrambling to locate a cardiac defibrillator machine. Jeanette's former schoolmates seemed perfectly content to stand there and gawk at their fallen monarch.

"What'd you do it for?" Tom asked.

Quickly, Savannah replayed the recent conversation between herself and her tormentor in her head and decided there was no part of it she cared to share with the world.

Heaven knows, they'd already heard way too much.

"You know Jeanette," she said. "Pick a reason. Any reason."

On the sidewalk, the stricken Jeanette began to stir. She sat up, put her hand to her left cheek, and massaged it for a moment. Dazed, she looked around, trying to reorient herself to her surroundings and the situation.

Dirk whispered to Savannah, "It's alive! It's alive!"

"Yeah," she replied. "Talk about mixed emotions."

Tom put his hand on Savannah's elbow, then gripped it tightly. "Savannah, you assaulted her. You know I'm gonna have to arrest you for that."

Savannah couldn't help being at least moderately amused as she watched Jeanette struggle to get her skirt down and her beehive updo straightened. "She assaulted me first," she told him.

He looked doubtful. "I don't see a mark on you."

"Not all injuries leave a mark, Tom. You know that." Savannah looked up at him, her eyes searching his for understanding.

She found it. The stern look on his handsome face softened, but he said, "That might be true. But if she decides to press charges, there won't be much I can do about it."

Savannah pulled her arm out of his grip and took a few steps toward Jeanette.

This time it was Dirk who grabbed her. "Leave her alone, Van," he said, "unless you want to spend the rest of our Dixieland vacation in the Crowbar Hotel."

"I promise, I'm not gonna ruffle a hair on her head. We're just gonna have us a little girl-to-girl chat. I'm not stupid enough to smack her around right under the noses of two fine policemen like yourselves."

When they both cut her withering sideways looks, she added under her breath, "Well, not more than once in an evening."

She walked over to Jeanette and knelt down on one knee beside her.

The instant that Jeanette focused on Savannah's face, she

appeared to become instantly aware of her circumstances and in total recall of former events. "You hit me! You knocked me down! You slapped the tar outta me! How dare you!"

"Now, now," Savannah said in her most soothing cop voice. "I didn't hit you, darlin'. My hand just kinda slipped, and your face got in the way."

"Hand slipped, my hind end! You attacked me, and I'm gonna press charges. I'm gonna—"

Savannah lowered her voice and leaned close to Jeanette's ear. "Hush. You need to stop running your mouth for once and use your head. I'm not about to plead guilty to anything involving the likes of you. Which means it'd have to go to trial. You just remember all the stuff you said right before . . . before my hand got that little spasm. The little trick you liked to play with your underwear. The fact that you fooled around with a guy you weren't the least bit interested in marrying, just so you could be one up on a girl you didn't like. That sort of thing goes over well in a small, conservative town like this."

Savannah glanced up at Tom, who was hovering over them. She wasn't sure if he could hear what she was saying or not. So she leaned even closer to Jeanette's ear and whispered, "And while you're testifying, be sure to add the part about how the sheriff's lousy in bed. He'll probably be sheriff for the next hundred years or so. Should make things nice for you, living hereabouts."

Her piece said, Savannah stood and brushed the dust from her knee.

Jeanette struggled, trying to rise, as well.

Tom offered his hand, but she slapped it away. "Just leave me alone. All of you yahoos. Just leave me the hell alone. The day I need help from any of y'all is the day I go lay my head on a railroad track somewheres. You're all just a bunch a hillbilly hicks. And that goes for you, too, Savannah. You may have moved off to California and become some kind of hotshot private detective, but you're still just a white trash kid with a drunk mother and a whore for a father. We all know that."

Dirk took a quick step toward Jeanette and raised his hand. Savannah grabbed it, gave it a squeeze.

"That's all right, darlin'," she told him. "It doesn't matter what the likes of her says about me. Or about anything else, for that matter. She's an idiot, and a mean one at that. Besides . . ." She flexed her right hand, which was still stinging. "I reckon she's had enough for one day."

Chapter 5

"So this is the infamous Lookout Point, huh?" Dirk asked as he pulled the rented car to within a few feet of the cliff's edge, parked, and turned off the headlights and the engine. "Somehow I was expecting more."

"Like what?" Savannah asked as she breathed in the pine-scented, sultry night air through the open passenger window.

"I don't know. Maybe something to look out at?"

She laughed. "It's not what you're looking out *at*. It's who you're looking out *for*." When he gave her a still-confused look, she pointed down the road they had just traveled. "From up here," she said, "you can see for over a mile behind you. You can *look out* for your parents, your school principal, your next-door neighbors, your pastor, or anybody else who might catch you foolin' around."

Dirk looked over his shoulder, down the road, and at the dark pine forest around them, then at the cliff ahead. At the bottom of the ninety-degree embankment lay a quiet lake. "I guess the water's kinda nice," he said grudgingly. "You know, with moonlight shining on it and all that stuff."

That's my guy, Savannah thought. *Always the romantic.*

"It's probably got frogs in it, though," he added. "Snakes, alligators, shit like that."

She sighed. "You're kinda killin' the mood here, boy."

"Sorry." He paused, thinking. "The trees smell good."

"Much better."

He unfastened his seat belt, reached over, and released hers. "I was kinda surprised you still wanted to come up here after that whole Jeanette rigmarole back at the school."

"All the more reason to make the trip," she replied.

He gave her a long questioning look. "Just so's I know, did we come up here to celebrate or for me to comfort you?"

"Well, we don't exactly have to break out the sparklers and party hats, but I'm feeling pretty fine. I've been itching to smack ole Jeanette upside the head for almost as long as I can remember. Since kindergarten, at least, when she started making fun of my bologna and mayonnaise sandwiches."

"I love bologna and mayonnaise sandwiches."

"Every day? Every single day of your childhood? And nothing else, not even an apple or a banana?"

"Okay. Point taken."

"Anyway, it was a long time coming. I do feel kinda guilty for hitting her instead of just telling her off. Everybody knows you're not supposed to lay hands on another person in violence, no matter what the provocation."

"Must've been some pretty nasty provocation."

"It was. That's why I'm not going to go mope around, hanging my head, staring at the floor, wringing my hands with shame."

"You'll find a way to handle all that guilt?" he asked with a grin.

"'Tis a hardship, but I'll bear up. I'm nothing if not resilient."

He pulled her into his arms and gave her a kiss. "I hate to admit it, but I was proud of you," he whispered against her cheek. "I was worried my wife was going to spend the next five or so years in jail, and I'd have to do my husbandly duty to her between iron bars. But I was proud of you."

She laughed and returned the kiss. "Why, thank you, kind sir. How's about we climb into that backseat and you can show me just exactly how proud you really are?"

"Mighty proud, Miss Savannah," he said, faking her Southern accent. His hands began to wander. His lips, too. "Powerful proud. And growing prouder by the moment."

"Is it just me," Savannah asked as she handed Dirk his briefs and continued the search for her panties on the rear floorboard, "or didn't backseats of cars used to be bigger?"

As he wriggled into his underwear, he accidentally poked her in the eye with his elbow. "Oops. Sorry. I think it's sorta like airline seats. We've gotten a little bigger, and they've gotten a whole lot smaller."

Savannah had donned her bra and was situating the "girls" in their individual cups when she heard something.

A splash.

A *big* splash.

She was pretty sure the sound was from the lake below.

"Did you hear that?" she said, sitting up and straining to see over the front seat and the car's hood to the cliff and the lake beyond.

Dirk paused, his pants half on, and listened. "No. I didn't."

"Well, I did. Loud and clear."

"My ears are still ringing."

"Ringing?"

He chuckled. "Yeah. A few minutes ago, this woman was screaming lusty obscenities in my ear. It's gonna take a while for me to get my hearing back."

Normally, she might have chuckled and uttered yet another dirty sweet nothing for his benefit, but she was sure of what she'd heard.

She got out of the car, wearing only her bra and panties and Marietta's heels, and walked over to the cliff's edge. Peering over the embankment, she saw only still, dark water, sparkling with a fine dusting of moon silver.

Dirk joined her, buttoning up his shirt and stuffing the tails of it into his trousers. "Normally, I wouldn't complain, because you look pretty hot there, kiddo," he said, giving her a long, lascivious body scan up and down. "But are you at all concerned that somebody might see you?"

"Who? The frogs? The snakes? The alligators?"

"Yeah, okay. Never mind."

The moon began to disappear behind some thick, ominous-looking clouds, so she had to strain to see any movement on the water, on the shore, on the road below.

Then she saw it. A set of lights. Taillights. One red light on each side.

On the right, a second red light shone momentarily next to the red taillight, then went dark just as the car disappeared around the curve at the bottom of the hill.

"There! Did you see that?" She grabbed Dirk's arm. "There was a car on the road."

He looked where she was pointing and shook his head. "Sorry, babe. I didn't see anything. But after tonight's festivities, I suppose we might not be the only ones up here cleaning the pipes. Old acquaintances renewed and all that stuff."

"And the splash?" she asked.

"Maybe it was a fish."

"It must've been a really *big* fish. Like Jaws or Moby Dick."

Suddenly, Savannah felt a large cold drop of water on her shoulder. Then another. Within seconds, it was as though they were standing in a giant shower with the tap turned on full force.

They raced back to the car, slipping and sliding on the muddy Georgia clay. By the time they dove into the automobile, they were thoroughly soaked.

"At least I have some dry clothes to put on," Savannah said, reaching into the backseat for her dress. "You, on the other hand, look like a drowned rat in a suit."

He was holding up one leg, then the other, looking at the mud splattered all over his trousers. "Yeah, yeah. Just tell me this Podunk town has a dry cleaner."

Indignant, she replied, "Of course. Do you really think we wouldn't have at least a couple of . . ." She sighed. "Okay, there's one. Three towns over."

"That's what I figured," he grumbled as he started the car and turned the windshield wipers on full speed.

As he began to navigate down the hill toward the main road, the vehicle slipped sideways, off the pavement and into the weeds. After the third slide, his mutterings and grumblings turned to full-fledged cursing as the car's tires spun in the mud.

"I wouldn't say it was a bad idea, coming up here with you," he said, "'cause we had a lot of fun. But let's just say, this sudden monsoon is a pain in the ass, and the thrill's fading fast."

"I tend to agree," she replied. "Only it's not the rain that has dampened my spirits. I can't get over that noise I heard."

"What? That so-called splash?"

"It wasn't 'so-called.' It *was* a splash. A big one. And I think it came from right around there," she said, pointing to an area ahead and to the right of the road.

Like the place farther up the hill where lovers enjoyed increasing their town's meager population, the spot ahead was clear of trees and brush and provided an unobstructed view of the lake below.

More than a few of McGill's residents had been conceived there, as well. It was the number two favorite make-out spot and was frequently used when the primary nook higher up the hill was occupied.

"Pull over," she said as they drew closer to the place in question. "I want to check it out."

"Check what out?"

"Right there. Where the splash came from."

Dirk slowed slightly. "I'm not pulling over anywhere. If I get off this road, we'll get stuck in the mud up to our axles and die up here."

She rolled her eyes. "That's a bit overly dramatic, don't you think? The most dangerous things in these hills are raccoons and the occasional bobcat, and we're both armed."

"And rattlesnakes and copperheads and cottonmouths and—"

"Okay, okay." Savannah could feel her skin crawl. She hated snakes and avoided thinking about them whenever possible. "I'm sure they're all safely tucked into their nice, dry snaky houses for the night."

"Watching TV or playing video games with their kids, right? I think I've heard this little fantasy of yours before."

"Hey, it works for me. Okay?" She reached over and poked him in the ribs. "Stop. You don't have to pull over. Just stop."

"Savannah, you're not goin' on one of your wild-goose chases out here in a dark Georgia woods in the middle of a downpour."

"Dirk," she said in a deadly serious voice, barely above a whisper, "if you don't stop this vehicle this very second, I swear, I'm gonna give you grief about it all night long. I'll be lying there in bed next to you, tossing and turning and mumbling to myself, frettin' up a storm, and wondering what I might've seen if you'd only just stopped and humored me for one teeny, tiny second."

He slammed on the brakes. The car slid a couple of feet and came to an abrupt halt.

"There," he snapped. "Happy?"

"Plumb ecstatic."

"Good."

She knew he was mad. He was huffing and puffing like a bulldog who had just run a marathon, and unless they were in the final throes of passion, that was hardly ever a good sign.

Casting a quick sideways look at him, she was pretty sure she could see tendrils of smoke curling out of his nostrils. His face was an unpleasant shade of green in the dim glow of the dash lights.

"I'm just going to be a minute. Really," she said in a voice far too sweet. "You'll see."

He muttered something under his breath that she couldn't understand, and she figured that was probably a blessing.

She had managed to get her dress halfway on, but she quickly peeled it off again and laid it across the console between them.

"What the hell are you doing?" he said. "You asked me to

stop so you could look and see . . . I don't know. . . . What? The splash you heard before? Well, I stopped. So *look*!"

She pointed to her side window, where nothing was visible but thick condensation on the inside of the car and rain streaming down the exterior. "Now you tell me. Can you see anything out that side window, boy? Can you? No, you can't. Even with those windshield wipers flappin' to beat the band, you can't see diddly-squat out the front, either."

"Don't you dare roll that window down."

"I'm not going to. Sheez. What kind of nitwit do you think I am?"

"Actually, I'm still trying to figure that out," he grumbled.

"I heard that."

"And will probably give me grief about that tonight, too, when I'm just trying to sleep. I put up with a lot off of you, girl."

"I know, sugar. It's 'cause you're so sweet and love me so much."

He growled.

She reached for the door handle and started to pull it.

"No!" He reached across her and grabbed her arm. "You are *not* getting out of this car, Savannah. You are *not* going out in this storm."

She pulled the handle. The door swung open a couple of inches. The cold rain blew in and pelted against her side, stinging her bare skin.

He's right, whispered an inner voice. She recognized the voice immediately. It was her higher spiritual self speaking. *Your husband is being sensible . . . for once. Follow his sound advice.*

Then the other voice spoke. And it didn't whisper. It was loud and obnoxious. *Are you kidding? This is* Dirk *you're dealing with*, it said. *If you admit he's right now, you'll never hear the end of it. In for a penny, in for a pound. For Pete's sake, just bite the bullet and do it.*

She steeled herself and flung the door open.

"I am *not* going to get out of this car and tromp around in the pouring down rain to protect you, Savannah," he shouted. "I'm not. You are on your own."

Grabbing her purse from the floorboard, she got out her Beretta and flashed it under his nose. "You didn't hear me requesting backup, now did you? If I chance to run into any marauding bobcats or rabid raccoons, I'll dispense with 'em all by my lonesome. That goes for copperheads and rattlers, too. So don't get your pecker stuck in your zipper over me."

As she hurled her reluctant body out of the car and into the chilling rain, again attired in only her lingerie and Marietta's hooker heels, she heard her husband say, "Okay, but if you slip and fall off that cliff and break your neck, don't you come running back to me. . . ."

"We shall never speak of this night again. Never. Ever. Understood?" Savannah said as she sat in the passenger seat of the rental car, shivering, her teeth chattering, water streaming off her hair, her bare feet and legs covered with mud up to her knees. She was holding her purse in her left hand and one of Marietta's sandals in her right.

Only one.

Dirk stopped the car in front of Granny's house and turned off the engine. Chuckling gleefully, he said, "Right. Get real. You know I'm going to torture you with this every day for the rest of our lives. No way *this* gets brushed under the rug."

She thought it over. Readjusted her expectations.

"Okay, I'll make you a deal. You don't tell Granny one word of what actually happened tonight—none of it," she said, "and you'll live to see the morning light."

"You got it, kid."

They found Gran wide awake and sitting in her comfy chair, reading her Bible. On the side table next to her was a crumpled tabloid newspaper. Granny considered both to be infallible sources of all things true.

"What in tarnation happened to you?" she said as she caught sight of her oldest granddaughter and her grandson-in-law. "Considerin' the lateness of the hour, I was halfway through plannin' your funerals, but I didn't reckon it'd be as bad as all *this*!" She waved a hand, indicating Savannah's sodden attire, dripping hair, and mud-caked legs.

"I'm so sorry, Granny," Savannah replied, lingering on the doormat. "We had a bit of car trouble and—"

"Don't go giving me that hooey. You never could lie worth a plug nickel, gal, so don't even bother."

Gran raised one delicate eyebrow as she took in every detail of the twosome's appearance. "*Okay*," she said once her evaluation was finished. "After the reunion shindig, you went up to Lookout Point for some hanky-panky, got caught in the rain and stuck in the mud."

Dirk turned to Savannah. "How'd she know where we were?"

Savannah sighed. "The color of the mud. It's redder up there than anyplace else in the county. Right, Gran?"

"Absolutely. I knew ever' time any of you kids went up to that den of iniquity to fornicate—or to come too dadgum close."

Savannah gave her grandmother an affectionate smile. "And only somebody who had visited that 'den of iniquity' would know such a thing. Right, Gran?"

Granny sniffed. "I've heard tale. Or maybe I've been up there once or twice in my time. But only with my husband, so . . ."

Nudging Savannah in the ribs with his elbow, Dirk said, "I can see now where you get your detecting skills."

Savannah nodded. "Let's just say, it wasn't a particularly windy day when that apple fell off the tree."

"The only question I have is," Gran continued, "why are you, Miss Savannah, so much worse off than your husband? He ain't the kinda man who'd have his wife get out and push a car that's mired in the mud. Hmmm."

Savannah sighed. "Gran, just once in a while, don't you reckon *some* things could remain a mystery?"

"Those are the words of a person with secrets to hide, so I'd say that whatever occurred, you, girl, were the culprit." Gran turned to Dirk. "If you would please, grandson, carry your wife into the bathroom yonder and hose her off in the shower."

Dirk gulped. "Carry her?"

"Most certainly. I sure don't want those muddy feet of hers on my clean floor."

Savannah grinned at him. "You carried me over the threshold on our honeymoon night."

"But that was one step."

Her grin started to fade. "Are you suggesting, big boy, that I'm a mite too heavy for you to hoist?"

"Why no. Not being a completely stupid man, I wouldn't dream of suggesting such a thing."

With only a slight groan, he scooped her into his arms and headed toward the bathroom. There was a brief moment of high drama when he tried to maneuver them both through the narrow doorway leading into the bath, but in the end, no romance novel hero had ever done it better.

As they disappeared into the bathroom, he added, "Let's just say, when I married you, babe, I got my money's worth."

Chapter 6

During her career as a law-enforcement officer, Savannah had been required to perform the sad task of informing the next of kin when their loved ones had passed. It had been her least favorite part of being a cop.

In the performance of that depressing duty, she had seen a wide range of reactions, from stoic bravery to numbing shock and uncontrolled hysteria.

But never in all her years had she witnessed the complete breakdown and devastation of a human being who had received bad news—until she told Marietta that her sexy, strapping sandals were a goner.

"No! No! It can't be true! Oh, Gaawwd! Tell me it ain't true!" Marietta shrieked, collapsing across Granny's sofa. Dramatically sprawled, legs apart, turquoise leopard-print knickers exposed, she pressed the back of her right hand to her forehead, while clutching the arm of the sofa with her left. "I can't believe it! I just can't believe it!"

Although Savannah had asked Dirk to be present when she broke the news to Marietta, she didn't blame him for jumping up from Gran's chair and hightailing it out the front door at the first sign of her sister's indecent exposure. Almost everyone who knew Marietta Reid was far more acquainted with her lingerie collection than they chose to be.

When someone misbehaved in that neck of the woods, it was commonly remarked that so-and-so had "shown their hind end." For some reason, Marietta took that phrase quite literally. Though usually only in the presence of males she found attractive.

"What's all the ruckus in here?" Gran said, charging into the living room, a dish towel in her hand.

When she saw her granddaughter draped across her furniture, writhing in distress like a cartoon blonde tied to a railroad track by a mustache-twirling villain in a long black cloak, she said, "Marietta, this had better be good, gal. You'd best have a powerful excuse for carrying on like a danged fool. And put your dress down and your legs together. We ain't having no hootchy-kootchy girl shows in my front room."

Marietta made a half attempt at correcting her posture, but the mournful wailing continued. Between sobs, she said, "You don't know what Savannah did, Gran. She totally annihilated my best pair of shoes."

"I know. I know. I saw."

"You saw?" Marietta turned on Savannah. "You let Gran see them, but you won't let me see them?"

Savannah donned her saddest, most compassionate face. "It's best," she said, "if you just remember them as they were. Trust me."

"But you let Gran see them! Maybe I can get them fixed."

Gran sat down abruptly on her chair, as though suddenly very tired. "Actually, Marietta, I saw one of them. And it was beyond help. You best work on gettin' over it."

Marietta fixed Savannah with an evil eye. "She did it on purpose. She murdered my shoes."

Gran wiped her face with the dish towel, settled back in her chair, and propped her feet up. Then she said in a calm, sweet voice, which Savannah wished she could emulate at moments of high stress, "Miss Marietta, I'm gonna say this to you one time. You need to listen and listen good. 'Cause if I have to get up from this chair on your account and go cut a hickory switch, you're gonna have something to bawl and carry on about."

Gran drew a deep breath and continued, "Girl, you gather your wits about you and mind your manners, or remove yourself from my house. Just as simple as that. You decide which it's gonna be. Right now."

Marietta bounced up from the sofa, having gone from grief to indignant fury in an instant. She snatched her purse off the coffee table. "Well! I know when I'm not welcome! Talk about adding insult to injury!"

As she marched toward the door, Gran added with equal grace and composure, "Okay. You've made your choice. And I'll thank you not to return to my home until you've had a change of attitude."

Marietta's exit was punctuated by a door slamming that rocked the house and rattled the glass knickknacks on a nearby shelf.

"I'm sorry," Savannah began. "I never meant to—"

"Of course you didn't." Gran sighed and closed her eyes for a moment, looking oh, so weary.

It occurred to Savannah that sometimes—times like these, when there were conflicts in the family—Gran actually looked her age. And that angered Savannah.

The thought that her grandmother would be troubled at all, especially by something like a pair of stupid hooker heels, seemed wrong to Savannah on so many levels.

"I can't take it like I used to," Gran said after a moment. "On the other hand, I reckon I could. But I choose not to."

Savannah sat on a chair near Gran's, reached over, and took her hand between her own. As always, she was surprised at how soft the older woman's skin was. Like a baby's. And she wondered, as she always did, why it should be so, that human beings were their softest at the beginning and the end of their lives.

"I don't blame you," Savannah said, stroking her grandmother's arthritic fingers. "Marietta knows better. You taught her better."

When Gran opened her eyes, Savannah saw tears brimming in them, and she felt like her heart would break.

"I tried to teach you all the same. The Lord above knows I did. But with some, it took, and with the others, it just didn't so much. I don't understand that. 'Train up a child in the way he should go,' the Good Book says, 'and when he is old, he will not depart from it.'"

Savannah shrugged. "Well, maybe Marietta's not old enough. Maybe she'll turn around yet."

"When she's ninety?"

Both women chuckled.

"Maybe she's a late bloomer," Savannah said.

"Might be, but either way, I'm afraid it won't be in time for me to see it."

"I wouldn't say that. I reckon that from up there in heaven, you'll be able to look down on us and see what's going on. If anybody can, it'll be you, keeping an eye on us, making sure things go well for us, if it's in your power to do so."

Gran squeezed her hand. "You know me well, Savannah girl. I reckon I won't ever be done raisin' you younguns."

Savannah looked into her grandmother's eyes, which were

the same shade of brilliant cobalt blue as hers, and said, "If someone had told you and Grandpa all those years ago what lay ahead . . . the heartaches you'd have with my dad, all us grand-kids, and the fact that you'd have to raise us, do you reckon you and he would've still gone up there that night to Lookout Point?"

Granny threw back her head and guffawed, the hearty sound of her laughter filling the little house, as it had for as long as Savannah could remember.

When she'd finally recovered herself, she said, "Lawdy, girl, the things you come up with sometimes. If I'd said somethin' like that to my grandma, she would've slapped me neckid and hid my clothes."

She wiped her tears of laughter away with a corner of the dish towel. "But in answer to your question, you're darned tootin' I would have. Your grandpa was one fine-lookin' hunk o' masculinity in his day, with a fierce, passionate nature. Knowin' what I know now, I would've raced that man to the top of that hill. And once I got him there and all to myself, I would have turned him ever' which way but loose."

As Savannah stood at the counter of her grandmother's kitchen and stirred the enormous bowl of carrot cake batter, she felt an almost overwhelming sense of guilt.

Living in a seaside resort town like San Carmelita, with its almost constant onshore ocean breezes, she had forgotten what summer afternoons in Georgia were like. Summer after-noons in almost any part of good old Dixie, for that matter.

As rivulets of sweat dripped into her eyes, stinging them, and streamed down the back of her neck, she silently cursed herself for not having gifted her grandmother with some sort of air conditioner over the years. While Gran claimed to be perfectly fine without one, Savannah couldn't imagine that any-one enjoyed being in a humid, one-hundred-degree room, let alone baking in one.

She vowed that as soon as she returned to California, the first thing she would do was order one of those energy-saving window units for Gran. Maybe even two. One for each end of the house. And then she would send her a couple of checks during the summer months to cover the extra expense on the electric bills.

"Man, if I'd known it was this hot here in this house today, I wouldn't have offered to come over and help y'all bake Gran's birthday cake," said her sister Vidalia from her position at the end of the table, where she sat, watching Savannah mix the batter and Alma gather the ingredients for the cream cheese frosting.

"Me either," said Jesup as she performed her most arduous chore of the afternoon—hoisting some iced tea to her lips and guzzling half the glass. "That's one of the main reasons I moved outta here and in with Darrell Abney. At least his trailer's air-conditioned."

"Those Abneys spend more time in jail than out," Savannah said over her shoulder. "Why didn't you buy Gran an AC or, better yet, get a place of your own?"

Jesup looked totally confused and more than a bit scandalized. "Now, why would I want to do a thing like that? I'd have to pay rent."

"I don't know," Savannah said. "A sense of independence maybe? The satisfaction that comes from knowing that you're an adult, that you're making your own way in the world?"

Jesup gave a snort and took another guzzle of iced tea. "If I get down in the dumps and wanna feel better, I go get another tattoo. Perks me right up. Don't tell Gran, but I've got 'em all over my butt now. Both cheeks. The one on the right's a big rooster, and the left one's of a devil—red face, horns, and everything—stickin' his tongue way out. You should see it."

Savannah rolled her eyes. "No, thank you. Lovely as it sounds."

As she poured the batter into the greased cake pans, Savannah could smell the fragrance of the cinnamon and other spices, as well as the pineapple and coconut. She could almost taste the cake now.

Maybe Jesup should take up baking as a way to fight depression, she thought. *It's less expensive, and Gran's not as likely to throw a conniption and faint dead away if she catches sight of her bent over in the shower.*

"Tattoos don't come cheap," she observed. "Who pays for yours?"

"Darrell's gonna give me one for my birthday. After that, I think I'm gonna dump him and take up with his brother Richie. He's got a job."

"Good idea. At least you have a fiscal plan for your future."

Alma giggled and shot Savannah a sly grin.

"What?" Jesup said. "Why are you laughing, Alma? Is she making fun of me?"

"Savannah wouldn't make fun of you," Alma replied.

"Only every time she opens her mouth to say somethin'," Vidalia added. "She's always been a smart aleck and a half."

The normally docile Alma whirled around, armed with a silver package of cream cheese in each hand. "Don't you say nothin' mean about Savannah! I'd hate to have to whup you, Jesup, but I will."

"Yeah, yeah." Jesup waved her off with one hand while refilling her tea glass from the nearby pitcher. "I'm scared plumb spitless. You're gonna beat me to a frazzle with some cream cheese.

I'm pretty sure you'd get the death penalty for that." Jesup saw something through the kitchen's screen door that caught her attention. "Speaking of the law, guess who just pulled into our backyard driveway."

Even before she looked up, Savannah had a feeling. For as long as she'd known him, she'd had a certain feeling when Tom Stafford was nearby. Apparently, being happily married to someone else hadn't changed that.

No sooner had Savannah popped the two round cake pans into the oven than her own special "someone else" came charging through the back door. The grimace on his face, the same one he got when he took a swig of sour milk, told her that it was, indeed, Sheriff Tom Stafford who had come calling.

"It's him," he announced as he rounded the table and joined Savannah, who had turned to wash her hands at the sink. "And he's got his Mr. Serious puss on."

Savannah's pulse rate increased by twenty points or so. She could feel the blood pounding in her ears.

"Reckon it's about last night?" she asked Dirk.

"I sure hope not. Otherwise, this five-star resort vacation of ours might be on its way down the crapper."

"What about last night?" Jesup wanted to know. "What happened last night?"

"I know," Vidalia stated. "I heard all about it this morning at the nail salon."

"Wait a minute," Dirk barked. "This wide-spot-in-the-road town has a frickin' nail salon?"

"Yeah. Three of them," Savannah replied. "And that doesn't include Marietta's hair salon. Why?"

"Why? Because I just drove forty-five minutes one way to take my suit to the dry cleaners. How can you have three nail salons and a hair salon and no dry cleaner?"

Jesup waved both hands. "Hold on a minute. I want to hear about what happened last night. What did they say there at the salon, Vi?"

"It's going to have to wait," Savannah said as she watched her old beau walk up to the screen door and stand there, filling its frame with his oversized, overly muscular body. He had his burly arms crossed over his chest, and as Dirk had observed, he was wearing his most officious scowl.

She recognized it immediately.

It was the look most lawmen—and women—wore when they truly meant business.

They practiced it in the mirror more often than they practiced their marksmanship at the shooting range.

She gulped and thought, *Oh, goody.*

Chapter 7

Over the past twenty-plus years, Savannah had often wondered if Tom Stafford still had feelings for her. And she'd hoped he did, if for no other reason than that her vanity demanded it.

After the decades she had spent pining over him, it seemed only fair that memories of her had haunted at least a few of his nights.

She didn't require much. No hand-wringing, midnight floor pacing, or suicidal regrets. Just a bit of tossing and turning, some pangs of conscience, and a bit of wondering about what might have been.

At the reunion the night before, she had seen him casting wistful glances her way, and she could have sworn she saw regret in his eyes.

But that was last night.

Now he was sitting in her granny's chair, on the edge of the cushion, leaning toward her, his green eyes boring into hers. From her seat on the sofa she could have reached over and touched him.

But she had never been less inclined to do so.

Gone was Tommy, the sweet boy who had snuggled with her, kissed her, and made passionate love to her in the peach orchards. Sheriff Tom Stafford was a man now, fully overgrown, wearing a khaki uniform and a star on his chest, which he appeared to take too seriously.

"Don't go battin' them big blue eyes at me, Savannah Reid," he was saying. "And don't go givin' me no abbreviated answers to my questions. I want to know exactly what you did from the time I last saw you until this minute right here. And don't leave out nothin'."

Dirk had been quiet for too long. He reached over and put his arm around Savannah's shoulders. "My wife already answered your questions, Stafford," he said. "Until you say why you're interrogating her, she's done talking unless she's got a lawyer present. Got it?"

Tom never took his eyes off Savannah. "Is that true, Savannah? Are you the kind of wife that does everything her husband tells her to do? You never seemed like that kinda gal to me."

She knew he was just trying to make her mad, to get her riled up so that she would say something she hadn't intended to.

And it was very nearly working.

But not quite.

She fixed him with an even stare that matched his own gunfighter eyes and said, "You tell me why you want an accounting of my whereabouts beyond what I've already told you, or I'm going to lawyer up."

A look of impatience and frustration crossed Stafford's face, but he quickly wiped it away. "You two are cops. Well, you are, Coulter, and you used to be, Savannah. You know I don't have to tell you nothin'."

"And we all know that goes both ways." Savannah sat back

on the sofa, crossed her legs, and try to appear as nonchalant as possible. "What's going on, Tom? Has Miss Prissy Pot decided to press charges, after all?"

"Yeah," Dirk interjected, "'cause if that's the case, you saw it all happen there at the school. Why does it matter what we did or didn't do after the reunion last night?"

Tom looked from one to the other. Savannah could practically see his mental wheels whirring as she searched her own mind for an answer to his line of questioning. Finally, he took a deep breath and said, "Jeanette's not pressing charges for anything. Least wise, I don't think so."

"Then what's all this about?" Savannah asked.

"She's missing."

His words hung in the air, heavier than the summer humidity.

"What do you mean, 'missing'?" Savannah asked, breaking the silence.

"Just that," he replied. "She was supposed to bring that new purple Cadillac convertible of hers to the dealer this morning. She'd made a big stink about the fact that she was comin' by. Something about her not liking the leather on the backseat. But Arthur says she never showed. When I called the house— the big Barnsworth mansion south of town, where she's still livin', even though he's dead—the maid answered and told me she hasn't seen her all day. And her bed hasn't been slept in."

"Maybe she got lucky after the reunion and forgot about the leather on her backseat," Savannah offered.

"She didn't show for her pedicure at the nail salon."

"Which one?" Dirk grumbled under his breath. "You have so many."

Savannah gulped as a sinking feeling swept through her.

Someday the world might stop turning. The seven seas might dry up, and time might come to an end. But the vain and meticulously groomed Miss Jeanette would never, ever miss a pedicure.

"Damn," Savannah whispered.

Tom heard her. "Yeah."

They all three sat in ominous silence.

Jeanette Barnsworth had gone missing. Within hours of an altercation with Savannah. In the presence of witnesses.

In the presence of law enforcement.

A softer look crossed Tom's face, and he even gave Savannah a slight smile. "You know I'd rather be anywhere but here right now, don't cha, girl?" he said, his deep voice tremulous. "I care about you and your family. I really do. The last thing I want to do is accuse you of anything. Let alone somethin' like murder."

"Then *don't* accuse her," Dirk said, his own voice hard and cold. "Dammit, man, if you're such a good friend of hers and this family, then cut her some slack. If you know Savannah as well as you claim to, you know she has never done anything criminal in her life, let alone a homicide."

Tom bristled. "I'm being a better friend to her than you think. If it was anybody else, I would've at least dragged them into the station to question them. And I'd probably have them behind bars. So you better just cool your heels, buddy, and stay out of this."

"That's asking a lot, Tom," Savannah said. "You're a good old boy yourself. Chivalrous and all. If your old lady was in the same predicament, there's no way you'd stay out of it. You'd be right there in the thick of things, stirring up as much trouble as you could."

He thought it over for several moments, then said, "Okay. Tell me the truth, the whole truth, and nothin' but the truth about what you did last night, and I'll leave you alone. At least for now."

Savannah could feel her pulse racing and her body starting to tremble as she struggled to make what might be one of the most important decisions of her life.

As a private detective, she told lies. Many lies. Everything from little white fibs to big, black, soul-threatening whoppers, and that hadn't bothered her conscience. At least not enough to cause her any lost sleep.

That was just part of the job.

But in her personal life she tried to be as honest as possible. Even if it was embarrassing or got her in trouble or might be hard for another person to hear, she almost always chose to tell the truth.

If Granny Reid had taught her nothing else, it was the value of honesty and forthright speech.

Other than smacking Jeanette Barnsworth's jaws, she had done nothing wrong the night before. And she certainly hadn't murdered anyone. Why not just tell the truth and let the chips fall where they might?

Because she had been a cop, and she knew how cops thought.

If she were Sheriff Tom Stafford right now, and if she knew for certain that Jeanette Barnsworth had been murdered last night, she would, without a doubt, know who her number one suspect was.

The woman who had harbored resentment toward the victim for decades. The woman who had exchanged harsh words with the victim the evening of her disappearance. The woman who had assaulted the victim only a few hours before she disappeared.

Savannah Reid.

And then there was the splash.

Savannah couldn't get that sound out of her mind. She knew she would hear it for the rest of her life.

Out there on that hill, amid the fragrant pine trees, in the midst of nature—an unnatural sound.

Even then, it had chilled Savannah's soul to hear it. And now that she knew her childhood enemy was missing, had probably come to a bad end, some part of her knew the sound she'd heard was connected to that disappearance.

She hadn't seen anything last night, when she had gotten out of the car and walked around in the pouring rain. She had even peered over the edge of the cliff to the lake below and had seen nothing unusual. But something deep inside her knew Jeanette Barnsworth, or what remained of her, was at the bottom of that cliff.

She looked into the eyes of the man she had loved for most of her childhood and for more of her adulthood than she wanted to admit, even to herself. She saw his affection for her and his hope that she would give him a solid alibi, something he could use to exclude her as a suspect.

She also saw his suspicion and his determination to follow his duty wherever the evidence might lead.

She thought of the sandal that had slipped off her foot as she trudged around in the mud. The high heel she had not been able to find in the rain and the storm. The highly identifiable shoe she had just worn to a party with one hundred or more of her fellow schoolmates in attendance.

The shoe was still there somewhere, waiting to be found by the all too observant Sheriff Stafford or one of his deputies.

She drew a deep breath and said, "Okay, Tom, you want the truth? Here it is. After my little squabble with Jeanette there by the back door of the school—"

"When you knocked her out cold."

"I didn't hit her that hard. She's obviously got a glass jaw. Anyway, after my conversation with you, Dirk and I walked to our car and drove away. We came back here to Granny's, took a shower, and went to bed."

He stared at her so intently that she felt like he was climbing right inside her, into her mind and soul. It was all she could do to hold the gaze and not to look away.

Finally, he said, "That's it? That's all?"

She nodded.

He turned to Dirk. "And you stand by that, Coulter? That's your statement, too?"

"Absolutely." Dirk stood and pulled Savannah to her feet. "If you don't mind, Sheriff Stafford, we're going to get on with our day, and I suggest that you do the same."

To Savannah's surprise and enormous relief, Tom stood, as well, and walked to the door. He stood there for a moment, as though considering whether to say anything more. But in the end, all he did was give her a long, sad, and hauntingly tender look before opening the door, walking out, and closing it quietly behind him.

Savannah turned to Dirk and saw every fear that she was feeling in his eyes.

He held out his arms to her.

She fell into them, buried her face against his chest, and began to cry.

Chapter 8

Needing a bit of privacy to discuss their course of action, Savannah and Dirk decided to leave the tiny house, filled with listening ears, and take a drive around the countryside.

Whether their destination would be Lookout Point and whether their mission would include the retrieval of a certain lost sandal—those would be the two major talking points of their intended discussion.

All went as planned when they were sneaking out of the house, but Granny nabbed them just as they were about to get into the car.

"I don't mind telling you," she said as she snatched the keys out of Dirk's hand, "that I am highly perturbed and disturbed." She turned to Savannah, blue eyes blazing. "I'm hearing from your sister that after the get-together at the school last night, you slapped ole Jeanette plumb silly."

Savannah shrugged and muttered, "Didn't take long. She was most the way there already."

"I'm sure it didn't. That girl's always been dumb as a box of hair. But that's beside the point, and you know it. I always taught you kids that it's wrong to lay hands on another person in a spirit of violence."

Savannah sighed and repeated the time-worn admonition. "Never lift your hand to another human being, unless they hit you first. Then beat the tar outta 'em, so's they know not to ever do it again."

"It appears your memory's better than your self-control."

"Gran, you don't know what she said to me before I smacked her. I had good reason."

"I'm sure it was something vile and nasty. I also know that there's more than one way to assault another person—and not all of them have to do with slaps and punches. I know that words can be the cruelest weapons of all. But for your own sake, if not for hers, you shoulda kept your hands to yourself."

Dirk stepped forward and gently patted Granny's shoulder. "What you're saying is true, Gran. And I'm sure that Savannah regrets what she did. But, frankly, that ship's done sailed, and we have bigger fish to fry right now."

"So I gathered. I can't say's I'm accustomed to entertaining the county sheriff in my front room. What did he want with you?"

Savannah weighed the pros and cons of telling the same set of lies to her grandmother that she had given Tom Stafford. But she knew better. Gran was far more astute than Tom, good cop or not, would ever be.

Besides, Gran had seen the red mud. Gran knew about Lookout Point.

Plus, there was that other pesky detail: Gran was the closest thing Savannah had to an alibi, false though it might be.

"He told us that Jeanette's missing," Savannah said. "Apparently, nobody's seen her since she left the school last night."

"Right after you cleaned her clock for her," Granny supplied.

"Exactly," Dirk said. "If it turns out that she really is missing, and there's no innocent explanation for it, that's not gonna look good for Savannah."

Savannah's heart ached as she saw the full realization of the situation register in her grandmother's eyes. To be the cause of pain or concern for the woman she loved most on earth was almost more than she could bear.

"I'm so sorry, Gran. You are absolutely right. I shouldn't have hit her, no matter what she said. If I could take that moment back, I'd do it all so differently. I'd just tell her to kiss my rear end, and walk away."

"I know you would, sugar," Granny said. "What's done is done. And as your husband just said, we got other fish to fry, and they might turn out to be whoppers."

Savannah couldn't disagree. "I suppose they might. Hope for the best, prepare for the worst, and all that."

Gran nodded. "That's just what we'll do. And all's going to turn out well, because other than smackin' her somethin' fierce, you didn't do anything wrong, let alone illegal, last night."

Savannah wasn't sure if it was a question or a statement. But she answered, anyway. "That's absolutely true, Gran. Whacking her was the worst thing I did to her or anybody all night long. I swear it."

"I believe you, granddaughter." Gran reached out, placed her hand on Savannah's cheek, and gave her a sweet smile. Then her expression turned somber and all business. "I reckon when Tom Stafford and y'all were havin' your little chitchat there in my front room, he must've inquired as to your whereabouts last night, after the party."

Savannah gulped. This was going to be the worst part. "Yes. He did mention it."

"And what did you tell him?"

"I told him that after the reunion we drove back to your house, took a shower, and went to bed."

Gran was silent for a while. Then she said, "Did he ask you what time you got back here to my house?"

"No," Dirk answered. "He didn't. Obviously, Tommy boy's not as good a cop as he thinks he is."

Or he's afraid he might hear something he doesn't want to, Savannah thought, *like that his old girlfriend killed somebody. His old girlfriend whom he still has some feelings for.*

But she didn't share her ruminations with Gran and Dirk. The last thing she needed now was for Dirk to get any more jealous than he already was.

Meanwhile, Gran wasn't saying anything. But Savannah could tell that she was weighing the situation and reaching a decision.

Finally, she spoke, and the deadly serious tone of her voice sent a chill through Savannah's soul. "Okay. If Sheriff Tom Stafford all of a sudden becomes a better cop and asks you what time it was when you got back here, you'd best make sure that I know what you told him. As it stands, I'm not sure what time you came home. I didn't look at the clock when you walked through the door. So, whatever time you say it was, that's what we're goin' by."

Savannah stood there, looking at her grandmother, who, as far as Savannah knew, had never told a lie in her life. And her heart ached that she was the cause of her being in this position.

If necessary, her grandmother would lie to protect her. Because she loved her, and because Gran knew she hadn't killed anyone. Knowing that made Savannah feel warm and safe and terrible all at the same time.

She tried to speak but couldn't for the tight knot in her throat.

Dirk spoke for her. In a quiet, gentle tone, he said, "We left the reunion about eleven, Granny. If Sheriff Stafford asks when we got back here, we'll probably tell him around eleven fifteen . . . more or less."

Gran nodded once, then turned and walked slowly back to the house. As Savannah watched her, she noticed that the usual spring in her step was gone. She didn't look like Granny Reid. She looked like a tired old woman.

And Savannah wished the ground would open up and swallow her.

"Where's a good old-fashioned Georgia sinkhole when you need one?" she muttered.

"What?" Dirk asked.

"Nothing," she replied with a sigh. "Let's get going."

"We can't keep driving in circles, Van," Dirk told her as, once again, they left McGill's city limits and headed down a monotonous county highway that led through nothing but endless cotton fields. "We have to decide. Are we going to go up there or not?"

Savannah reached over and turned the car's air-conditioning up a notch. Then she readjusted the vent so that it would blow directly on her face. She was beginning to think she would never be cool and comfortable again. How had she stood this weather as a child?

You stood the heat and humidity because you didn't have a choice, she told herself. *But you do now,* her inner voice added. *And you'd better make the right one, or you may live to regret it.*

"Let's just run through it one more time," she said, "in case there's something we forgot or something we didn't think of."

"There's always something to forget. Always something you don't think of," Dirk replied with a sniff. "The prisons are filled with guys who thought they'd thought of everything."

She shot him an irritated look. "Gee, thanks."

"I guess that didn't help much, huh?"

"You think?"

He reconsidered. "But all those dudes in jail, they're not nearly as smart as you and me. We can probably think of everything."

"Seriously, Dirk. Watch what you say. I'm not doing so well right now. I don't recall when I was this scared. I can literally feel my guts shaking inside me. Did you ever feel like that?"

He nodded solemnly. "A few times. Right before I got the runs, so watch out. If you need me to pull over so's you can do your business there in the cotton patch, just let me know."

Savannah felt her last thread of patience snap. "I mean it, Dirk. This is not the time to be funny. I'm so not in the mood."

He looked confused. "Funny? I, oh, yeah. Okay."

They traveled on in silence past a few more fields. Finally, he said, "Let's run over it one more time."

Steeling herself, she said, "Yeah. And then we're going to decide. Okay? Because I can't stand this sitting-on-the-fence business much longer."

"All right." He reached into his pocket and pulled out a plastic zip-top bag full of cinnamon sticks and tossed it into her lap. "Gimme one of those things, would ya?"

As she handed him a stick and he poked the end of it in his mouth, it occurred to her that the stress of the situation might cause him to relapse with his smoking.

Was there no end to the consequences of a single slap down?

"Okay," he said. "If we don't go up to Lookout Point and find your shoe—"

"And Jeanette's body is at the bottom of that cliff, and the cops find the sandal—"

"You're dead meat."

"Delicately put."

"And true," he said.

"Or maybe it's all just a bunch of hooey, and Jeanette shacked up with somebody last night somewhere and hasn't gotten back to town yet. In which case, I have nothing to worry about."

"Or she was driving home from the reunion, had some kind of hemorrhage in her brain as a result of you hitting her, drove off the road and into a ditch, and nobody's found her yet."

She gave him another dirty look. "Gee, we can only hope."

"You're so sure you heard that splash—"

"I did. And soon after it, I saw a set of taillights going down the hill. Like somebody dumped something into the lake and then took off."

"Or got finished with their make-out business and went home."

"Nobody was parked in that lower spot when we drove by, going up the hill," Savannah said. "I know. I looked."

"So they got there after we did and finished quicker than us." A self-satisfied smirk crossed his face. "Not every guy takes his time and stops the elevator at every floor like I do."

She rolled her eyes. "That's what I've always loved about you, your sexual prowess and your humility."

"If we go up there now," he said, "we're going to have to traipse all around in the mud to find that shoe."

"Since when were you worried about getting your old sneakers dirty?"

"Since I realized that we'd be leaving a bazillion footprints in the dirt. How long do you think it would take your old honey to pour some plaster in those prints, then come knocking on Granny's door, wanting to check out my sneakers and your loafers?"

"Good point," she conceded. "But what if the shoe's lying somewhere close to the road? What if we can just lean over and pick it up?"

"That's kinda a big *if*, but I suppose it's possible."

"We'll leave tire marks on the road."

He shook his head. "I don't think so. Water was running down that road like a river last night. And it was still raining when we went to bed there at Granny's. The mud's probably all washed away."

They reached a T in the road. Dirk stopped the car, and they sat there for a long time, deciding.

"Which way, kiddo?" he said. "Turn left, circle back to town, forget the whole thing, and take our chances? Or turn right and head up to Lookout Point?"

As it did in moments of high stress, time seemed to slow for Savannah. A thousand thoughts raced through her mind, but she spoke only one word.

"Right."

"You got it, babe," he said as he took the chosen road. "I'm glad you said that. I figure we have to at least try. If something goes wrong, we'll find a way to live with it. But if everything goes in the toilet, and we didn't even give it a shot . . ."

When she didn't reply, he reached over and nudged her arm. "We'll be careful," he told her. "Besides, you mark my words. This is all just a bunch of crap. Jeanette's gonna turn up, fine and dandy. And before sunset, Stafford'll be knocking on your grandma's front door, apologizing to us and asking for an invitation to her birthday party. Right?"

Savannah wanted to answer him, to tell him that she absolutely agreed, and that this was all much ado about nothing.

But she couldn't.

She'd heard that splash.

All she could do was give him a halfhearted nod.

"This place looks a lot different in the daylight," Dirk told Savannah as he stopped the car near the lower-level make-out spot. "It was a lot more romantic in the moonlight and then in the pouring-down rain, with you running around in your Skivvies."

She groaned and shook her head. "At least you have some fond memories of the occasion. I'd hate to think this was all for naught."

They cast some furtive glances up and down the road and, seeing that all was clear, got out of the car.

As they walked to the edge of the pavement, which was, as he had predicted, clear of all mud, Savannah began mumbling under her breath.

"You told me to tell you when you're talking to yourself," he said. "You're doing it again."

"I'm not talking to myself. Not this time, anyway," she told him.

"Practicing your defense speech?"

"No, Mr. Smarty-Pants. If you must know, I was praying."

"Praying? It's not that desperate yet, is it?"

"Gran taught me that it's best to start praying before things turn desperate. You know, get a head start on it."

He nodded thoughtfully. "That makes sense, I guess. Then if everything goes to hell in a handbasket, you've got some retroactive prayers already racked and loaded. Can't hurt."

"I don't think Gran used those words exactly, but that was the gist."

They stood at the pavement's edge and stared into the area beyond, between the road and the cliff's edge. Just off the road there was soft red mud galore. Other than a few tracks, which Savannah was pretty sure had been made by a rabbit, the surface was unmarked.

"There's no way we could walk on that and not leave our signatures," Dirk observed.

"No kidding," she replied. "We might as well write our names and leave our handprints, like the movie stars at Grauman's Theatre."

Looking around at the lush green forest and through the break in the trees where the lake waters glittered in the sunlight, Dirk said, "It is kinda pretty up here. Smells nice, too. This is what pine trees *really* smell like. Not that junk in the spray cans that you use in the bathroom after you—"

"Do you mind? Can we discuss the finer points of room deodorizers *after* we find Marietta's stupid shoe?"

"Oh, yeah. Okay. Here, let's get some sticks to poke stuff with."

After selecting a couple of small, straight branches from the other side of the road, they walked back and forth along the edge of the pavement. Every few feet or so they used the sticks to gently lift a pinecone, a clump of leaves, or a discarded beer can. After looking under and around the items, they carefully returned them to their resting places and continued their search.

When twenty minutes or so had passed, Savannah stopped to wipe the sweat off her face and catch her breath. She could feel that her bra cups were saturated and the freshness from last evening's shower was long gone. She'd need another one as soon as she got back to Gran's.

Then she considered the nonexistence of shower facilities at the city jail and renewed her search. She even "racked and loaded" a few more prayers in the process.

At the thirty-minute point, she was about to scream with frustration when she heard her husband say, "Hey, babe. I've got good news and bad news. Which do you want first?"

"The bad. I always want to get the worst out of the way."

"Okay. It's at least ten feet away. Maybe twelve."

"What? Oh! Oh! You see it?" She ran over to him, as excited as a kid on an Easter egg hunt, if finding the egg was a matter of life and death.

"Yeah. That was the good news."

"Where is it?"

"Over there, by that broken log with the moss on it."

After a few moments, she spotted the shoe—a bit of rhine-stone sparkle in the greenery. "I see it," she said, less enthusiastic than before. "It looks like the strap's tangled around the log."

"That was my second bit of bad news. I didn't want to hit you with it all at once."

"Thank you."

"You get depressed easy."

"Yeah, well . . ."

"Especially since you started this 'change o' life' business."

She turned to him, gave him a long, hard look, and said, "You know, statistics show that women commit more murders during menopause than at any other time in their lives."

"Really? Is that true?"

"If you keep talking about how cranky I am now that I'm in it, you might just find out."

He gave her a grin and a wink. "Let's see if we can find us a twelve-foot stick. Unless you wanna fool around again, and then we could use my—"

"You're gonna die, boy. You're tap-dancin' on a tightrope over a swamp with a hungry momma alligator right under you."

"A menopausal alligator."

"Those are the worst kind, and don't you forget it."

After finding several long limbs, only to discover that their choices were mere inches too short, Dirk finally located one that would reach the sandal. But it took another twenty minutes of futile and frustrating attempts before Savannah was able to hook the end of it through the shoe and out its open toe.

Carefully and ever so slowly, scarcely daring to breathe, she pulled it free.

"Now, don't drop it," he advised as she balanced it on the forked end of the stick and eased it toward them an inch at a time.

"Any more useful advice like that," she said, "and you get this stick in your left ear."

"Empty threat if ever I heard one."

By the time several more stress-filled minutes had passed, she had the sandal more than halfway to the road. For the first time since Savannah had seen it, seemingly beyond their reach, she began to think their little foray into the dark world of crime-scene tampering might prove to be successful, after all.

Then she heard it.

And felt it.

A buzzing, like that of an angry bumblebee, in the back pocket of her jeans. Along with a cheerful little jingle that she had found particularly irritating, so she'd chosen it as Vidalia's ringtone. Overly excited, frenzied, and frenetic, it had seemed appropriate at the time. And even more so now.

"Shoot!" she said. "Dang Vidalia's mangy hide. That girl always did have lousy timing."

"I'll answer it." He reached toward her rear end.

"Don't you dare touch me! If that dingbat sister of mine makes me drop this thing . . ."

"You're right. Ignore it. Just keep doing what you're doing. You've almost got it."

She turned slightly to her left, bringing the end of the branch and the dangling high heel toward him. He wasted no time getting into a squatting catcher's position, as though preparing to receive a third-strike fastball.

The second it was within his reach, he snatched it off the limb, clasped it to his chest, mud and all, and let out a series of deafening celebratory yelps, which he usually reserved for when his favorite team won the World Series or one of his least favorite boxers hit the mat.

Savannah tossed the branch back on the other side of the road, then yanked the phone out of her back pocket.

"Yeah, Vi. What's up?" she asked breathlessly, trying to sound casual and not like a woman whose bacon had just been pulled, sizzling, out of a smoking skillet.

"I thought you wuz never gonna answer," Vidalia scolded. "It musta rang a dozen times or more."

"I was a little busy."

"Me too. But I still took the time to call you."

"Why?"

"Why what?"

Savannah had an awful thought. "Oh, no. You didn't let Gran's cake burn, did you? That was a scratch cake, girl, and if it's burnt, you're gonna be measuring all those teaspoons and quarter cups and stuff to make the next one."

"No. The cake's fine. Alma looked after it."

"Okay. Then what do you want?"

Savannah watched as Dirk opened the car's passenger door and tossed the muddy shoe onto the floorboard. Then he motioned for her to get inside. She did, and he closed the door behind her.

"What I want is to tell you some news that I just heard," Vidalia was saying. "It's about your long-lost friend Jeanette."

A thought, an evil thought, passed through Savannah's brain. *If that gal's not really dead, after all I just went through getting that damn shoe, I'm gonna kill her myself.*

But she quickly discarded it and said as demurely as she could manage, "Really? Do tell."

Vidalia happily obliged. "I just got a call from Butch. And he said that Tom called him a while ago there at the garage and told him to get hold of the biggest tow truck he could get his hands on, even if he had to go out of town to get it, and bring it up to Lookout Point."

Dirk had started the car, and they were descending the hill. But Savannah felt as though her stomach had already hit the bottom.

"Lookout Point?" she said, shooting Dirk a look of alarm.

Instantly, he was all ears.

"Yep," Vidalia continued. "Seems one of them Henderson boys, the least one, I think, was out there on the lake, fishing, first thing this mornin'. And he saw something in the water 'bout halfway up the hill there to the point. You know, where we all used to stop and smooch if somebody'd already claimed the spot at the—"

"Yes, yes, I know the place. What did the littlest Henderson boy see?"

"Something purple. There in the water. Well, actually, just below the surface of the water."

Savannah gulped. "Purple? Like the dress Jeanette wore to the reunion last night?"

"Oh, no. Something way bigger than that. Something like that big purple Cadillac convertible of hers."

It was only after she had hung up that Savannah realized she hadn't told her sister good-bye.

Like it mattered.

Like anything mattered right now. Anything that wasn't some gaudy, horrid shade of purple.

"What is it? What did she say?" she could hear Dirk asking as though from far away. "Come on, Van. Talk to me."

"That was an even bigger splash than I thought," she whispered, more to herself than to him.

"What the hell are you talking about, woman? Spit it out! I'm dyin' here!"

But she never answered him.

Because they had reached the bottom of the hill, and there, blocking their path, was a big black-and-white patrol car with its red and blue lights flashing. Two other similar units flanked it on either side.

And inside the center car, glaring at them thorough his dark wraparound sunglasses, sat one very angry Sheriff Thomas Stafford.

Chapter 9

After Savannah's initial thought, which included a string of colorful curse words, it occurred to her that they should have put the muddy high heel in the trunk. Or, at least, she should have shoved it under the seat beneath her.

But Sheriff Stafford's radio car was much too close to their own vehicle for her to perform any furtive movements. Especially the shoving of evidence under a seat. If there was a gesture that every street cop knew when they saw it, that was the one.

As if reading her mind, Dirk said, "Don't lean down. He'll see you."

"I know. I won't."

"What are we going to say if he asks about it?"

"If all else fails, we might have to tell them the truth."

"Hell, I hope not. Surely, it won't come to *that*."

With her foot, Savannah nudged her purse closer to the shoe, partially, but not completely, concealing its sparkly muddiness.

At that moment she felt the passing urge to snatch Marietta bald.

Her and her stupid shoes.

If only she'd been wearing her sensible black pumps, they never would've fallen off her feet, and she wouldn't be sitting here, doing the High Noon Gunslinger Stare Down with Tom Stafford.

Then things went from bad to worse.

"Driver and passenger," Stafford shouted as he opened his door and stepped out of his unit. "Exit your vehicle. Slowly."

Savannah saw to her shock and horror that he had drawn his weapon and was pointing it at them.

As he had directed, she and Dirk cautiously and calmly got out of their car.

"Raise your hands," he demanded.

Savannah noticed that the other two deputies, who had also left their vehicles and were standing on either side of Stafford, had not drawn their weapons. She knew both of them and at one time had been their friends. Rather than meeting her eyes, they were staring down at ground in front of them and looking miserable.

She and Dirk followed Stafford's directions and raised their hands.

But one quick sideways look at Dirk told her that he was furious. As was she. Never in her wildest fantasies had she ever imagined that this moment would come, that her childhood sweetheart would be holding her and her husband at gunpoint.

"Oh, come on, Tommy," she said, half joking, half pleading. "What's going on here? What's this all about?"

"Shut up and get down on your knees. Both of you. Right now."

Savannah's temper soared. She dropped her hands down

to her sides and started walking toward him. "I most certainly will *not* get down on my knees. What the hell's wrong with you, boy?"

She heard Dirk call her name and registered the alarm in his voice. But she ignored him. Walking up to Stafford, she pushed his pistol aside and stood so close that her chest brushed his.

"You oughta be ashamed of yourself, Tommy Lee Stafford," she shouted up into his face. "How *dare* you draw a gun on me! Why, I should slap you upside the head for pullin' a stunt like that!"

To her surprise, and certainly to her relief, he reholstered his weapon. He even removed his sunglasses and stuck them in his shirt pocket.

Now that she could see his eyes, she knew that her words had had their intended effect. He *did* look ashamed.

She decided to press her point a bit further. "If you wanted to talk to me or my husband, you could've just walked over to our car and done so in a civil manner. You don't have to treat us like armed and dangerous felons."

She realized she had gone a little too far when his face turned red again with anger.

"For all I know, the two of you *are* felons," he yelled back. "Cold-blooded murderers, armed and dangerous. What the hell are you two doing up here at my crime scene?"

She shrugged and tried to look as innocent as a kindergartner with a candy-smeared face. "What crime? What scene?"

"I think you know. I think you knew this morning, when I was talking to you both there at your grandma's house. I think you were lying your asses off to me, and you both know how much we cops just *love* gettin' lied to."

He pushed her an arm's length away from him and gave her a head-to-toe scan that was much more thorough than that

105

given by any airport security apparatus. She felt naked and exposed—and not in any sexual sort of way.

It was far worse than that.

Then he turned to Dirk, who had walked up to join them, and gave him the same once-over.

"What's that mud on the front of your shirt?" he asked Dirk.

Dirk looked down and shrugged. "I don't know. Dirt, I guess. There seems to be a lot of it around here. Along with pine trees. You should probably check me for pine needles, too."

"Don't get smart with me, Coulter. You know what I mean."

Savannah tensed, expecting Dirk to flare up.

But he didn't. He gave Tom an even, calm look and said, "No, actually, I *don't* know what you mean, Sheriff Stafford. Maybe you should explain why you ordered my wife and me out of our car at gunpoint and are making a big deal about the fact that I have some mud on my shirt. I don't know about here in Georgia, but in California there's nothing illegal about driving down the road or getting dirty."

Savannah took a step back from Tom and was trying to decide what to do next when they all heard the chugalugging of a large vehicle coming in their direction.

A moment later, it rounded the curve in the road, and an enormous tow truck appeared, with her brother-in-law at the wheel. Butch pulled up behind the parked cop cars and sat, looking at the assemblage, a worried expression on his usually placid face.

"All right," Tom said, turning to his deputies. "We got our truck and work to do. Stick him in your car, Jesse. And, Martin, you put her in yours. Then let's get to it."

Savannah's heart sank. The last thing she wanted to do was spend the next few hours caged in the back of a hot patrol car, separated from Dirk.

She reached over and poked Stafford in the ribs, what she hoped was a reasonably companionable gesture, but not overly familiar. "Come on, Tom. Seriously. We were just taking a little drive today. You know, checking out the local hot spots."

"Yeah," Dirk interjected. "We'd already taken in all the museums and the ballet and opera, and this make-out spot was the last on our to-see-and-do list. How were we supposed to know that you boys were coming up here to . . . well . . . do whatever it is that you've gotta do?"

When Tom didn't answer right away, Savannah could see that he was thinking it over. Perhaps even leaning toward leniency. She hoped that his former affection toward her would win out over his cop's instincts.

Apparently, it did, because he said, "We got a tip that there's a car, a purple car, in the water at the bottom of the cliff. A Cadillac convertible."

"Do you reckon it's Jeanette?" Savannah asked.

Tom gave her a derisive sniff and said, "Well, now, you tell me, gal. How many purple Cadillac convertibles you figure we got in the fine metropolis of McGill? In this whole dadgum county, for that matter? Of course it's her car. Once we get it pulled to the top of the cliff, I reckon we'll find out if she's in it or not." He looked back and forth between her and Dirk. "Unless the two of you wanna go ahead and tell me right now. I've got a feeling y'all have known since last night."

Savannah locked eyes with him and said with all sincerity, "Tom, I swear to you, neither one of us has any idea whether or not Jeanette's in that car. I give you my solemn word on it."

A sense of relief swept over her as she uttered the words. It felt good to be able to tell the truth for a change.

And Stafford seem to register her emotion, as well.

"All right," he said. "I won't lock you up in the cages. But don't you leave, either one of you. And you stay out of our way. You hear?"

Savannah gave him the benefit of one of her dimpled smiles. She figured Dirk would be okay with it, under the circumstances. "We hear you, Sheriff," she said. "Loud and clear. And if you need any help, we could always—"

"I won't. I done warned you. Stay out of my way, or by gum, you'll wish you had."

Savannah sat on the hood of her rental car and thanked the heavens above that she wasn't stuck in the back of a hot, stuffy cop car. Two hours had passed, and absolutely nothing had been accomplished.

Dirk sat next to her, less patient, less grateful.

"If this is the way law enforcement operates around here," he grumbled, "I'm surprised the crime rate is as low as they claim. These stooges couldn't catch a dog with one leg."

"Maybe not, but these stooges, as you call them, have still got badges and guns with bullets. I'd keep my voice down if I were you."

Sheriff Stafford and Butch were arguing, as they had been for hours, about the feasibility of pulling Jeanette's convertible out of the lake and up the cliff.

"Sheriff," Butch was saying, "I know you want to get your hands on that car, but I'm telling you now, it ain't gonna happen."

Tom Stafford was pacing back and forth at the edge of the pavement, his hands thrust deep into his trouser pockets and an ugly scowl on his face.

Savannah knew the look. She knew the pacing. And she knew that this was Tom at his worst. She didn't envy her calm, peace-loving brother-in-law.

What Butch had been trying to explain to the sheriff for far too long would have made sense to anyone else. Anyone except a police officer who was determined to recover what might be the most important piece of evidence in a homicide investigation.

She understood Butch's misgivings about the recovery. But she totally related to Tom and his desire to have that car on dry ground.

"This here cliff ain't all that stable nohow," Butch was telling him again. "And now that it's been rained on and all softened up, there's no way it'd support even the weight of this truck, let alone the strain from lifting that heavy car, too."

"Then stay back here on the pavement," Tom argued.

"I done told you, the cables ain't nearly long enough to reach all the way across here to that cliff and then way down to the water."

"No, no, no. There has to be a way. We've got to get it up here," Tom shot back. "If you don't know how to do it proper like, then just say so."

Butch bristled, and Savannah saw he was clenching his fists.

That's not good, she told herself. *Only one member of the family should be in trouble with the law at a time.*

She slid off the hood and walked over to stand beside Butch, who was saying, "It ain't a matter of expertise, Sheriff. I know how to operate a tow truck and get most anything out of anywhere. But I'm telling you, unless you can work some miracle and get the National Guard or an army helicopter up here to lift it out or whatever, that car's stayin' put."

With his piece said, Butch spun around on his cowboy boot heel and, with stiffer posture than she had ever seen on him, marched over to the tow truck and drove away.

Turning to Tom, she said, "I don't want to butt in here. However, I was thinking that—"

"Since when don't you wanna butt in?" Tom shot back. " 'Butt in' is your middle name, gal. Always has been."

"Hey, watch it, buddy," Dirk said, walking up behind Savannah. "That's my wife you're talking to. Keep it respectful."

"Or what?" Tom demanded, seemingly eager to turn his anger and frustration elsewhere.

"Or you'll regret it," Dirk replied, his tone more relaxed and less confrontational than his words.

Savannah took a deep breath and plunged, once again, into the deep end. "As I was going to say, why don't you send down a diver and see if there's even a body inside the car? If there's not, then maybe bringing the vehicle to the surface isn't as much of a priority as you think."

Dirk considered her words and nodded. "She's got a point there, Stafford. You're all in a dither, thinking this is a homicide, and you don't even know yet if she's dead or not."

The sheriff continued to pace for a while longer. Then he said, "That's easy for you to say. 'Just send a diver down.' This ain't California. And we ain't just got a diver or two lollin' around on every street corner, at our beck and call."

"Then why don't you send a couple of your deputies down?" Savannah suggested. "I don't know how far below the surface it is, 'cause you won't let us walk to the edge of the cliff and look. But from what you said, I gather it's not down very deep. You might not even need scuba gear. Maybe a couple of you guys could just hold your breath and take the plunge."

Stafford perked up a bit and turned to his deputies. They both began to shake their heads as they took a couple of steps backward.

"No, no, sir," Jesse said. "I can't swim worth nothin'."

"I sink like a tombstone," added Martin. "You might as well

just take me out on a boat, tie an anchor around my neck, and sink me."

Savannah listened and watched Tom's dismayed reaction. She knew that he, too, wasn't a particularly good swimmer. He was reluctant to venture outside of a private pool.

Dirk, on the other hand, was far more graceful in the water than he would ever be on land.

"Sounds like it's you and me, Sheriff," he said, peeling off his Harley-Davidson T-shirt and handing it to Savannah. "Let's scramble down that cliff to the water and take ourselves a swim. Who knows what we'll find?"

Savannah knew it cost Dirk a lot to make that offer. He might be Aquaman in the water, but he was deathly afraid of two things: chickens and heights. Undoubtedly, he had to be terrified to "scramble" down that cliff for any reason. But she knew he was trying to ingratiate himself to Tom at any cost. For her sake.

She made a silent vow to think of some kinky new bedroom activity to reward him.

Early in their marriage she had discovered that positive reinforcement and all that good stuff worked on husbands, too. That was how she'd gotten him to be more careful about hitting the center of the toilet and not the surrounding landscapes.

It was surprising what a man would do in exchange for some bedtime adventure.

"How do I know you're not just trying to get me down there so's you can drown me?" Tom asked him, ever the suspicious cop.

Dirk laughed and shook his head in disbelief. "In front of two of your deputies and my wife? Get real. If I was going to do you in, I'd probably just wait until a dark and stormy night and throw you off a cliff into a lake somewhere."

Nobody spoke.

Nobody breathed.

Finally, Dirk said, "I'm kidding. It's a joke. And here I thought you Confederates had a sense of humor. Sheez Louise." He reached over and slapped Sheriff Stafford soundly on his big, broad shoulder. "Let's get down there, Sheriff, and see what we can find."

Once the course of action had been decided, it didn't take long for Tom to remove his own shirt and for both men to climb down the cliff. At the bottom, they took off their shoes and socks, stuck them on an outcropping, and dove into the water.

Tom had left instructions for the other two deputies to keep an eye on Savannah, but neither of them dared to stop her when she stepped to the edge and watched the activities below.

She, too, could see the purple vehicle submerged in relatively shallow water only a few feet from the base of the cliff. But the area was in the shade and was dark, so she couldn't make out any details of what lay below. Most importantly, she couldn't tell if the car was inhabited or not. And she wasn't altogether sure she even wanted to know.

She could feel her heartbeat increasing by the moment as she watched Tom and Dirk take deep breaths and plunge beneath the surface over and over again. Each time the two men stuck their heads above the water, they spoke to each other, but Savannah couldn't tell what they were saying.

Finally, it was Tom who came up for air and shouted out to those standing above. "She's here. Send down a body bag."

Jesse scurried away and returned a few moments later with

a bag and some heavy ropes. He tossed down the bag, and Dirk, who had come up for air, caught it.

Savannah felt as though she was living some strange, awful dream. The worst was true. Jeanette was in the car, after all. At least her mortal remains were.

Savannah couldn't believe it. Not even when she saw Tom and Dirk struggling to balance the body in the water and place it in the bag. The limp, sodden mass didn't look like Jeanette, in spite of its purple dress. But then, dead bodies seldom looked like they had when inhabited by living beings.

Savannah had come to accept that as a fact, though she had never come to terms with it emotionally. For her, death was and, she suspected, always would be the most perplexing of life's mysteries.

Once the body was inside the bag, and the zipper was securely closed, Jesse tossed down the ropes, and Tom and Dirk tied them tightly to both ends.

"Okay, haul her up. Careful like," Tom shouted to his deputies.

They did, but even with Savannah helping, it wasn't easy. Although Jeanette was a fairly petite woman, it was more difficult than Savannah had anticipated to deliver the body to the top of the cliff in a gentle, respectful manner.

But once the deed was accomplished and the bag was lying on the ground at the top of the cliff, Martin and Jesse busied themselves by loosening its ropes. When those bindings were free, the deputies tied the ends of the ropes around two trees and passed them back down to Tom and Dirk.

Dirk and Tom put on their socks and shoes and, aided by the ropes, began the arduous climb back to the top.

With the men all occupied, Savannah stood next to the

bagged body and felt a strange moment of connection with the woman she had once known all too well.

For some reason, she felt as though she should say something to her. But what? "I'm sorry you're dead. I'm sorry you were such a jerk when you were alive." Neither comment seemed adequate or appropriate, so Savannah let the moment pass in silence.

It was all she could do not to reach down and unzip the bag. It wasn't that she wanted to view the body up close. But she was almost frantic with curiosity, wanting to see if there was any clear cause of death.

But with Dirk and Tom pulling themselves up and over the edge of the cliff, this wasn't the time to be interfering with evidence.

Dirk tossed the rope aside and walked toward her, drenched and covered with mud. In all the years they had worked together, she had seen him angry, worried, even traumatized. But she had never seen that particular type of fear in his eyes. He looked like he had just suffered some sort of horrid paranormal experience.

She hurried to him and took his hand. "Hey there. Are you okay?" she asked.

"Yeah. I guess." He wiped the water off his face with the back of his hand and shuddered. "Let's just say I don't wanna be a recovery diver when I grow up someday."

Tom nodded as he walked over to the bagged body. "No kidding, huh? That was downright creepy. It never occurred to me that dead folks look a lot deader in the water." Kneeling beside the bag, Tom unzipped it halfway. Savannah found that she had a much clearer look at her old schoolmate than she wanted.

Jeanette would not have been pleased with the way she

looked in death. Her skin had a ghastly white, opaque appearance and was badly wrinkled. Her eyes were open. Her facial expression registered surprise and horror.

Savannah could tell just by looking at her that Jeanette had not died peacefully.

Her hair was plastered flat against her head, and some of the lake's grasses were intertwined with her ringlets, like so many tiny green snakes. She was no longer wearing her tiara.

"Maybe she was drunk and just drove right off the cliff," Martin said. "We'd probably have found some tire tracks if it hadn't been for last night's awful downpour washing everything away."

Tom was carefully brushing Jeanette's hair away from her forehead with his index finger. "We'll have Herb check her blood alcohol level, but this wasn't your average car wreck."

"How do you know?" Jesse asked.

"Because she was buckled in her seat down there in that Cadillac," Tom said. "Nice and tight."

"So?" Savannah couldn't help asking.

"That gal never put on a seat belt in her life. The county's budget got balanced every year with the money we made from me writing her tickets. And . . . because she's got a bullet hole right here in the side of her head."

Savannah caught her breath and peered down at the body, trying to see where he was pointing.

Sure enough, directly over her left temple area was a small, round, neat hole.

Something about the wound looked strange to Savannah. But when she leaned down and tried to get a closer look, Tom yanked the zipper on the bag closed.

"We'll know more once Herb's done with his autopsy," he said.

"Mr. Jameson's going to do the postmortem?" Savannah asked. "Isn't that going to be a bit rough on him, what with him having been her boyfriend and all?"

Tom stood and shrugged. "That's the way it is in a small town. We don't have the luxury of having strangers do our dirty work for us. We've gotta take care of our own."

"Yeah," Dirk interjected, "but there's the little matter of him being under suspicion about his last autopsy. Wasn't there some talk that he might've rigged his findings to suit the widow here?"

Tom looked quite annoyed as he slipped his uniform shirt on over his wet, muddy torso. "Why don't you just let me take care of my own investigation, Detective Sergeant Coulter?" he said.

Dirk put on his T-shirt. "And you're most welcome, Sheriff Stafford. Anytime you need somebody to climb a cliff with you, jump in a lake, and fish out a gross dead body, you just feel free to kiss my lily-white ass."

The two men stared at each other, and Savannah was disheartened to see that whatever recently developed camaraderie they might have built over the shared experience of the recovery had disappeared before their hair had even dried.

"Where's your weapon, Sergeant?" Tom asked Dirk, his voice hard and clipped.

Dirk waited a couple of beats before answering just as sternly, "Locked in the glove box of my rental car. Why?"

"I'll need to see it." Tom turned to Savannah. "And yours, too. I assume since you ain't got a badge no more, your carry permit is all up to date."

Savannah glared at him, thinking that there was more than one lily-white butt in the vicinity that he was welcome to pucker up to. But her anger cooled a bit when she remembered that her Beretta was in her purse, and the purse was resting on the car's floorboard, right next to Marietta's cursed high heel.

"Of course my permit is current. Do you really think the airline would've let me fly with it otherwise?"

"Maybe," Tom replied. "If you fluttered those big blue eyes of yours and grinned with those cutesy dimples, you could probably make a guy believe most anything. Like that you and your old man went right home after the reunion last night."

Dirk started to offer a retort, but Tom was already walking away from them, heading for their rental car. Savannah and Dirk exchanged a quick look of alarm, then hurried after him.

"Just for the record," Dirk said as they caught up with him at the vehicle, "neither one of us has given you permission to search anything."

"Yeah, and I'm just gonna worry myself sick about that," was Tom's reply as he yanked open the passenger door.

He pulled the car keys out of the ignition and unlocked the glove compartment. In a moment he had Dirk's Smith & Wesson revolver in his hand and was sniffing the barrel. "This weapon's been recently fired," he announced.

"It sure has," said Dirk. "I go to the range regularly. Went two days ago, in fact. Right before we left California."

Tom handed the revolver to Jesse, then reached down to the floorboard for Savannah's purse. As Savannah watched his hand closing over her bag, she had the same sensation as when she dropped a glass and watched it fall to the floor, beyond her reach. A feeling of utter helplessness. A sense that fate was already in motion and beyond her control.

But he didn't seem to notice the shoe as he lifted the purse, opened it, and took out her Beretta. She knew what was coming next. As was their habit, she had accompanied Dirk to the firing range the day before their flight.

"This one's been fired, too," he said.

She couldn't resist a bit of sarcasm. "I hope you aren't suggesting that we *both* shot Jeanette. There's only one hole in her head."

Tom didn't reply, but he gave the Beretta to Jesse, as well.

It was when he tossed Savannah's purse back onto the floorboard that he saw the shoe. He froze, looking at it for what seemed to Savannah like one and a half eternities. Finally, he reached down, hooked his finger through one of the straps, and lifted it out. Dangling it in front of her face, he said, "Why, lookie here. Cinderella done lost her slipper at the ball last night."

Don't put it together, Tommy, she silently pleaded with him. *Don't figure it out. Please be a bad cop just this once. Not the smart, observant one you've always been.*

"This is one of the shoes you were wearing last night," he said. "Where's the other one?"

"Back at Granny's," she replied. "That one fell off when I was getting out of the car last night. I just tossed it back in there."

"So you got this shoe all muddy there in your granny's driveway?"

"Yes."

He closed his eyes for a moment, as though he had just absorbed a sharp blow to the ribs.

Or a direct stab to the heart, Savannah thought.

When he opened them, he looked at her with an expression that was as sad as any she'd ever seen on his handsome face. "Why, darlin'?" he whispered. "Why'd you have to go and lie to me? I would've given you every benefit of the doubt. I'd have moved heaven and earth for you, but, damn it, gal . . . you had to go and lie to me."

Dirk stepped between them. "What makes you think she's lying to you? It's some mud on a shoe, not a fingerprint in blood."

"It's *Lookout Point* mud . . . red as a clay flowerpot," Tom told him.

Turning to Savannah, Tom said, "In the years you and me was keepin' company, how many times did we check to make sure we didn't have any Lookout Point mud on our shoes when I took you back home to your granny? With those eagle eyes of hers, I even had to make sure none of it was on my tires. Do you really think I'd forget a thing like that, Savannah? Never, girl. I've not forgot a thing about those years we was together."

His words found their way to her heart, as she was sure he had intended them to. She said nothing, and the tension in the silence around them rose with each passing second.

Under no circumstances would it have been easy for her to listen to her boyfriend talk about the "good old days" in front of her husband. But with the added burden of her being under suspicion for murder, it was almost unbearable.

Just when she thought she was about to burst into tears, start screaming, or begin banging her head against the nearest pine tree, Tom turned and handed the shoe to Jesse.

"We're taking both of those weapons and that high heel into evidence," he told his deputy. "Now, if y'all will excuse me, I'm gonna phone Herb Jameson and get him up here to pick up this body. And then I'm gonna try to find somebody in this county who gives a damn that Jeanette's dead and inform them of her untimely passing."

He started to walk away. Then he turned back to Savannah and Dirk and added, "Don't think 'cause I ain't haulin' you two in that you're in the clear. If either one of you dares set foot out of this town, and I have to come after you, God help you."

"Sounds like he means it," Dirk said as they watched Sheriff Tom get into his car and drive away.

"He does," she replied. "Believe me. Every word."

Chapter 10

In anticipation of the fact that there would be a crowd the size of an army at Granny's for dinner, and to save her the effort of cooking for everyone on the eve of her birthday, Savannah and Dirk had stopped by the local pizza parlor and had purchased a mountain-high stack of pies.

Now "the gang," which included every Reid who was in town and not incarcerated, was around the table and lining the counters, gobbling down the goods.

Even Marietta and her two boys were present. Although her offspring had entered the surly, adolescent stage of life, they were still tolerable. And Marietta was less agitated than when she'd huffed and puffed her way out of Gran's house.

Apparently, she'd done some of the soul-searching and attitude adjustment that Granny had required to gain re-admittance. Marietta was fairly adept at readjusting her attitude when free food was within reach.

"I was relieved to hear that the two of y'all were gonna be able to join us tonight," Butch said as he stuffed his face with a garlic knot. "When I heard the sheriff done nabbed your guns and is holding them as evidence, I figured y'all might be eating supper in the penitentiary tonight."

Savannah groaned, made a face at Dirk, and said, "So much for keeping any bad news under wraps until after supper time." She turned to Butch. "How did you know about that? By the time Tom confiscated our weapons, you and that whale of a tow truck were long gone."

Butch shrugged. "I'm good buddies with Martin's wife's second cousin, Kenny. He told me when he came by the garage and asked me to fix a flat for him. Third time this month he's had a blowout. That boy never has learned the virtue of bitin' the bullet and paying for a set of new tires."

"Reckon that explains everything," Savannah said. She looked at Dirk. "He knows Martin's wife's second cousin."

Dirk nodded, chewing thoughtfully. "Who's a menace to society, driving around on bald, patched tires. Glad we cleared that up."

Vidalia decided to jump into the conversation. "I heard that he confiscated Marietta's shoe, too. Took it into custody, so to speak."

Savannah cast a quick look at Marietta, hoping she hadn't heard. But of course she had. Marietta never listened to anything important that was told to her. However, if a word of gossip or a whisper of bad news was uttered three counties away, she caught every word.

"My shoe got *arrested*?" she said, spitting meatball pizza bits across the table. "My very best, sexy, strappy, rhinestone-studded sandal is in the hands of the law? Is that what you're telling me, sister of mine?"

Vidalia munched on happily, seemingly unaware of the emotional trauma she had just inflicted. "Yep, that's right. Sheriff Stafford's got it locked up nice and tight in a safe there in his office." She turned to Savannah. "And before you ask, big sis, I know this because Martin's wife's youngest sister is president of the PTA, and I ran into her at school this afternoon, when I was registering the twins. She told me all about it. And that the principal's foolin' around with the school secretary again. He keeps this up and he's gonna get hisself fired, for sure."

Dirk shook his head. "Is that all you guys do around here? Gossip?"

"What else is there to do?" Gran said, refilling his glass of iced tea. "Since the UN moved its headquarters outta here and set up shop in New York, and our philharmonic symphony hightailed it off to Boston, it's been a little dull here 'bouts."

"I'm tellin' ya," Butch added, "when our Rockettes up and deserted us for Radio City Music Hall, I 'bout bawled my eyes out."

"Okay, okay." Dirk held up his hands. "I got it. You're in the midst of a cultural dry spell."

"My high heel is in Tommy Stafford's safe?" Marietta's lower lip was starting to tremble, and her eyes were filling with tears. "Was it as muddy as the other one? By the way, where *is* the other one? Where did you put it, Savannah? You didn't throw it out, did you?"

Gran reached across the table and shook her finger in Marietta's face. "Marietta, don't you start up with that nonsense again. If you do, I swear I'll send you home without your supper."

From his place at the counter, Marietta's oldest son turned around and tapped Gran on the shoulder. "Granny, if Momma has to go home without her supper, do we have to go, too?"

His brother piped up. "Yeah, Gran. You wouldn't throw us out along with her, would you? We hardly ever get pizza anymore. All she makes is bologna sandwiches."

"Of course not, darlin'. If your momma gets throwed out on her ear, y'all can stay. Somebody'll give you a ride home. I promise."

"I'm gonna go see that Tommy Stafford first thing tomorrow morning," Marietta was muttering. "If I explain to him that it's not even Savannah's property, maybe he'll give me my shoe back. I always did think he was a little sweet on me, you know, once him and Savannah parted ways."

Savannah had never been happier to feel a butt buzz in her life. And when the merry little song that represented Tammy Hart began to play on her phone, she thought she was going to burst into tears of happiness.

Instantly, she yanked the phone out of her rear jeans pocket and said, "I'm so sorry, Gran. I know how you feel about cell phones at the supper table, and I absolutely agree. But this is Tammy, and I've been waiting for her to get back to me. It's important."

Gran gave a dismissive wave with her pepperoni and onion slice. "Go. Do whatcha gotta do, girl. But that Hawaiian pie might be all gone by the time you get back. Who would've thought that ham and pineapple would taste good on a pizza? Goes to show, you're never too old to learn something new."

"Don't worry, babe," Dirk said, transferring a slice of it to his plate. "I'll save this piece for you."

As Savannah left the table and headed for the front of the house, she mumbled, "Sorta like leaving the biggest, hungriest pig to guard the trough."

When she reached the living room, Savannah plopped herself in the accent chair next to Gran's. Certainly Granny's was the most comfortable chair in the room, but unless her grandmother specifically invited her to sit in it, Savannah didn't feel right doing so.

It was all about respect. As far as Savannah was concerned, Granny deserved all the love and honor that a granddaughter could demonstrate. And Savannah was determined to do so whenever possible.

"Hi, kiddo," she said, answering the call. "Whatcha doing out there in that mild, moderate, and not steamy hot climate?"

There was a giggle on the other end, and Savannah could just see her sweet friend, in all her golden California beauty, sitting at the rolltop desk in her living room. No doubt, she was working away, performing acts of love and service for the Moonlight Magnolia Detective Agency.

If Tammy wasn't using her sharply honed technical skills to hack into bank accounts, medical records, and confidential Facebook postings, she would be cleaning out the office garbage can and dusting off the ancient computer monitor. No task was too big or too small in the pursuit of justice. And like Savannah, Tammy derived her greatest pleasure from nabbing bad guys and protecting good ones.

Tammy Hart's first love had always been what she called sleuthing. Although, now that she was crazy about Savannah's brother Waycross and was five months pregnant with their child, her priorities had been reordered, and detective work had slid to number three on her list.

"I got your message," Tammy said. "Apparently, I can't let you out of my sight for one minute without you getting into trouble."

Savannah chuckled. "As if having you around has ever kept me out of trouble."

"Good point. So what's happened down there? You said in your message that the mean girl you hated got killed, the sheriff thinks you had something to do with it, and he confiscated your gun and Dirk's, too. And something about Marietta's muddy shoe?"

"That's about it in a nutshell."

Savannah lifted her feet and placed them on a nearby ottoman. Suddenly, she was feeling very tired. But that was hardly surprising, considering her past twenty-four hours.

"I need to send you some names of people I'd like for you to run checks on, if you aren't too busy entertaining my brother and having a baby."

"Your brother's working on something, and he won't let me tell you about it."

"Sounds intriguing."

Tammy snickered. "Oh, you have no idea. You'd think he was guarding some national secret. And the baby's fine. It's been fluttering around a lot inside there, like a big butterfly."

"Enjoy those flutters while you can. Vidalia says in the third trimester it feels like they are doing a *Riverdance* routine on your bladder."

"That's okay. I'm looking forward to it all."

For a moment, Savannah considered the differences between her sisters and her best friend. The climate wasn't the only sunny thing that Savannah loved about California.

"Is there anything special that you'd like for me to find on these people when I run my checks?" Tammy asked.

"Just the usual," Savannah replied. "Financials, criminal backgrounds, juicy personal stuff. If any of them ever tossed somebody they didn't like over a cliff, I'd sure want to know about that."

"You got it. Send me the names, and I'll get right to it."

"Don't push yourself. It can wait till morning if you need to take a nap or something."

Tammy laughed. "You're doing your big sister, mother hen

routine on me, Savannah. I ran my usual five miles with your brother this morning, and I was doing my yoga when I got your message."

"Sorry. There for a moment I forgot who I was talking to. I'll dispense with my mother hen clucking."

"I doubt that. I don't think you can help it. Force of habit and all that." She paused. "Wait. Hold on a minute. Waycross just walked in."

Savannah listened while Tammy spoke to her brother. "It's Savannah. Can I tell her? Can I? I'll swear her to secrecy. Okay, cool!"

In a moment, she was back. "He says I can tell you, but just because we know you're good at keeping secrets."

"Eee! I know what it is! You found out if the baby's a boy or a girl, and you're going to tell me."

"Yes, we did find out, but we're not even going to tell you which. You have to wait until it's born, like everybody else."

"Then what's the national secret?"

"We're flying out there to see you all."

"When?"

"In six hours. We're taking a red-eye to Atlanta. We wanted to be there with Granny for her birthday, anyway, but now that we know you're wanted for murder—"

"Suspected of, not wanted."

"Whatever. Waycross just stuck the suitcases in the car. So, when we get there, I'll be able to tell you all the good dirt I dig up on those names you're going to send me."

Tears filled Savannah's eyes. The stress of the past twenty-four hours spilled in liquid form down her cheeks. "I'm so glad you're coming, honey. You know, if you're sure you're up to it and—"

"Cluck, cluck."

"Okay, okay. I'm stopping. Just have a safe journey, and be sure to get out of your seat every few hours and walk around, because—"

"You're hopeless."

"I know. I am. And so, so grateful that you're coming. You have no idea." She sniffed and wiped her eyes. "Now, I have a weird favor to ask you, and I have to ask you because if I ask my bashful brother, he'll die of embarrassment."

"Ooooh. Sounds interesting."

"If you have time before you leave, could you please run over to that big porn shop—"

"The new one on Lester Street, with the two mannequins in the window?"

"I don't know about the mannequins, but yes, it's on Lester."

"The mannequin on the left's wearing a red feather boa and crotchless, edible panties, and the other one is in black bondage garb and is holding a cat-o'-nine-tails whip with feathers on the ends. I think their sign says they're open twenty-four hours a day."

"Hmm. I see you've noticed the place."

"Not really."

"Uh, well, if you don't mind, go inside and . . ."

"I'm sorry about your slice of pizza," Dirk said as they cuddled beneath Granny's tulip quilt that night. "I don't know what happened to it. Maybe one of Marietta's boys nabbed it when I wasn't looking."

"Yeah, right. Whatever."

It was the third time since they'd gone to bed that he'd offered a theory concerning the Case of the Missing Hawaiian Pizza Slice.

She had heard about all she wanted to on the subject, but

was trying to be sweet and loving and not to blurt out the words, "You know you ate the damned thing, so just hush up about it."

It wasn't easy being a good wife.

On the other hand, he had been the perfect husband today, risking his life, his limbs, and even his freedom to stand beside his wife. So it wasn't a good time to get snippy with him over pizza.

Even Hawaiian with extra pineapple.

A woman had to choose her battles.

"Don't worry about it," she said, laying her hand on his chest and snuggling her head against his shoulder. "I wasn't hungry, anyway."

"I know what you mean," he said. "After seeing that Jeanette gal all dead and white and wrinkly, her hair and clothes and the weeds and stuff all floating around her there in the water . . . It was like something out of a horror movie. I could hardly eat anything, either."

"I'm sorry you had to go through that, sweetie," she said. Then she added mentally, *Too bad your loss of appetite didn't keep you from snarfing down my pizza.* "If it helps, I was really proud of you," she told him. "And, by the way, you've got better abs than Tom."

"Really?"

"Definitely. Way more cut. And he's got some major love handles going on there." She coughed. "His pecs aren't as good as yours, either."

She was lying through her teeth, but she was counting on the male ego, in all its strength and glory, to aid her in carrying it off.

"Gee. Cool."

He sounded extremely pleased.

Mission accomplished.

"How did your phone conversation with Tammy go?" he asked.

"Great. She told me a secret, but I swore I wouldn't tell anybody. It's a surprise."

"Her and Waycross are flying here tonight."

She raised her head and stared at him. By the glow of Gran's "praying hands" night-light, she could see the big grin on his face. "How do you know about that?"

"A couple of days ago, I was walking by the office desk, and Tammy was looking at something on the computer screen. She shut it off right away, so I wouldn't see it. Then she went in the kitchen to blend up some of that stupid green guck she drinks for lunch."

"You turned it back on and looked."

"Of course I did. Two coach-class tickets to Atlanta. Red-eye, tonight."

"Granny's going to be so pleased."

"She will." He hugged her closer. "And you'll be happy to have your favorite brother and the ding-a-ling here, considering all that's going on."

"Don't call her that."

"She calls me Dirko, and she says it like she means 'total idiot.' "

"I don't think that's an exact translation. More like 'complete and utter dumbbell.' "

"And that's better?"

She sighed. "I believe so. In her mind, anyway. Let it go, darlin'. Take a lesson from me and try not to worry about what anybody thinks of you. It's a waste of time and energy. Not to mention the scars it leaves on your heart."

He toyed with her hair for a while, running his fingers through her ringlets. Finally, he said, "I'm sorry she hurt you so bad, darlin'."

Tears welled up in her eyes once again. This time she let them flow. "Well, she's dead now, isn't she?"

"Very. Believe me, if you'd seen her floating in that water—"

"And years ago, I'd have been happy about that."

"I doubt it. You were probably just as sweet when you were a kid as you are now."

In spite of her dreary mood, she nearly laughed aloud. Of all the adjectives she might have used to describe herself, *sweet* wasn't on the list.

"I just feel sad and a wee bit relieved that she's gone," she said. "But mostly, I feel aggravated at myself for letting her get to me the way she did. Even last night, when I hit her, it was because I'd let her get under my skin. Now she's gone. And I'll never have the opportunity to look her straight in the eye and say, 'You can think whatever you want to about me. You can say anything you choose to. But your nasty words are going to roll off me like water off a fresh-waxed Chevy coupe. You'll never hurt me with them again. I'm a good person. At least I try to be. And that's good enough.'"

He leaned down and kissed her on the forehead. "It's not important whether she heard what you just said or not, babe. She wouldn't have taken your words to heart or changed her rotten ways or apologized. Even if you could've said all that directly to her, you wouldn't have gotten any satisfaction out of it."

"Probably not. I don't think self-improvement was a priority of hers. She thought she was pretty perfect as she was."

"The person who needed to hear you say that just did. *You*

needed to hear Savannah, the woman, defend Savannah, the kid. And you just did." He turned her face so he could look into her eyes. "Feel better?"

"Yes," she said, meaning it from the depths of her little girl heart. "I do. Thank you."

"You're welcome, darlin'," he said. "Good night."

He stroked her cheek for a while with his forefinger, waiting for her response.

But Savannah was already asleep.

Chapter 11

"Happy birthday to yooou. Happy birthday to yooou. Happy birthday, dear Granny! Happy birthday to yooou!" The festive song filled the small house as soon as the first light of dawn touched its windows.

Gran was an early riser. If her grandchildren, their spouses, and her great-grandchildren wanted to preserve the age-old tradition of treating her to breakfast in bed, they had to roll out early and get cracking.

In what had formerly been called "the older girls' bedroom," she was lounging like pampered royalty on the feather bed, propped up on lace-trimmed, embroidered pillows. Her sparkling silver hair was neatly brushed, and she wore her pink satin quilted bed jacket and her best cubic zirconia stud earrings.

When Savannah peeped into the bedroom to see if she was ready, it occurred to her that Queen Elizabeth herself had nothing on Granny when it came to receiving visitors graciously in one's bedchamber.

The great-grandkids arrived first, carrying a saucer on which slices of banana, apple, and orange had been lovingly placed in decorative layouts. This year, the array included roses made of strawberries, inspired by a fancy fruit-cutting class Marietta had taken at the local library.

Next came Jesup and Cordele with sweetened coffee topped with fresh-whipped cream and sprinkled with cinnamon.

Savannah and Alma had been assigned the most difficult chore, the main course, which included eggs fried to perfection, without a hint of a "ruffle" around the edges; crisp bacon; succulent sausages; totally lump-free cream gravy; and fluffy, "float out of the basket and into your mouth" biscuits.

Vidalia and Marietta supplied dessert—oatmeal cookies from the Burger Igloo, McGill's one and only café.

When Gran was finished, had wiped her lips with a rose chintz napkin, and had overseen the removal of the dishes, she tried to shoo them out of the bedroom.

"I have to get up and get dressed," she protested. "I don't care what you say. I'm not going to loll about in bed all day long like a lazy floozy. I've got too much to do and too little time to get 'er done. All of you, skedaddle. Right now!"

Savannah grinned and said, "But there's one more course we want to serve you. And then you can get up and dance a jig if you've a mind to."

"Another course? Lord have mercy, I couldn't eat another bite if my life was hangin' in the balance."

"But you're going to like this course. It's very sweet, and I guarantee you have room for it. If not in your tummy, in your heart."

Gran looked suspicious. "What's that supposed to mean?"

Savannah moved aside and motioned to the doorway. "It came about ten minutes ago, a special arrival from California."

Tammy and Waycross stepped through the doorway and into the bedroom.

Tammy looked beautiful, her pretty face glowing, her long blond hair glimmering in the morning sunlight, her baby bump showing just enough to be adorable. Waycross was wearing a shy grin on his freckled face, his own copper curls in magnificent disarray from him having slept, or at least having tried to, on the plane.

"Hey, Granny," he said. "You didn't really think we'd miss your birthday, didja?"

"We had to be here to celebrate with you." As she patted her belly, Tammy added, "All three of us."

Gran flew out of the bed and raced across the room to enfold them, and as many of her other loved ones as her arms could hold, in a rapturous hug.

And they all danced a jig together.

With the Reid clan all milling about the house, hovering over Gran, stuffing their faces with tasty edibles and swilling iced tea by the gallon, Savannah had to take Tammy into the backyard to get a moment alone with her.

They met behind the vegetable garden, in the midst of Gran's flower garden, between her Mister Lincoln and John F. Kennedy rosebushes. The scents from those snowy and scarlet blossoms, along with those of her deep purple, pink, and white peonies nearby, filled the moist air.

"This is sooo pretty back here," Tammy said, looking around and soaking in the colors, the perfumes, the beauty of the blossoms waving in the gentle midday breeze. "It reminds me of your backyard. Which reminds me . . . Your neighbor, the busybody one, was happy when I asked her to feed the kitties and water your yard."

Savannah rolled her eyes. "Of course she is. She gets to come into my house and snoop around, knowing I'm on the opposite side of the country." Quickly, she added, "Not that I'm ungrateful, mind you. Cleo and Di adore her, and she doesn't just bop in and play with them. She stays, fixes herself something to eat, watches the food channels on my TV, takes a bubble bath in my tub."

"She bathes in your tub? Seriously?"

"Yes. The last time she kitty sat for me, she informed me beforehand that she has a strong preference for my lilac-scented bubble bath. So I made sure there was plenty of it on hand. Hey, what are you gonna do? Good kitty sitters don't grow on trees, you know."

Savannah nodded toward the white plastic bag that Tammy was holding under her arm. "You got a chance to go shopping for me?"

"I did. I hope you like what I got. I wasn't sure. . . ." Tammy opened the discreet garbage bag and revealed a pink paper bag inside with a NAUGHTY LADY'S NOOK logo on it.

Both women looked all around, checking their surroundings thoroughly, before Savannah reached inside, opened the pink bag, and took a peek.

"Perfect," she said. "How much do I owe you?"

"A fortune," Tammy replied. "This stuff doesn't come cheap, you know."

Savannah reached into her front jeans pocket, pulled out a wad of cash, and pressed it into Tammy's palm. "There. And thank you."

"Anytime."

Savannah took the bag from Tammy and tucked it under her arm. "By the way, did you get an opportunity to run those checks?"

"Of course. I had a four-and-a-half-hour flight with nothing to do."

"I figured you'd sleep, what with you expecting and all."

Tammy gave her the "Don't mommy me" look.

Savannah held up a hand in surrender. "Okay, okay. What did you find out?"

Tammy pulled her electronic tablet from out of nowhere and began scrolling down the screen. "Jeanette Barnsworth wasn't as rich as she might have let on to you and the rest of the town," Tammy said. "In fact, she was deeply in debt. Apparently, she had a bit of a spending addiction."

"But her husband was rich."

"He was. Filthy rich. But he didn't get that way by burning through money the way his wife did. He had her on a tight budget. She spent every penny of it and had run her credit cards sky-high. It was only a matter of time until he was going to find out about it."

"If he died," Savannah mused, "she could settle her debts and go on the spending spree of a lifetime. Plus, he'd never have to find out she'd run up the bills. Both are solid motives for murder."

"You'd have a hard time proving it." Tammy found the file she was looking for and showed it to Savannah. "That's his autopsy report. Natural causes. Respiratory failure after a bad chest cold."

"Any illegal drugs or pharmaceuticals mentioned?"

"None."

"Of course."

"Whether there was or not, the mortician could have lied about it. And that would be equally hard to prove."

"Unless you could somehow hack into the records of the lab

that did the actual processing and get that original report to compare."

An evil smile crossed Tammy's otherwise lovely and angelic face. She twirled a lock of her hair and giggled. "Ahhh, how I love a challenge. Consider it done."

"How about the mortician's financials?"

"Solid down the line. Though he did make some purchases, like a new Cadillac, which he paid for with cash. And I didn't see that chunk of change anywhere in his accounts beforehand. He also bought two first-class tickets to the Bahamas."

"The names on the tickets?"

"Herbert Jameson and Jeanette Barnsworth," Tammy answered. "And he'd prepaid for an all-inclusive stay at a luxury resort there. A pretty tidy sum and nonrefundable."

Savannah thought back on how Herb and Jeanette had interacted with one another at the reunion. Herb had been clingy and adoring; Jeanette condescending and standoffish. It seemed to her that he had had high hopes, hopes that were destined to be dashed. "I think ole Herb was headed for a reality check," she said.

"Maybe he got it before she died," Tammy suggested. "That might be a motive for murder, too."

"The last I saw of them, as we were all leaving the reunion, he was the one issuing the walking papers. I think he figured out things weren't going well when she yelled at him right there in front of God and everybody and said that he was old and impotent."

"Another motive for murder."

"Folks have killed for a lot less. That's for sure." Savannah glanced over Tammy's tablet screen. "Who else have you got there?"

"Well, since we think Jeanette might've killed her husband

for his money, I looked for heirs to see who might inherit the goodies if Jeanette died."

"Good idea. And?"

"His only surviving blood relative is his half sister, Imogene Barnsworth. She lives over in Sulfur Springs."

"Hmmm. She can't have a lot of extra spending cash if she lives there. I think if you took everybody who lives in Sulfur Springs, held them up by their ankles, and shook 'em, you wouldn't get a dollar's worth of change for your efforts."

"She's in her seventies, living in a nursing home. I'm sure some extra money would go a long way toward making her a lot more comfortable."

"But an elderly lady in a nursing home doesn't make your best murder suspect."

"I'd still talk to her if I were you," Tammy said. "She might know something."

"I'm going to. But the first thing on my list is to go to the funeral parlor and have a chat with Mr. Jameson. If he'll see me, that is."

"Do you want company?" Something about Tammy's lackluster tone and the sleepy look in her eyes told Savannah that hers was an offer the young mother-to-be was hoping she would refuse.

"No, sugar. You go stretch out on Granny's feather bed and have yourself a nap, if you can get some sleep in that house with all the ruckus going on."

"That's okay. I'm going to have Waycross take me back to our hotel room."

"Hotel? What hotel? Oh." Savannah gulped. "You two checked into the No-Tail Motel?"

"Yes. It's all we could find."

"Did the, um, name tip you off that maybe . . . ?"

"I did wonder about that. But then I saw the logo on the Web site. It's of a cute little dog with a teeny bobbed tail. I think that's where they got the name."

Savannah looked at her a long time, then nodded solemnly. "Okay."

As the women walked through the vegetable garden on their way back to the house, Savannah said, "If the other folks staying at that motel are too noisy, turn up your radio real loud so you won't have to listen to 'em."

"Will do."

"And be sure to lock your doors and windows nice and tight, and prop a chair under the doorknob."

"Why?"

"That no-tailed dog might be vicious."

"Oh. Right."

As Savannah and Dirk drove away from Granny's house, with Savannah at the wheel, Dirk sat, shaken and pale, in the passenger's seat. He wiped the sweat from his brow with the tail of his T-shirt and said, "I gotta tell you, Van, you scared the hell outta me back there."

"I'm so sorry, darlin'."

"When you said that business about going to see Jameson all by yourself, my whole life flashed in front of me."

"It was awful of me. I don't know what I was thinking."

"Well, I know what *I* was thinking. I thought you were gonna leave me there with that houseful of women and kids all by myself."

"Please forgive me. It must've been horrible. Soul scarring, in fact."

"It was. All that talking, talking, talking. And about absolutely nothing. And the fighting about every stupid little thing. How did you ever survive, growing up in that?"

"I went for a lot of walks. I like to wore this road out," she said, pointing to the narrow dirt driveway they were traveling from Gran's front door, through the cotton fields on either side, to the paved highway.

He settled back in his seat, then rummaged around in the glove compartment and retrieved his bag of cinnamon sticks.

"I felt like a guy on death row who'd gotten a reprieve from the governor when you called Butch and asked him if I could come over there to the garage and help him out."

"It was the least I could do, sugar, under the circumstances. You should've known that I'd never do a thing like that to you—leaving you alone with my family. At least not that many of them at once." She reached over and squeezed his knee. "After all, I promised to love, honor, and cherish you."

She gave him a sideways glance, and when she saw the sappy look of unadulterated love on his face, it was all she could do not to snicker.

Her big, brave hubby could face down a gang of bank robbers and hardly break a sweat. But confronted with the prospect of being alone in a small house with a gaggle of gabby, loudmouthed, quarrelsome women, he fell to pieces.

She turned the car onto the highway and headed for the three-block-long stretch of stores and businesses that constituted downtown McGill, Georgia.

When they entered town and Savannah pulled into the parking area beside Butch's garage, Dirk pulled the cinnamon stick from his mouth and tossed it onto the rear floorboard.

"Your brother-in-law *does* know that I'm pretty much clueless about cars, right?" he asked. "I mean, I don't have the first idea how to help him fix a double clutch."

Savannah laughed. "That's okay, sugar. He's not working on a double clutch. He's probably got his feet propped up on his desk, sipping sodas and looking at girlie magazines."

"Really?" Dirk looked impressed. "How do you know?"

"Because there's no such thing as a double clutch."

"You're kidding."

"Nope. It's code."

"For what?"

"For 'I don't want to be around my wife's crazy relatives, so I'm pretending I have to work.'"

"All right! See ya later, babe! You're the best!"

Before she could assure him that, yes, she *was* the absolute best, he had given her an enthusiastic kiss on the lips, had bounded out of the car, and was scurrying up to the garage office in search of cold, free soft drinks and PG-rated pornography.

Chapter 12

During the drive from Butch's garage to the mortuary, Savannah thought of at least twenty different possible ways to gain access to Jeanette Barnsworth's remains.

In feasibility, they ranged from highly iffy, like just asking Herb Jameson very sweetly and fluttering her eyelashes, to downright silly, like climbing through a window, scrounging around the mortuary and locating the body, then sneaking a peek.

She'd already decided against Plan B. The last time she squeezed through a window, lost her balance, and hit the floor on the other side, she'd cracked a rib and torn her favorite pair of slacks.

Besides, a peek wasn't going to do it, anyway. She'd already had a peek there at the lake. What she needed was the autopsy report, if Jameson had finished it. And even more unlikely, if he would share it with her.

If she was the coroner, and the number one suspect asked for a look at the body, she would have laughed in their face and shown them the door. How could she expect Mr. Jameson to do anything else?

It wasn't going to be easy to get the information she needed. But then, when was a homicide investigation ever simple? She supposed some cases were. But she'd never had any of them.

By the time she arrived at the funeral home, she'd decided upon a fairly straightforward plan. She was going to ask Herb Jameson with all the Southern belle sweetness and gracious female persuasion she could muster.

And if that didn't work, she'd mow over him like a giant John Deere combine harvester.

She wasn't proud. Whatever the job took, she was up to it.

She wasn't going down for a murder she hadn't committed. Especially Jeanette's. Not after all those years of resisting her homicidal fantasies and urges to do exactly that.

The funeral home's colonial façade gave the place an elegant, yet imposing appearance. The stark white walls, the black shutters, and the graceful columns spoke of formal finality. But the colorful flower beds that edged the perfect lawn lent a warm personal touch.

She drove from the circular brick driveway to the less decorative, more utilitarian paved road that led to the side and back of the establishment. A triple-vehicle garage had two doors open. Inside one she could see the long black hearse that had carried many people she knew, and some she loved, to their final resting places. In the other was Herb's new Cadillac.

Apparently, he hadn't returned it, as he had threatened to at the school. At least not immediately.

Savannah was a bit disappointed to see both the hearse and Herb Jameson's personal car. One part of her—the sneaky but more forthright part—had been hoping to find the mortician gone from his business. The more she thought about trying to talk her way into the place, the more an old-fashioned break-ing and entering seemed preferable.

She parked the rental car near a side door, which she hoped was less used than the others, and got out. Mentally crossing her fingers, she walked up to the entrance, hoping against hope that the local custom of not bothering to lock one's door extended to the neighborhood mortuary.

She stifled a yelp of glee when the knob turned and the door swung open. It didn't even creak.

So far, so good, she thought.

Having been to the back area of the mortuary once before, when trying to clear her brother of a murder charge, she knew the way.

Down the narrow hallway, with its drab walnut paneling and dark blue carpet, was the preparation room, which was some-times used for autopsies. In a small community where homi-cides were almost nonexistent, there was no need for a full-time coroner. So on the rare occasion when one was needed, the local mortician might be pressed into service. And such was the case with Herb Jameson.

When she had consulted with him before regarding the homicide her brother was accused of committing, she had found Jameson to be surprisingly knowledgeable in the foren-sic sciences. She hoped he would be as efficient in this case, because the truth would lead Tom Stafford to the real killer and away from her.

Savannah felt a pang of anxiety when she heard a noise that sounded like the clanging of metal instruments being tossed into a tray. After years of watching Dr. Jennifer Liu, San Carmelita's medical examiner, perform autopsies, she was quite familiar with the sound.

But even though she wasn't looking forward to the conversation she was about to have, she was glad that the autopsy was still in progress. She wasn't too late, after all.

Although Granny's teachings about good manners dictated that she knock before opening the closed door, Savannah decided to take a slightly more aggressive approach. She opened it just enough to stick her face through and only then gave it a light triple knock.

Herb Jameson was dressed in disposable paper overalls, complete with matching booties over his street shoes. On his face was a surgical mask. His hair was netted, and his hands were gloved. He stood beside a large stainless-steel table, upon which lay the earthly remains of Jeanette Barnsworth.

"Excuse me, Mr. Jameson," she said. "It's me, Savannah." She eased her head and one shoulder inside the room. "I know you're terribly busy, so I won't take up much of your time. I was just wondering if . . . well, how your autopsy's coming along. And if you need any help. If you do, I'd be happy to lend a hand. You know, clean your instruments or—"

The look he gave her was far less friendly than any she had ever received from him before. "Thank you, Savannah. I appreciate your offer," he said, with absolutely no gratitude whatsoever in his tone. "But I don't think Sheriff Stafford would approve of me allowing his main suspect to handle the victim's body. Some might call it a conflict of interest, don't you think?"

Savannah fought to keep her sweet face from sliding off and gentled her tone when she said, "I understand perfectly, Mr. Jameson. But surely, no harm would be done as long as I don't touch anything."

She stepped all the way into the room and gently closed the door behind her. After taking only one step in his direction, she stopped and said, "See? I can stand right here with my hands in my pockets, and that shouldn't cause any problem at all. From here I can just ask my couple of questions, and if you don't want to answer them, you just say so, and I'll be on my way."

After badgering you half to death, she silently added, *and only if you chase me out of here with one of those big, sharp scalpels of yours.*

When he didn't answer, she continued to press. "All I want to know is if you've determined a cause and manner of death yet. That's it. That's all."

He peered at her over the top of the surgical mask in much the same way she studied a suspect she was interrogating. And as she tried to resist squirming inside her jeans, she decided it was a lot more fun to be the interrogator than the one getting squeezed.

"Are you telling me, Savannah," he said, "that you have no idea how this young woman died?"

She fixed him with her most sincere, determined gaze and replied, "That's *exactly* what I'm telling you, Mr. Jameson. I have no idea whatsoever how she died. If it was an accident—"

"It was *not* an accident," he said, interrupting her. "She was murdered."

Savannah winced. Expected or not, the words were hard to hear. "That's tragic," she told him. "I truly hate to hear it. No one deserves to leave this earth that way."

"At least we agree on that," he replied.

"If you've already determined the manner of death, then you must know the cause, too."

"Yes, I do. It was drowning."

"Drowning? Wow. Really?"

"You seem surprised."

"I *am* surprised. There at the lake, Sheriff Stafford, his

deputies, my husband, and I all expressed the opinion that she was dead before she went into the water. Probably from that injury to her temple."

"But none of you are coroners, now are you?"

"No. We aren't. And I'm not questioning you, sir. I'm sure you have good reasons for why you arrived at that ruling."

"Of course I do."

"Then would you mind sharing your findings with me? It will all be a matter of public record soon, anyway. Why would it matter if I find out now or later?"

He peeled the surgical gloves from his hands and tossed them into a bright orange trash can with a BIOLOGICAL WASTE sign on the side. Then he turned to Savannah, and in a voice that sounded both weary and sad, he said, "Her lungs are water-logged, and I found the presence of more water in her stomach. She was alive when she went into the lake."

"But what about the bullet wound to her temple?"

Jameson removed his mask, and Savannah was grateful. It made him look more like the man she had known and liked as a child. Her friends' kind and gentle father. And less like the coroner whose ruling might send her away for murder.

"It isn't a bullet wound," he said simply.

Forgetting her promise to stand still in one place, Savannah took a couple of steps closer to the body and stared at the neat, round hole on the side of the head.

"You're right," she said. "When I first saw it there at the lake, I caught only a glimpse of it. But even then, I thought it looked strange. Not like your usual GSW. There's no gunpowder stippling around the wound."

"Though there wouldn't be if the shooter was standing far enough away," he replied.

"True. But where's the black edging? I don't think I've ever seen a gunshot wound without those dark edges that a bullet makes when it burns its way into the flesh."

"Like I said, it isn't from a bullet. It's a puncture wound."

"How deep?"

"About five centimeters."

"Could the head injury have occurred when she went off the cliff, like in an accident? Maybe something in the car caused it. A metal rod perhaps?"

"No. Definitely not. The wound occurred antemortem."

"How long before death?"

He shrugged. "There's no way to tell for sure. A half an hour? Perhaps more. There's definite swelling, bruising, and blood inside the brain, surrounding the wound. And that would have taken some time to occur, unlike the drowning, which would've been much faster." Pausing, he shuddered. "Though not fast enough. I'm sure she suffered terribly."

"But if the head wound came first, maybe she wasn't conscious. . . ." She paused. "You know, for the drowning part."

"Maybe. Maybe not. People assume that every brain injury is instantly fatal. It isn't. She may have been fully aware and suffering through the whole thing."

Savannah saw an intense pain in his eyes, and she reminded herself that at least until last night, this man had feelings for the woman on his autopsy table. She couldn't imagine autopsying anyone she knew, let alone cared for.

"I feel terrible that someone did this to her, Mr. Jameson," she told him. "I feel sorry for her and for you. It's awful, losing someone you're close to."

He turned his back to her and busied himself with placing the remainder of his soiled instruments and tools into a stainless-steel tray.

While he was occupied and was not watching, Savannah

took the opportunity to take another step closer and get a better look at the small, round wound.

"What do you suppose the weapon was?" she asked.

When he didn't answer, she thought perhaps he hadn't heard her. So she said, "The shape of the stab wound . . . It doesn't look like a knife was used."

"It wasn't a knife," he said, his back still turned to her. "And she wasn't stabbed. She was struck. Very hard. With an object that was flat on the end, not pointed."

"Like a screwdriver?"

"No."

Savannah searched her mind but could think of nothing. "Then what?"

He turned around and once again gave her that dark, penetrating look. "My best guess is that the puncture trauma to her head occurred when she was hit with a shoe. Or more specifically, the heel of a shoe."

Savannah's head started spinning. So did the room. She felt as though she had to sit down before her knees buckled beneath her and she fell.

"A heel?" she asked, hearing the trembling in her own voice.

"Yes." His voice sounded as cold and dead as the woman on the table before them. "Jeanette was murdered with the heel of a woman's shoe. A high heel. A stiletto."

Chapter 13

As a resident of Southern California, Savannah had experienced more than her share of earthquakes. She was all too familiar with the physical sensations they produced: the queasiness that went far deeper than the average upset tummy, the loss of equilibrium, the sinking feeling that the ground beneath your feet was about to rise up and smack you in the head. Not to mention the pure panic of it all when you realized that your world, as you knew it, might literally be coming apart at the seams.

As she stood there in the middle of Jameson's preparation room and heard the words "high heel," she experienced all those earthquake sensations and more.

In less than a couple of seconds, her imagination had generated more than one horrific scene that would most likely be part of her future: Sheriff Thomas Stafford reading that ruling on the coroner's report, members of the jury listening to Herb Jameson testify as they stared at the muddy high heel that was Exhibit A on the evidence table.

One look into the mortician's eyes told Savannah that he was all too aware of the high heel, her high heel. The shoe that was now in Sheriff Stafford's possession.

She swallowed hard and wished that she was still standing closer to the door, so she could reach over and grasp the knob for support.

"I know how it looks, Mr. Jameson," she said. "Believe me. If I were you, I'd be thinking the same thing. But I assure you that I didn't kill her. And I'm begging you to help me find the evidence I need to prove it."

She searched his face for any sign that she might be winning him over with her entreaties. But she saw only condemnation and anger.

"If you truly came here for answers," he said, "which I do not believe for one moment, then you have them, and you should leave. But if you came here to convince me that someone, anyone, other than you murdered this young woman—cruelly, painfully—then you've wasted your time and mine."

"I'm very sorry you feel that way, Mr. Jameson," she said.

"I'm sure you are. I'm sure you'd have been much happier if I hadn't figured out what you did and what you used to do it."

He ripped the disposable overalls off, wadded them into a ball, and tossed them into the wastebasket with the rest of the soiled garments. "Let me tell you something, Miss Savannah. This may be a small rural town. And you may look down your nose at us and think we're a bunch of bumpkins. But some of us here in McGill happen to know our business. And some of us know it well. So, country bumpkin or not, you're not going to murder one of my people—let alone a woman I cared about—and get away with it. Not while I'm coroner in this town."

Savannah couldn't remember a time when she had felt so much fear and sadness wash through her so quickly and take possession of her spirit and mind so totally.

To her horror, she burst into tears.

It was the last thing she wanted to do, sobbing her face off in front of this man. A man whose respect, even affection, she had always delighted in having.

Now it appeared he was her worst enemy.

Unable to think of a single thing to say, she headed back to the door. But before she was able to escape the room, her accuser, and the terrible sight of Jeanette's dead body, she heard the mortician say, "Yes, Savannah Reid, you'd better run. I talked to Tom Stafford on the phone not an hour ago. I told him what I found, what my ruling's going to be. He was on the other side of the county when we talked. But he said he was heading back here quick as he can."

Savannah didn't reply, but she could practically feel the blood draining from her own face.

"That's right," Jameson said. "The sheriff's coming for you. Says he'll have a warrant in his hands. And you're going to pay for what you did. You're going to pay for killing this beautiful, vibrant young woman. And it won't be just a prison sentence, either. The last time I checked, the state of Georgia still has capital punishment. If I have anything to do with it, and I will, you'll get the death penalty."

Savannah ran from the room.

She raced down the dark, claustrophobic hallway, with its walnut paneling and navy blue carpet. She made it out the seldom-used side entrance and into the parking lot . . . before she fell to her knees and threw up her part of Granny's birthday breakfast feast.

* * *

When Savannah arrived at Butch's garage to collect Dirk, she didn't get out of the car. She just beeped the horn and waited for him to emerge, figuring that the fewer people who saw her with swollen, teary eyes and a red nose, the better.

Funny how a bit of news, especially about murder, can make it from one end of town to the other at the speed of pizza delivery, she thought as she waited. She could practically hear the gossip as it flew through the air over her head.

"Hey, I heard Savannah Reid was bawling like a lost pup right there in front of Butch's garage. Made a fine spectacle of herself, she did!"

"Yes, I heard that already. Thelma Sullivan says it's 'cause she's about to be arrested for endin' ole Jeanette Parker. Oughta give her a medal instead of the 'lectric chair, if you ask me."

Savannah couldn't help grinning at her own extravagant fantasies. *Don't worry, darlin'*, she told herself in her best big sister manner. *You won't get the electric chair. Hell. They don't use those things anymore. They'll put you down with an injection, like a toothless old hound dog with a chronic bladder infection who's taken to peeing on the carpet.*

Oh, shut up. You aren't helping.

To pass the time and possibly distract her racing mind, she turned on the radio and caught the middle of a news story. "Execution of convicted husband murderer Penelope Barbera was postponed today because of questions about whether the drug to be used to end her life is humane or constitutes cruel and unusual—"

"Ugh!" She turned it off, took out her phone, and called Dirk. "Your limo has arrived," she said. "Are you ready to go?"

"Naw. Me and Butch are fixin' this double clutch. We're up to our elbows in grease."

"Now ain't the time, darlin'. You need to shake a leg and get yourself out here."

"Okay." He snickered. "Want me to bring you a soda? Wait a minute. Butch says around here it's called pop."

"Yes. A ginger ale if you've got one."

"You want a candy bar?"

"No. I'd probably throw it up, like I did my breakfast."

There was a long silence on his end. Then he said, "Bad news from Jameson?"

"The worst."

"I'll be right out."

Three seconds later, she saw the office door fly open. Dirk ran out, a soda bottle in each hand. Butch emerged behind him but stayed in the doorway, a worried look on his face.

It touched Savannah's heart to see her brother-in-law so concerned about her. While they'd never had the opportunity to really develop a close relationship, they had always liked each other and gotten along well. Savannah considered him a saint for putting up with Vidalia's mercurial moods. A less even-keeled fellow would have flown the domestic coop long ago.

He gave her a half wave, and she returned it as Dirk dove headfirst into the car. She decided to move along before Butch's curiosity got the better of his good manners. The last thing she needed was an overly concerned relative asking questions.

In that regard, she already had her hands full with Dirk.

The instant he got into the car, he gave her a quick, thorough once-over. Unhappy with what he saw, he said, "What's the matter? What did Jameson say? How bad is it?"

"Let's get out of town first," she said as she took a long swig of the lemon-lime soft drink he had handed her. No doubt, it was the closest thing to a ginger ale in Butch's minimally stocked soda machine.

"Out of town?" he complained. "I have to wait until we're *out of town?*"

"Think about the town you're in before you get too frazzled there, darlin'."

"Right. I forgot. This is one of those 'sneeze and you'll miss it' communities."

That limited discourse had lasted long enough for Savannah to cross the boundary of the city limits and pass officially into the countryside. Several seconds later, they were surrounded by nothing but cotton fields.

She pulled the car over to the side of the road and drank a bit more soda. Then she turned to Dirk and said, "Remember in our marriage ceremony, that business about 'for better and for worse?'"

"Yeah."

"Well, call it a hunch, but I reckon this would qualify as 'worse.' Maybe even 'worst.'"

"I can hardly wait to hear it. Spit it out, kid."

Savannah took a moment to compose herself. She knew that a concise accounting would alarm her husband less than one containing all the nasty details.

The last thing a worried hubby needed to hear was something like "The coroner said he was absolutely certain I'm the murderer, and he intends to do everything he possibly can to make sure I get the death penalty."

Just the facts, she told herself. *Give him just the facts.*

She drew a deep breath and plunged ahead with her abbreviated story. "Cause of death—drowning. Manner of death—homicide. Antemortem wound five centimeters deep, caused by a narrow cylindrical object with a blunt end."

"A high heel?"

It wasn't easy being married to a homicide detective.

She nodded. "Jameson seems to think so."

He groaned and slumped in his seat. "Shit."

"My thoughts exactly."

The hot noonday sun might have been a blessing for the occasional snake who climbed up out of the roadside ditches onto the hot asphalt to catch a few rays and work on his tan. But as Savannah and Dirk traveled that highway on their return trip to Granny's house, Savannah cursed the blazing heat. She cursed the sunbathing reptiles, the cotton fields where she had worked so hard as a child, and in general, this part of the world, where it seemed nothing good ever happened to her.

"That isn't entirely true," she muttered to herself. "Gran's good."

"You're doing it again," Dirk told her.

"Talking to myself?"

"Yeah. Not that I particularly mind it, 'cause I talk to myself, too."

"You most certainly do. All the time."

"Yeah, but you start talking halfway through your thought, instead of at the beginning, like you're supposed to. And that drives me crazy, wondering what the heck you said, or didn't say, before it."

"Ugh. I didn't realize there are rules governing how one should talk to oneself."

"I just made it up. And 'one' should not say 'oneself,' either. It sounds uppity."

"Okay. I shall try to remember that, too."

" 'Shall' is kinda uppity, too."

"Shall I tell one what one can do to oneself and with what?"

He reached over, placed his hand on her knee, and gave it a

squeeze. "Don't worry about it, babe. You've got a lot on your mind. I was just kidding."

And she did have a lot on her mind. Mostly the intersection up ahead, where the highway and Gran's driveway met.

The intersection where Sheriff Thomas Stafford's patrol car sat hidden in a copse of trees and bushes.

"Dadgum," she said. "He got that warrant awful quick."

She felt Dirk tense beside her and heard his breath quicken. "You let me handle this," he said. "I'll be happy to tell him where he can stick that warrant of his."

"I'm sure that would make you happy, big boy," she replied. "But I'm also sure that's not the best way to handle the situation."

"I don't have a lot of alternatives, since he took my weapon." He sighed. "I've got some bullets I could throw at him, but he probably wears a vest."

"I appreciate the thought," she told him. "And I know you'd even be happy to insert those bullets manually, but I'm going to ask you for a really big favor."

He gave her a frown, which told her that he wasn't expecting to like what he was about to hear. "*Okay.* Lay it on me."

"I want you to stay in the car while I talk to him. I want you to let me handle this, one hundred percent, by myself."

"You're right. I don't like it. You're my woman, and I'm going to protect you."

She sighed. "I understand that you love me, darlin', and you want to take care of me. But now's not the time to get all caveman on me—"

"Caveman's got nothing to do with anything. If things were turned around, you'd be the same way, gettin' into my business whether I wanted you to or not. That's what you and me do. Especially when it's important stuff. And we did it even before we got married. It's about being partners."

He had her there. They both knew she'd be acting the same way he was, or worse, if their roles were reversed.

She tried a different approach. "It's true, sugar. I take back the caveman comment. But I know this guy way better than you do, and I know how to handle him."

"You didn't seem to be handling him all that well back at the lake."

She pulled the car off the highway and stopped about twenty feet away from Stafford's patrol car. "Give me a chance to see what I can do by myself. If it starts going badly, I'll give you the sign, and you can come charging in with the cavalry and rescue me. Okay?"

He seemed to hesitate, which she decided to interpret as acquiescence. "Thank you. I appreciate it. You just sit tight now."

She started to get out of the car, but he grabbed her arm. "What's the sign?"

"Our usual one."

"The one you do when you're mad at me? Where you scratch your nose with your middle finger?"

"That's the one."

Chapter 14

As Savannah walked toward Tom Stafford's car, hidden among the trees and the bushes at the end of her granny's drive, she couldn't help remembering all the times she had done this very thing in years past.

Under very different circumstances.

How many times had she gone for a walk, only to meet him here for some quick stolen kisses, caresses, and whispers of sweet nothings?

As she approached his car, it occurred to her that if she was remembering, perhaps he was, too. And maybe that would help.

It couldn't hurt.

If she had to be arrested, surely it was better if the officer was someone she'd once loved.

And she was pretty darned sure that Tom had loved her, too, all those years ago. Infidelities aside. She'd seen it in his eyes, heard it in his voice, felt it in his touch.

Yes, he had been stupid and had ruined their chance for

happiness together. But Savannah had never doubted that she was important to him.

Not important enough to keep his zipper closed, unfortunately, she reminded herself. But important, nevertheless.

As she approached his vehicle, she saw that he was wearing his dark sunglasses, and she wished that she had hers on, too. If there was ever a good time to hide, surely this was it. She opened the passenger door and slid onto the hot black seat. The leather burned the back of her thighs through the thin fabric of her slacks as she settled into place.

For a long, awkward moment, neither of them spoke.

Then he said, "How do?"

With a neutral civility that matched his, she replied, "Fine. You?"

"I've been better," he said. "I've never particularly enjoyed arresting a former girlfriend for murder. Call me old-fashioned, but it just doesn't feel very chivalrous."

"No problem. Just don't do it. You know in your heart she's innocent, anyway."

"I do?"

He turned to face her, and even through the dark glasses, she could tell that he was studying her, appraising her. She figured that must be a good thing. Perhaps he hadn't fully made up his mind yet.

"You know I didn't kill anybody," she said.

"I do?"

"Stop saying that."

"Sayin' what?"

" 'I do.' We ain't exactly getting married here."

"We could have, if you hadn't gone and tore outta here like a wildcat with its tail on fire the first time we had a fight."

"It was a *big* fight, Tommy."

"I remember. You threw stuff at me and everything."

"Just think, now you could probably arrest me for that. Call it domestic violence or whatever."

To her surprise, he reached over, took her hand, and folded it between his. "I wouldn't arrest you for anything, gal. Not unless I absolutely had to. I hope you know that."

She could feel her face turning red as she snatched her hand away from him. Glancing over at Dirk, she wondered what he was thinking. Whatever it was, she was pretty sure it involved blood being shed.

Tom's, of course.

"You know," she said, "that it never would have occurred to Herb Jameson that Jeanette's head wound was caused by a high heel unless somebody told him that you'd confiscated one from me."

"Probably not."

"Then what does that tell you?"

"That it's a darn lucky thing I caught you red-handed with the murder weapon. Otherwise, I might never have solved this case."

"You still haven't solved it, peckerhead. And with me in jail, I'm not going to be able to help you solve it, either."

"Who ever asked you for your help, gal? I don't need your help or your boyfriend's—"

"Husband's."

"Whatever. I've got the warrant in my pocket. The judge seems to think we've got a case."

"Which judge?"

"The Honorable Judge Andrew Lund."

"Judge Lund? But that's a conflict of interest. The Lunds are second cousins twice removed from the Parkers."

"Around here that's as unrelated as anybody gets."

"So does that mean you're going to arrest me?" She didn't bother to fight the tears that quickly sprang to her eyes and rolled down her cheeks. There was no point.

"I don't have a choice. You two gals had bad blood between you for years."

"And *you* had nothing to do with that?"

"Yeah, I did. Okay? I'm sorry, Savannah. But what happened with her and me, which, by the way, didn't amount to a hill of beans—"

"Except to me."

"Yes, except to you. And then to me, after you dumped me for doin' it. But all that's got nothin' to do with the price of rice in China or me arresting you for killing her. You assaulted her only an hour or so before she disappeared. You lied to me and obstructed my investigation. You gave me an alibi that you knew damned well was false. And then I caught you, clear as day, at the scene of the crime, retrieving the murder weapon. What the hell am I supposed to do, Savannah? What would you do if you were me?"

I'd arrest my own butt, she thought. *No doubt about it. I've arrested people with a lot less.*

But nobody I'd made love to.

Passionately.

In a moonlit peach orchard.

"I understand how bad it looks," she told him. "And I accept responsibility for what I did wrong. I never should have lied to you. The minute you said Jeanette was missing, I should have told you everything then."

"Yes, you should have. But you didn't. So tell me now."

"Will it do any good?"

He chuckled wryly. "Well, it ain't gonna do no harm, is it?

I've got the warrant in my pocket, and I'm getting ready to cuff you, stick you in the backseat, and cart you off to jail. Can't get much worse than that, now can it?"

"Good point." She dragged her fingers wearily through her hair and began. "After we left you there in the school parking lot, Dirk and I drove up to Lookout Point."

"To celebrate slapping the devil outta your old enemy?"

"*In spite of* the stupidness I'd done. We'd already planned on it before I smacked her."

Tom turned his head and looked out his side window. Savannah sensed he was hurt or angry that she had taken her husband up to *their* place. But considering his history, he hardly had reason to complain.

"Go on," he said gruffly.

"We went up there. We fooled around and—"

"For how long?"

"I don't know. Forty-five minutes. An hour maybe." *A lot longer than you and I ever did, Mr. Quickie*, she added smugly to herself. "Just as we had finished," she went on, "I heard a loud splash coming from the lake."

"Which direction?"

"Down the hill. Then it started to rain. We got back in the car and drove down there. When we reached the lower make-out spot, I made Dirk stop. I wanted to check the area."

"Well?"

"Nothing in the clearing there leading to the cliff, and nothing in the lake. If the car was there already, I wouldn't have seen it. The moonlight was gone. The clouds were getting heavy, and it was really dark. But I did see a car on the road at the bottom of the hill."

"Did you recognize the car?"

"No. I just saw the rear lights. The left brake light was out.

Hey, have you written any fix-it tickets for left brake lights lately?"

He thought for a moment, then shook his head. "No. Afraid not. What else?"

"It was pouring, the ground was soggy, and I lost my sister's shoe in the mud. Then we drove back to Granny's, showered, and went to bed. So see? I didn't exactly lie to you. I just didn't mention the Lookout Point pit stop."

He turned to her and looked intently into her eyes. "I wish you'd told me everything when I first questioned you, and don't pretend that just because the words that came outta your mouth were true, you were being honest with me. You deceived me, and you meant to. That's lying."

Savannah's temper flared. "And you can keep telling me that until the cows come home to roost, but if you'd been in my place, knowing what we know about the law and how it jumps to conclusions sometimes, you'd have done the same thing. Don't tell me you wouldn't have, 'cause you're not that much better of a person than I am, Tom Stafford."

"Cows come home to roost?"

"You know what I mean."

"I wish you'd told me the truth."

"And if I had," she said, "you tell me what would be different right now. You'd still have an arrest warrant in your pocket and be getting ready to cuff me and take me in. In fact, you might have even done it then and there. So, if I'd bared it all and confessed that I'd fooled around with my husband at Lookout Point, what difference would it have made?"

He gave her a sad look, then said softly, "Maybe I'd trust you right now. Maybe I'd think you're still the woman I loved."

She didn't know what to say to that, so she sat in silence, staring down at her hands, which were folded in her lap.

"I'm sorry, Savannah," he said. "I'm arresting you for the murder of Jeanette Barnsworth. You have the right to remain silent. Anything you say can and—"

"Whoa! Wait a minute. Tommy, please. Wait a cotton-picking minute."

He was taking a pair of cuffs off his belt. "I'm sorry, baby, I can't—"

"Yes you can. It's Granny's birthday. We're having a party for her in a couple of hours. The cake's baked and everything. Let us have the party, please, Tom. At her age, we never know how many more we'll have with her. I swear to you, on all I hold dear and sacred, if you give me the rest of this day and this night to spend with my family, I'll turn myself in first thing tomorrow morning. I mean it. I will."

He wouldn't look at her. He fumbled with the cuffs, toyed with his keys, put on his sunglasses, then took them off again.

"All right," he said finally. "For Granny's sake."

"Thank you, Tom!" It was all she could do not to kiss him right there, with her husband looking on.

To her shock, it was he who leaned over and kissed her.

Once. Lightly. On the cheek.

"And," he continued, his voice tremulous with emotion, "because I owe it to you for what I did. To you. To us."

"I'm so grateful. And I promise I'll be there when you arrive tomorrow morning at nine o'clock."

"Seven thirty."

"Seven thirty?"

"Yeah. I'm the sheriff now. The boss. I have to do all the hard things." He looked at her, and she was sure she saw tears in his eyes. "Sometimes I hate my damned job."

She gave him a little smile. "You're just doing what you have to, Tom. Any lawman worth his salt would do the same thing. Don't feel too bad if you can help it."

She opened the car door and got out. Before shutting it, she said, "I owe you one, darlin'."

"No, Savannah. You don't owe me anything. At best, we're even." He smiled. "And after all these years, even that feels mighty good."

Chapter 15

In Savannah's opinion, the worst thing about growing up with a passel of siblings was the complete lack of privacy. In a family with nine children, everyone knew everything about everybody—from their toilet habits to their favorite piece of chicken, to who had a crush on whom at school that week. All the kids knew more about their brothers and sisters than they ever wanted to know.

The girls even knew whose turn it was to wear the panties with the faded blue rosebuds and the worn-out, unreliable elastic waistband. They knew because they had either worn them already, would wear them someday, or had them on at the moment.

So why did she think she could hide something as important as a murder warrant?

The moment she and Dirk stepped through the door, they were met with a frantic mob, which delivered a barrage of questions, bits of old news, and useless suggestions, all soaked in a deluge of tears.

"Did you know that the sheriff's out to get you?"

"I heard it's a murder warrant he's got in his pocket. The judge done signed it and everything."

"We could poke you in the back of Butch's pickup, toss some blankets on you, and sneak you out once it gets dark."

"Naw. There might be a roadblock where they're checking backs of trucks and car floorboards and such."

"They catch a lot of felons on the run that way. I saw it on *Cops*."

"Maybe Butch could rig up some sort of harness thingamajig and sling her under the truck. I don't think they look *under* trucks. Just *in* 'em."

"He couldn't go roarin' over any big bumps, though, or that might be the end of 'er then and there. Squashed flatter than a flitter."

Savannah held up both hands and yelled, "Stop! While I'm sure y'all mean well, you're fixin' to drive me crazy. What's all this talk about murders and warrants and arrest? We got a birthday party to throw here, and that's all that's important right now."

She shooed them away from her, then pointed to the sofa and assorted chairs. "Sit yourselves down and grab something good to eat. I just talked to Sheriff Stafford, and everything's under control. Let's get the celebrating under way."

Dirk put his hands on Marietta's back, spun her around, and gave her a push toward the nearest chair. "Savannah's absolutely right. Don't we have some presents to open or a donkey to pin a tail on or something?"

Savannah glanced around the room at her distraught and overly excited siblings. Only Gran, Tammy, and Waycross remained calm. And even they looked terribly worried and sad.

Gran pulled a footstool close to her chair, gave it a pat, and said,

"Come sit over here by me, granddaughter. We've gotta have us a serious heart-to-heart talk. And the rest of these knuckle-heads are gonna hush up, settle down, and listen."

Since Gran was wearing her "I mean business, so don't mess with me" face, Savannah immediately did as she was told and took a seat on the footstool. Dirk followed and stood behind her, his hands resting lightly on her shoulders. She leaned back against him, grateful for the comfort the simple contact offered.

Gran reached over and took Savannah's hands in both of hers. And for a moment, with the two strongest, most precious people in her life in front of her and behind her, Savannah felt that maybe there was hope. With the love and the strength of her family surrounding her, perhaps there would be an answer.

In her peripheral vision she could see Tammy and Waycross sitting to her right, and she felt their love and support radiating toward her, as well. She wasn't sure what she had ever done in her life to deserve such devotion from such truly good people, but she was infinitely grateful for it. And never more so than now, when she needed all the help she could get to tip the scales of Lady Justice in her direction.

"First of all, Savannah girl," Gran said, "get any ideas of birthday parties out of your head. There ain't gonna be no cel-ebrating done in this house until this mess with you is over and done with. Once we get you out in the clear, then we'll have double the reasons to hoot and holler and kick up our heels."

"But, Gran—"

"Not one more word about that, young lady. It's my birth-day, so the party's gonna be when I say. Not a minute before or after. We're gonna eat that fine cake you baked, though, while it's still fresh. And somebody else besides Savannah is gonna have to make me another one when the time comes. But other than that, us Moonlight Magnolia members have got serious business to attend to. If any of the rest of you wanna be temporary honorary members, then hang around and make yourself useful. As for the rest of you, thank you for coming to my home to honor me. I appreciate it, but we've got a murder to solve."

The Reid clan looked around the room at each other. At first, no one made a move. Then Marietta rose and picked up her bejeweled giraffe-print purse and slung it over her shoulder.

"I don't know about you," she said, "but I haven't got a clue as to how to solve a murder. I actually make it a point to steer clear of that kind of nonsense. It's bad enough that Savannah gets herself all wrapped up in junk like that all the time."

The others sat silently and watched her walk out the door.

Savannah felt mixed emotions, seeing her sister leave. She couldn't help being somewhat offended by Marietta's lack of concern. But, on the other hand, it was a relief to have her gone.

Domestic tranquility had never been Marietta's strong suit. And if they were going to get anything accomplished, they needed a peaceful setting and as little drama as possible.

Vidalia was the next one to rise. As she gathered her two sets of twins to her sides, she said, "I think I'll be getting along, too. The kids are cranky and need a nap. You don't want them hanging around underfoot. But if you'd save us all a big piece of that cake, we'd be most obliged." After being assured that her crew would not be dessert-deprived, Vidalia and her offspring made a hasty exit.

"Me too," Jesup said, springing to her feet. "I've got someplace important I oughta be."

"By all means, don't let us keep you," Savannah whispered.

Dirk's hands caressed her shoulders.

"I've got a test tomorrow I need to study for," Cordele said, rising and smoothing imaginary wrinkles from her baggy skirt. "But if there's anything y'all need, like pencils and notebooks to write on, just let me know."

Those two hurried out the door, as well.

The family members who remained in the living room wore somber but determined looks. There were the usual core members of the Moonlight Magnolia team: Savannah, Dirk, Granny, Tammy, and Waycross. And now their numbers had increased by one, little Alma.

"Don't worry," she told Savannah. "We've gotcha. And we've gotcha good. You ain't goin' nowhere, leastways not off to prison. It's bad enough that Macon ends up behind bars from time to time with his nonsense. And that Mom sleeps it off in jail once or twice a month. But you've always been good. You're not a criminal. You've dedicated your life to *catching* criminals."

"Thank you, sweetie," Savannah said.

"You don't have to thank me. I'm just saying what's true. And those of us sitting here, we're not going to let anything happen to you. You're ours, and we love you, and we've gotcha."

"That's right," Tammy said. "You put your life on the line time after time for us. Now it's our turn to help you. And we're more than happy to do it."

Gran added, "We've solved murders together before, Savannah girl, and with a lot less motivation than we've got now. Somebody must've killed Jeanette Barnsworth, and we know it wasn't you. We're gonna find out who it was, and then you'll be safe and sound, on the right side of iron bars, and with your good name cleared."

Savannah lost her battle with her tears as she placed her trust and her freedom into the hands of those she loved.

* * *

Unfortunately, the confidence inspired by her family's pep talk lasted only as long as it took Savannah to fill them in on the unpleasant facts concerning Jeanette's demise and the so-called evidence that, at least in the sheriff's and the coroner's opinions, pointed to Savannah being the killer. By the time all the gory details had been shared, she could tell that even their resolve was shaken.

When, finally, at one in the morning, everyone had decided to go to bed and get some sleep, Savannah was as frightened as she'd ever been. She knew more about the justice system than most people, and she knew that sometimes—not often, but sometimes—mistakes were made and innocent people were convicted.

She also knew that police officers, or those who had been cops in a former life, suffered terribly in prison. Their terms were often served under circumstances that were, literally, worse than death.

And that was assuming she escaped the death penalty for her "crime."

She pulled Gran's soft, tulip quilt up to her chin and snuggled over against Dirk, drawing strength and comfort from his closeness and the warmth of his body against hers.

"Only person in history to get the needle for slapping a smart mouth," she muttered to herself.

He heard and hugged her closer. "You're doing it again," he said, "but I caught your drift, even if you didn't say it all out loud."

"I'm sorry. I'm just worried. Really worried. I can't help it."

"I understand. I'm not exactly jazzed about all this myself, babe. Tomorrow morning I'll be driving my wife into town so she can turn herself in."

"I know. I shouldn't add to your burden with my complaints."

He kissed the top of her head. "Don't apologize for anything you say to me, Van. I'm your husband. Nothing's off-limits."

"Okay then. Here goes." She took a deep breath. "It's got to be bad when once she heard the evidence, even Granny asked me if I did it."

"She asked you once, because she had to, just to get it out of the way, if maybe you'd done that gal in purely by accident. She never asked if you killed her intentionally."

"If I can't convince my own grandmother who raised me . . ."

"But you did. She knew you meant it and so will anybody else who asks you. Your sincerity shines like a floodlight at a new strip mall opening."

She couldn't help chuckling. This man might eat cornflakes and read newspapers loud enough to wake a cemetery full of dead folks, but he could make her laugh at some of the worst times in her life.

As he ran his fingers through her curls and gently massaged her temples, she allowed herself to enjoy the moment as much as possible, considering her circumstances. Although she hated to think about it, this might be her last night to lie next to her husband and feel his caresses. She felt the need to make the most of it. Every single moment.

The sultry night air drifted through the open window nearby, lifting and parting Granny's lace curtains. Savannah felt the gentle breeze blow across her bare legs and wondered if Tommy Stafford's jail cell had a breeze. The last time she was there, some years back, the place was horrid. A sweat box, without a hint of fresh air, that reeked of urine, perspiration, and desolation.

Well, kiddo, she told herself, *you'll be finding out soon. Now, aren't you glad that you slapped Jeanette? Hope you had a good time, 'cause you're sure gonna pay for it.*

Long ago Savannah had realized that she had two inner voices. At least two. And over the years, she had become increasingly more grateful for one and more assertive with the other. The former spoke words of kindness, encouragement, and support. The latter was a witch with a nasty, scolding voice who never missed an opportunity to point out her shortcomings to her. Voice number two would expound upon those faults for as long as Savannah would allow her. And lately, with all that was going on, she'd had far too much to say.

"You just shut up already," Savannah told her. "Nobody yanked your chain. So keep your opinions to yourself."

"Just to make sure," Dirk said, "you're talking to someone in your head, not me, right?"

"Yes. The voice of my head that keeps telling me I messed up bad and now I'm screwed."

"You didn't mess up bad. You did what anybody with an ounce of gumption would've done under the circumstances. I don't know what that gal said to you, but I'm sure it was bad, or you never would've lifted your hand to her. The only one you're beating up who doesn't deserve it is yourself. So knock it off."

He kissed her on the nose and added, "As far as you being screwed, we'll see about that. First thing tomorrow I'm gonna be all over this case. All of us will be. And we're not gonna stop until it's solved and you're cleared."

"Tom's not gonna like that," she told him.

"I don't give a damn what Tommy boy likes or doesn't like. If I piss him off bad enough, he can lock me in a jail cell with my wife. I can think of a lot worse things."

"I've seen those jail cots of his," she said. "They're two feet wide, if that. We'd have to sleep double-decker."

He chuckled, the sound of it deep and masculine in the darkness. "So what? You and me, we've done double-decker plenty of times before. And speaking of . . . What you think, darlin'? Am I going to get lucky tonight or not?"

"Reckon we ought to. It might be the last time we get a chance to for God knows how—"

He pressed his fingertips to her lips, shutting off the rest of her words. "Don't say it, Van. I mean it. I'm gonna make love to you right now, just like I have many times before and just like I'm going to many, many more times. And not during some stupid conjugal visit, either. You got that?"

She smiled at him, and by the dim blue glow of the night-light, she saw him smile back.

"I've got it. I've got it," she assured him. "And now the all-important, burning question is, am I going to get it?"

He laughed again, and the sound of it went through her, sweeter and more sensual than any other form of foreplay

"Ah, brace yourself, darlin'," he said with a growl. "You're gonna get it *good*."

Chapter 16

The sweet intimacies of the darkness had faded all too soon, to be followed by a cheerless gray dawn. Morning had come far too quickly for Savannah's liking, and her dread of all the day might bring had kept her awake the entire night.

She was exhausted, too tired to breathe, and she hadn't even gotten out of bed yet.

That was never good.

As the first feeble ray of light shone through the lacy curtains, she heard some rustling in the kitchen. Soon the smell of fresh-perked coffee reached her nose.

No drip coffee for Granny. It had to be the "real" thing, made in a percolator and allowed to brew until it could crawl out of the pot and bench-press a Mack truck.

Savannah told herself the caffeine would help. Heck, it might even give her a pulse.

"You awake, babe?" she heard her husband ask.

She rolled toward him, took one look at his haggard face, and knew that he, too, had been awake all night.

"Yeah," she said. "I'm lying here wishing I'd paid more attention to Miss Puddiphatt in seventh-grade geography. Which do you reckon is closer to Georgia? Canada or Mexico?"

She was trying for a joke, but he didn't even smile.

"Probably six of one and a half dozen of the other. But if either one is where you wanna go, darlin', let's get moving. I'm with you all the way."

She studied his face a moment. "You're kidding, right?"

He shrugged. "Six of one and a half dozen of the other."

"Hmmm. Go on the run or put my trust in the American justice system. Are those my only choices? Really?"

"Don't you believe in the American justice system?"

"I used to, back when you were innocent until a jury decided you weren't. Nowadays, with folks being tried by public opinion in the press and the politicians weighing in before they've even had a trial . . . not so much."

"I hear ya. But things seem a bit backward around here. Maybe they're old-fashioned when it comes to stuff like that."

"One can always hope."

The aromas of baking biscuits and bacon drifted into the bedroom, mixing deliciously with the scent of the coffee.

"Shoot," Savannah said, throwing back her sheet and quilt and sitting up in bed. "Granny's making a full breakfast. I didn't want her to go to all that trouble. Especially when she probably didn't sleep a wink herself last night."

He caught her by the arm and pulled her back to him. "Leave her alone, babe. Let her do what she needs to do. It's important to her to make you a big breakfast. You know how she is. A wild tiger and a rabid grizzly bear couldn't keep her from sending you on your way with a full stomach. Especially *this* morning."

"That's true, God bless her." Savannah reached for his

hand. "We have to find out who did this murder. Who *really* did it. Because if I go away for it, it'll kill her."

"I know, sweetheart. I know. And we will. I'm sure of it."

Savannah breathed in the blended fragrance of the food and listened to Granny rattle her pans while humming one of her favorite hymns. Ah, the scents and sounds of Savannah's childhood.

She only wished that she was half as sure as Dirk was pretending to be that everything would turn out all right.

Somehow it seemed appropriate to Savannah that it was raining when she and Dirk drove up to the front of the sheriff's station in downtown McGill.

The sky was as gray and cheerless as her mood. And why shouldn't it be? Unless her luck improved considerably over what had come her way the past few days, this was the end of her life as she knew it.

Dirk parked the car at the curb in front of the small, two-story brick building that housed the McGill Sheriff's Station. He switched off the key, and in unison, they both glanced up at the second story, where the windows had bars.

The jail.

Savannah's new home.

They had arrived fifteen minutes early, as the last thing Savannah wanted to make Tom wait after giving him her solemn word that she'd be there on time. And yet, now that they were there, Savannah found that her feet refused to get out of the car and walk up to the station. The old, square brick building was so special to her, the place where, as a child, she had dreamed of being a police officer.

Who would have thought that a simple trip back here would

result in her being imprisoned in that building, in her being unable to return home to San Carmelita?

Sometimes, life took a strange turn when you least expected it. And there seemed to be no way to prepare for the twist. You just hung on and rode the roller coaster to the end. Like with any other thrill ride, there was no stepping off midway.

"It was hard to say good-bye to Granny when we left," she said, fighting back the tears, which recently seemed so near the surface at all times. "She took it well, though. Held up better than I did, in fact."

Dirk grinned wryly, looking in his rearview mirror. "That's because she was just pretending to say good-bye."

"What are you talking about?"

"Look behind us."

Savannah turned in her seat and peered out the car's rear window. At first she thought there was some sort of impromptu demonstration or parade forming on Main Street in McGill, Georgia. Then she realized it was just her relatives. All of them.

Having parked their assorted vehicles, they were tromping down the street in Savannah and Dirk's direction. When they reached their car, they surrounded it. Gran, Marietta with her two boys, Cordele, Jesup, Alma, Vidalia and Butch and their double sets of twins. And with them marched Waycross and Tammy. The Reid family, full blooded and adopted, in all their indignant glory, had come to, as Gran had put it, "walk our Savannah girl through her valley of the shadow of death."

Savannah appreciated the support, if not the melodrama.

She and Dirk stepped out of the car and stood with them in the pouring rain.

"You shouldn't have come out in this storm, Gran," Savannah said, enfolding her grandmother in a warm embrace.

"Of course I should. We have to show that snotty-nosed Tommy Stafford who he's dealing with. We're not gonna cotton to him giving you any grief. At least none that's not absolutely necessary. We aim to show him that you're well represented by your kinfolk, and he'd better treat you right, or he'll have us to answer to."

Savannah didn't have time to suggest that maybe a gentler, subtler approach might work better with Sheriff Stafford, because at that moment his patrol car pulled up in front of them.

Tom got out, wearing an oversized bright yellow rain slicker with wide silver reflector tape across the chest and around his equally oversized bicep areas. She'd seen him looking happier. Much happier, in fact.

He shook his head as he approached her. "What? General Sherman and his army weren't available, too?" he asked. "Good Lord, gal. I should've known you'd show up with a dadgum entourage."

Gran stuck herself between him and Savannah and glared up at him with fire in her eyes. "Don't you get smart, boy," she said. "We've as much a right to walk on this public road and sidewalk as anybody else."

"Actually, you don't have the right to walk *in* the road," he told her. "If one of you gets run over, I'll be the one fillin' out the paperwork."

Gran turned to her family members. "Sheriff says to relocate yourselves onto the sidewalk. And you better get a move on it, too, or he might arrest you. Seems he's gone from being a good sheriff to all arrest happy these days."

Savannah saw Tom wince. She said to Gran, "That's okay, Granny. Tom's just doing what he feels he needs to. Don't be too sore at him for fulfilling his duties."

G.A. McKevett

Granny sniffed, unconvinced. "If he was doing his job proper like, he'd have done solved this murder and found the real culprit, instead of laying the blame on you."

Dirk stepped forward. "I agree with Granny. A real cop would've done some actual investigating. Not just pinned it on the—"

"The most likely suspect?" Tom interjected. "Heaven forbid, Sergeant Coulter. If this was your case, you'd never do such a thing, I suppose."

Savannah felt her heart sinking, which surprised her, because she thought she'd already hit the bottom of the catfish barrel.

"Let's just go inside and get 'er done, Tom," she told him as the rain suddenly increased fourfold and the wind began to blow. "If we keep standing out here, you won't even have to try, convict, and execute me. I'll catch my death of cold and die of pneumonia."

Without cuffing her, for which she was most grateful, he led her to the front door of the station. Her faithful soldiers marched close behind, much to Tom's chagrin.

While she had to admit that they might be carrying the "unified front" business a bit too far, she had never felt so loved and supported.

When Tom opened the rusty old screen door for her, she couldn't help noticing and commenting on the patched holes in it. "Last time I was here," she said, "you were keeping the mosquitoes out with cellophane tape. I see you've graduated to screen patches held on with . . . What is that? Gray bubble gum?"

"Metal glue," he replied gruffly. "Move along before this storm washes us all down to the river." He opened the wooden door, with its peeling green paint, and nudged her inside.

Dirk followed close behind, a grim expression on his face.

Inside the stationhouse, the air conditioner was cranking full force, and Savannah had the creepy feeling that she had just stepped into a meat locker. Certainly, the office area had all the charm and ambiance of a pork processing plant. Dark, cold, and somehow sinister. Sparsely furnished with only the barest of necessities—a couple of desks, some folding metal chairs, a locked gun cabinet, a single computer, and a fax machine—it spoke of a no-frills, no-nonsense operation.

And she still loved the place.

Even arriving as an unhappy, unwilling guest of the county failed to lessen her affection for this simple building.

It was here that she had first dreamed the dream of becoming a police officer. It was this strong brick station that housed those heroes in blue who had rescued her and her siblings that night so long ago.

Of all the places on earth to face such degradation, why did it have to be here, in this place that was sacred to her soul?

With a deeply troubled look on his handsome face, Tom Stafford dismissed Martin, who was apparently the night-watch deputy. And once the younger man was gone, the sheriff reached into a cupboard and took out a large green plastic bag.

"Have a seat over there, Savannah," he said as he opened a drawer, searched through it, and pulled out a pair of flip-flops sealed in a clear bag.

She sat, as directed, and Dirk stood beside her chair, silent and vigilant.

Tom dropped the flip-flops onto the floor, next to her feet. Then he held the large green bag open in front of her. "I'm going to need your shoes and socks, your belt, if you're wearing one, and your jewelry. Also any cash you may be carrying on your person."

She knew the drill. In fact, she knew it so well that she had actually given herself a pedicure the night before. Heaven only knew when she would have the opportunity to again. And just because she was a jailbird didn't mean she couldn't have bright red, sexy toenails during her incarceration.

Marietta would've been proud.

She pulled off her loafers and dropped them into his bag. "I'm not wearing socks or a belt, and I'm giving my jewelry and my cash to my husband, if you don't mind," she told him.

She made a bit of a show about taking off the enormous engagement ring that her otherwise tightwad husband had bought for her. She made sure that Tom got a good look at it when she passed it under his nose and placed it in Dirk's hand.

She was mighty proud of that ring. A guy who made a practice of hanging up used paper towels to dry so that they could be used again and again and again had forked over a zillion bucks to buy her a doorknob-sized diamond.

If that wasn't love, what was?

Tom sealed the green bag, used a black marker to write her name on it, and stashed it inside the cupboard.

One by one, Savannah's family had entered the room, and they were standing shoulder to shoulder, a solid, silent wall of protestation.

Savannah heard one of Vidalia's older twins ask, "Is Aunt Savannah going to get her fingerprints made?"

"Yes, sugar," his mother told him. "I reckon she is."

"Is it gonna hurt?" he asked.

Savannah turned to him and gave him a wink and a smile. "No, puddin' cat, it won't hurt. Not a bit. You want to get your thumbprint done?"

"Hey, I don't know if—" Tom began to protest.

"Lighten up, Tommy. This is an informal proceeding, right?

I mean, how many times do you get to arrest a woman you almost married? And in front of the folks who were almost your in-laws, at that?"

Tom shook his head and ran his hand across his face. "You may find this all highly entertaining, Savannah. But I'm not the least bit happy about being put in this position. I'd rather swallow a gallon of hot sauce, without a single beer to wash it down, than put you through this in front of your family. In front of your new husband, too, for that matter. How would you feel if you had to do it to me?"

Savannah stole a glance at Dirk, whom she had never seen looking so miserable. She searched Tommy's green eyes and saw a world of sadness. She turned and saw that her grandmother was wearing the same grief-stricken expression as when they buried her grandfather.

No, this was no fun for anyone. And the sooner it was over, the better.

"You're right, Tom," she said. "Get me printed and searched. Then show me to my cell."

"I will," he replied. "And why don't you tell your family that they can go on home now? They made their point. They love you and are behind you all the way. They certainly didn't need to traipse down here in the rain to show me that. I never doubted it. Not now, and not in all the years I've known you and them."

Savannah gave her relatives, each in turn, a sweet, loving smile as she said, "Sheriff Stafford's right. Y'all should run along home now and get some rest. None of you had a good night's sleep, so you need to get caught up. Especially the kids and Granny and Tammy. I don't want anybody falling down tired on my account. I guarantee you the first thing I'm going to do when I get into that cell is take a nap. Y'all will be frettin' up a storm about me while I'm snoozing away. And what's the point in that?"

"Okay," Gran said. "If that's what you want, Savannah, then that's what we'll do."

She walked over to the sheriff and stood looking up at him, her body tense with anger and indignation. Tapping her finger on his broad chest, she said, "I'm going to tell you, Tommy Stafford, the very same thing that I used to tell you when you were a smart-aleck teenager and you and Savannah was keepin' company. You treat my granddaughter like the fine lady that she is, and you and me won't have no trouble. But if you act disrespectful to her in any way, shape, or form, I swear, I'll be on you like a big ole sticker burr on the heel of a cheap sock and ten times more painful. You got that, boy?"

Savannah thought that Gran's speech might make Tom angry, but it didn't seem to. In fact, she saw something twinkle in his eye, which might be a spark of humor or, at the very least, a great deal of respect and affection.

"Yes, ma'am," he said. "I'm going to make sure that she's well taken care of. It's the least I could do, considering the kindnesses you and your family have shown me over the years."

Gran lifted her chin a couple of notches, turned on her heel, and marched toward the door. But as she passed Dirk, she said over her shoulder, "You best see that you do, Sheriff Stafford. 'Cause if you don't, not only will you have to tangle with *me*, but this big boy here'll jerk two knots in your tail."

"Make that three," Dirk assured him.

Savannah watched her family file out the door, each shooting threatening looks at poor Tom.

She saw the way her old beau was avoiding Dirk's eyes as

he fingerprinted her and lightly skimmed his hands, palms out, over her body, pretending to search her.

Then he reached into his desk and extracted a set of keys. Without looking at either of them, he headed for the stairs that led to the jail on the second floor.

On the first step he paused and said, "I'm gonna go on up and make sure that cell's ready. A clean sheet and all that. That'll give you two a bit of privacy to say your good-byes. Don't take too long. Savannah, when you're ready, come on up."

When he disappeared at the top of the stairs, she and Dirk fell into each other's arms and kissed sweetly, then fiercely.

She tried not to cry. She didn't succeed.

Neither did he.

Finally, she said, "I guess I better go on up. He'll think we took off to Mexico."

Dirk nodded. "And the minute I get back to Granny's, I'll hop on the phone to Ryan and John and see if they have any ideas about how to get you a really good attorney and a bail bondsman."

After one more kiss, she stood still and silent, waiting for him to leave. Then she realized that as long as she was within his sight, he never would.

So she started up the stairs, slowly putting one flip-flop in front of the other. One, then the other. One, then the other. On legs that felt as though they were filled with lead and feet that seemed encased in cement.

Until she reached the top.

Until she heard the door softly close below.

Chapter 17

From the top stair Savannah looked down the narrow corridor with cells on either side and saw Tom holding an iron-barred door open for her. Apparently, her new living quarters were the second cell on the right.

The squalor of the place attacked her senses on so many levels as she walked that short distance. Overhead, naked low-wattage lightbulbs hung from frayed cords and cast their feeble illumination on the depressing scene.

The decrepit brick building might have been state of the art when it was constructed over one hundred years ago. But bare-minimum maintenance over the past century had taken its toll. The dark green army surplus paint had mostly peeled away from the walls and the iron bars, and rust and graffiti had taken its place.

The first two cells Savannah passed were occupied. She didn't find it particularly comforting that she recognized the guests in residence. They were regular partakers of the county's hospitality. They were minor offenders, and their transgressions could mostly be categorized as disorderly conduct while under the influence of alcohol or drugs.

"Right in here," Tom told her, indicating her cell with a dramatic wave of his arm. "Got 'er all ready for you. Fresh sheet and ever'thing."

"Gee, thanks," she replied. Once inside, she looked around. "Where's the 'everything'?"

"The toilet's clean. Don't gripe."

She took in the cot, which folded down from the wall, secured by chains on two corners; the ancient metal toilet; the filthy six-inch window, which was set far too high in the wall to be of any use, other than to let in a wee bit of light.

"Gee," she said. "It looked so much better on the Web site. Just goes to show, you book a honeymoon suite on the Internet, you never know what you're getting."

He didn't laugh or even smile. "Seriously, gal, this is the best one of the bunch. I did what I could for you."

"And I appreciate that, Tom," she said. "Truly, I do."

He left her standing in the middle of the cell and walked to the door.

As he let himself out, she said, "Just out of curiosity, and please don't take this as a complaint, 'cause far be it for me to bellyache when you're bending over backward to be nice, but what makes this cell so much better than the others?"

He gave her a nasty little grin as he turned the key, locking her inside. "It's the one most recently sprayed for bedbugs."

Savannah's neighbor across the corridor was a bit of a town celebrity. Yukon Bill held the record for the most nights spent in the county jail. Since he had turned eighteen and officially become an adult, Yukon had "slept off" at least half of his nights behind bars. He was now eighty years old.

The town had thrown him a party when he reached one thousand incarcerations. They had honored him with a parade at five thousand. Yukon was now over the ten-thousand mark, but the town had ceased to find his habits humorous and worthy of accolades—or even of acclaim that was satirical in nature.

Savannah could remember when Yukon Bill's waist-long beard was shorter and bright gold. Now every strand had turned to silver, and the wrinkles on his darkly tanned face had deepened to crevasses.

"Did you bring me a liverwurst sandwich?" he asked her for the third time in an hour.

"No," she told him. Again.

Apparently, Yukon had lost a bit of short-term memory, too.

"Why didn't you bring me a liverwurst sandwich?"

"I done told you, all I had was sardines and crackers."

"Oh, okay. Don't ever bring me sardines. Never did like those smelly things."

Savannah was lying on the cot, with her head toward the window and her feet toward the cell door. But when Yukon whipped out his equipment to "drain the dragon," as Dirk liked to call it, she decided to reverse her position and stare at the dirty, rain-streaked window instead.

Anything was better than watching the town drunk relieve himself. Especially since while he did so, he leered at her, smiling and showing his solitary yellowed tooth.

To her surprise, Savannah found herself longing for the segregated population of a state prison.

"Hey, girly," Yukon shouted her way. "How's about I ask the sheriff if you and me can share a cell tonight?"

When she didn't answer, he continued to present his case. "I may not be much to look at no more. But I still know a thing or two about how to please a lady."

Savannah rolled onto one side and pressed her pillow against her ear. "Lord, just take me now," she whispered.

"I know all kinds of tricks. You'd be surprised what a man can do with some know-how and a beard this long."

Savannah felt something snap inside her, and she was pretty sure that it was her last nerve. Jumping to her feet, she hurled the pillow onto the cot and marched over to her cell door.

"Tom! Yoo-hoo, Tom!" she shouted.

When there was no response, she yelled even louder, "Tom-m-y Stafford, you come up here right now, or I swear, I'm gonna eat this pillow and choke myself to death."

Still nothing.

"How do you reckon my family's gonna take it when you have to tell them I croaked myself in your jail?"

A minute or so later, she heard heavy steps, someone plodding up the stairs.

Eventually, he appeared at her cell, looking tired and aggravated. "What?" he snapped.

"I tried. Okay? I really did. But this just ain't gonna work."

"*What* ain't gonna work?"

She pointed to Yukon Bill, then to herself. "This. Him and me. I want a divorce. At least a different cell mate."

"Gal, your pancake ain't done in the middle. How can he be your cell mate when he's in a different cell?"

"Yeah, but he's still way too close. He's flashing me and making indecent proposals about his beard and how he wants to use it to have sex with me."

"What?" Tom whirled around to face Yukon, eyes blazing. "What are you thinking, you old geezer, showin' off your privates to her and talking dirty? You know better than to pull that crap in my jail."

"I was just takin' a piss!"

Savannah shook her head. "He was not. Well, he was. But he was also making it real obvious, dangling it out there in plain view. And he was enjoying it, too."

"Enjoying it?" Tom looked horrified. "You mean he was . . . I mean . . . it was . . . he had a . . . ?"

"No! For heaven's sake, he's an old fart. Probably hasn't had a—"

"Hey, hey," Yukon interjected. "I'm standing right here. Watch what you're sayin'. I get my feelings hurt easy."

Savannah reached through the bars and grabbed the front of Tom's shirt. "Come on, Tom. You've got to do something. Don't you have another empty cell?"

"Nope. This was it. We've had a run on *stupid* in the past forty-eight hours, so we're fuller than usual."

She tried another tactic. "I realize you don't have a gender-segregated jail here. But you've usually got a hooker or two locked up. Can't you stick me in with one of them?"

Tom looked doubtful. "I've got one female in custody on a drunk and disorderly, but I don't think you'd be happy with—"

"I'll take her! I will. Please, just move me away from Romeo here. Listening to him and, God forbid, looking at him constitute cruel and unusual punishment."

Tom sighed and reached for the ring of keys on his belt. As he unlocked her cell and opened the door, he said, "Now this is it. If you don't like your new accommodations, you just keep a shut mouth about it. This is the last time I'm gonna run up those there stairs to do your bidding. Hear me?"

She nodded vigorously and hurried out of the cell before he could change his mind. "I hear you, darlin'. Loud and clear.

I'll be quiet as a mouse peeing on a cotton ball for the rest of the night. I promise."

"Savannah Reid," he told her, "the day you get quiet, I won't even have to check your pulse. I'll know you're dead."

He led her all the way to the end and the cell on the left.

"I warned you that you weren't going to like this," he said as he turned the key and opened the door. "So you just move along right inside there and no more complaints. Come sundown, I'll be releasing Gilbert Hayworth across the way. And I'll move you over there for the night. That way at least you'll have your own cot."

"That's fine, Tom. I appreciate it. I didn't mean to be difficult. I'd just enjoyed as much of Yukon's company as I could stand without going completely—" Savannah froze, swallowed her words, and tried not to choke on them.

Her eyes had adjusted to the dim light of the cell. And she had recognized the all too familiar face and form of the woman standing with her back against the rear wall.

"Mom."

Chapter 18

"Well, well, well. Won't cha just look at this?" Shirley Reid said as she watched her oldest daughter take a seat on the cell's only cot.

Savannah felt her body ache, along with her heart, as she leaned back against the cold brick wall. Now she was completely convinced that this whole trip was nothing but an awful, prolonged nightmare. Surely, in real life she would never have this many strokes of rotten luck in so few days.

Locked in a jail cell with my beloved mother, she thought. *What's not to love about that?*

Savannah snuck one quick look at Shirley and was horrified at the change in her since the last time they met. If possible, her mother was even thinner than before, a rickety rail of a human being, with yellowed, crinkled skin stretched over bone. Savannah could see her ribs pushing against the worn denim fabric of her Western-style shirt. Her stiff-spined posture had disappeared, and her back was severely bowed, like that of a beast of burden who had carried far too heavy a load for much too long.

Heaven knows, it wasn't the burden of the nine children she brought into the world, Savannah thought. *A burden of guilt perhaps?*

But Savannah quickly reconsidered, reminding herself of who her mother was. Shirley Reid seemed to have an uncanny ability to deflect any blame that might come her way from either an external or an internal source. Everything negative that had happened in Shirley's world had originated elsewhere, and certainly not from her. At least in her own mind, she was a victim, used and abused by those she had loved and treated so well.

As she leaned against the wall and surveyed her daughter from head to toe, Shirley snickered, obviously enjoying herself enormously. "It appears what I've been hearin' 'bout you at Joe's is true, after all."

Savannah rolled her eyes. "Well, you know what they say. Anything you hear at Whiskey Joe's Saloon has to be the gospel truth."

Shirley laughed. "All I know is, here you are, coolin' your heels with me in a jail cell. And I don't figure it's for something as simple as drinkin' a little too much and disturbin' the peace, like I did."

Savannah tried to ignore her, but all of a sudden, having Yukon Bill for a neighbor seemed vastly preferable to her current situation. Of course, she couldn't call out for Tom again. Not after promising him absolute silence and contentment for the rest of the evening.

She tried to block out her mother's voice, but she knew that even if her ears and her mind could do so, her heart would hear every vicious, condemning word.

Some things just never changed.

"Who would've thought," Shirley babbled on, "that after all

these years of you and that sanctimonious grandma of yours bailing me out of jail, that you'd be right here with me. Only I'll be out first thing tomorrow morning, and word is around town that you may never get out. I reckon this time it's me looking down my nose at you for a change."

Savannah stood, walked over to the cell door, and turned her back to her mother. She gripped the bars so tightly that she could feel the flaked paint digging into her fingers and palms.

"So you killed that prissy little bitch Jeanette Barnsworth and dumped her and her ugly purple Cadillac in the lake. I never pegged you for a killer, but that just proves that you never know about somebody."

"I didn't kill her," Savannah said, trying to keep her voice even. Long ago, she had learned that showing any emotion, especially distress or pain, to Shirley simply brought on more abuse.

"I don't care if you did or not," her mother continued. "Jeanette always did look down on me, me and everybody else around her. She acted like she was so high and mighty, but she was nothing but a two-bit slut. Anytime she wanted to get laid, she'd come prancing into Joe's and pick up some guy. Any guy. And the lower on the totem pole he was, the better, as far as she was concerned. Yes indeed. When them high-society girls get horny, they don't go for their stuffy men in their pressed suits. They come across the tracks and go slummin' at Joe's. That's how they get their kicks. They're no better than any of the rest of us. Their shoes and jewelry might cost more. But that don't make them better."

Shirley walked over to the cot and sat down. "As far as I'm concerned, you did the world a favor, murdering that bitch."

"I told you, I didn't kill her. I slapped her. That's all."

"That's enough to get your butt arrested. You were stupid

to slap her, especially in front of other people. I'd never do a thing like that."

"No," Savannah said quietly. "You slap only your children. Or maybe hit your fellow bar patrons over the head with a beer bottle if you get drunk enough."

"Don't you get smart with me, young lady! I won't stand for it."

Slowly, Savannah turned and faced the woman who had struck her more times than she could count. The mother who had beaten her children with belts, switches, and anything else she could lay her hands on for such serious infractions as missing a bit of egg yolk when washing a plate or forgetting to call her "Shirley" instead of "Mom" in front of a male she was trying to impress.

"I've had a very bad couple of days, Shirley," Savannah said. "Very bad. And I'm in one helluva rotten mood. I'd advise you to tread softly with me."

"Or what?"

"Or you might regret it."

Shirley smirked. "You're gonna beat me up right here, right now? With a witness in the cell across the way? With the sheriff right downstairs, and you with a murder charge hanging over your head? I don't think so. No." She snickered again. "Whatever I wanna dish out, girl, you're gonna take."

Savannah rose, took a couple of steps toward Shirley, then stood, glaring down at her. The taunting look on the older woman's face disappeared.

Savannah leaned down and whispered, "What I had in mind can be done very quietly. And it doesn't leave any marks. So, go on. . . . Dish out what you've got, and then we'll see how much you can take. I promise it won't hurt any worse than getting whupped half to death with a wooden coat hanger."

Shirley jumped up from the cot, ran to the bars, and shouted, "Sheriff Stafford! Sheriff Stafford! Get up here quick! I mean it. I'm gettin' death threats here! Get a move on!"

Tom Stafford and Savannah stood in the corridor between the cells, their every movement being watched and their every word overheard by the prisoners inside those cells.

This was turning out to be one of the more entertaining days to spend in the McGill jail in a very long time. Each inmate was glued to his or her bars, straining to hear every word and see what was going to happen next.

Tom bent his head down to Savannah's and through gritted teeth said, "What the hell am I going to do with you, gal?"

She raised one eyebrow and propped her hands on her hips. "Tommy, climb down off that high horse of yours. You knew darned well that wasn't going to work before you stuck me in there with her."

"I was hopin'." He sighed. "Seriously, I'm running out of places to put you. I oughta poke you in the cell with Yukon and let him have his way with you."

"Don't even joke about something like that."

"You promised you'd be good."

"I tried."

"Obviously, not hard enough." He gave her a look that was half annoyance and half affection. "You always did have a streak of pure ole contrariness a mile wide."

She grinned up at him and even employed her dimples. "You could just let me hang out downstairs with you."

"You're a murder suspect!"

"I know, but I'll be good."

"Like you were up here?" He shook his head. "And what if you decide to make a break for it the minute my back's turned?"

"You could always handcuff me to the radiator."

"I was just kidding about the radiator."

"It ain't turned on. Don't bitch."

She wriggled her arm, trying to find a less miserable position to sit in with her wrist fastened to a large metal pipe that was only an inch or so from the floor.

What she would have given for the universal cuff key in her nightstand table back at home! Or even a sturdy paper clip or a plastic straw, for that matter.

Unable to imagine herself relaxing on a Mexican beach or skiing down a Canadian slope without her loved ones, she had no intention of trying to escape. But she would have loved to have uncuffed her own wrist, then reattached herself to something a bit less ridiculously awkward. How fun it would be to surprise Mr. Smarty-Pants, who was pretending to work on her case by shuffling papers around on his desk.

She was about to raise yet another outcry when the front door of the station house flew open and Dirk rushed inside, accompanied by Granny and Marietta.

Dirk marched up to Tom, a stack of papers in his hand. "Okay," he said. "I've got it all here. And you'd better be happy with it, because I paid a fortune to get all this crap faxed here from California in record time."

Dirk turned to Savannah. "And you can thank Ryan and John, who pulled some strings, or it would've taken a week or more."

He slapped the first document down on the desk in front of Tom. "This," he said, "is from the county recorder of deeds for

Savannah's house, showing there aren't any judgments or liens against it." The second document quickly followed. "And that shows the true market value of the place. And this"—he threw down another piece of paper—"is a certified copy of the deed." He took a deep breath, stuck his thumbs in his belt, and lifted his chin. "So, Sheriff Stafford, consider her bail posted and let 'er out. Pronto."

"Yeah, pronto," Granny said.

Nodding, Marietta added, "Yeah. What they said."

Slowly, Tom picked up each piece of paper and scrutinized it with great deliberation, nodding and muttering to himself. Then he stacked them carefully, paper clipped them, folded them neatly, and handed them back to Dirk.

"That's impressive," he said, "you gettin' all that together so quick. And, Savannah, it appears that real estate's a lot more expensive there in Southern California than it is here. I'm proud you've done so well for yourself."

Savannah held her breath. She could smell a big "but" coming.

"But," he said, "the property's out of state."

"So?" Dirk said, his face turning an ugly shade of red.

"We don't accept out-of-state properties for surety."

"Why on earth not?" Gran shouted. "What's the difference if it's here or there? It ain't like it's gonna run off or nothin'."

"It might fall in the ocean, though," Marietta added, "you know, if they have that Big One earthquake thing they're always talkin' about, and the whole state of California just cracks off and floats away into the—"

Gran shot her a stern look, and she shut up.

Dirk leaned far over Tom's desk, until the two men were nearly nose to nose. "Don't tell me that I can't bail my wife out of jail with a house worth thirty times what it says there in your standard bail schedule. Do *not* tell me that!"

Tom looked up at him calmly and said, "I'm sorry, Sergeant Coulter. But that's exactly what I'm telling you. I don't make up the rules. And I can't break them. Not even for as fine a woman as . . . your wife."

Savannah thought Tom was going to choke on those last two words. And in that moment she knew, if she'd ever had doubts before, that Tom Stafford was still very much in love with her.

For all the good it did.

Granny pushed her way around Dirk to stand beside the desk. Reaching into her purse, she said, "I had a feelin' this sorta thing might happen. So I brought the same kinda papers, only they're to *my* house." She shoved the documents in Tom's face. "And, young man, the last time I checked, my house *was* in the fine state of Georgia."

Tom took the paperwork from her and perused it, as well. He avoided her eyes when he handed it back to her and said, "I'm sorry. While I appreciate the fact that you're trying to help your granddaughter, your property value just ain't high enough to do the trick."

To Savannah's sorrow, she saw tears fill Granny's eyes.

"Are you telling me," Gran said, "that the home I raised two families in ain't worth enough to get her out?"

"I'm sorry, Granny. I truly am."

But Gran wasn't moved. "Until you let my grandbaby out of this jail of yours, you can just call me Mrs. Reid."

"I understand."

Marietta wriggled her way forward and, to Savannah's shock, began to rummage around in her giant rhinestone-encrusted giraffe bag. "As it happens, I have a property that I can throw in the pot, along with my grandma's. Between the two, I'm sure it'll put you over that danged limit of yours."

"Since when do you have property?" Tom asked her as he took the papers from her hand. "Aren't you and your boys livin' in one of old man Landers's duplexes out there by the cotton gin?"

"Yes, we're renters. But that's the deed to my business. My hair and nail salon. And as you can see right there, it's worth a small fortune."

Tom squinted as he read the property report "This was signed by Wanda Blaylock. Isn't she one of your very best customers?"

"Yes, she is. Comes into my place for nails and hair three times a week. I keep her looking gorgeous. So she, of all people, should know full well how valuable it is."

Tom sighed, snatched Gran's papers out of her hand, and clipped them to Marietta's. "Okay," he said. "I reckon between the two, it'll come close to coverin' it."

Cheering erupted. But it was short lived, because Sheriff Tom Stafford rose from his chair, held up both hands, and shouted, "That's enough! Quiet! The sooner y'all settle down, the quicker I can process her outta here."

He turned to Savannah. "And as far as you go, gal"—he stuck his finger in her face and waggled it—"you've been nothing but a royal pain in the ass from the minute you got here. I *cannot wait* to be shed o' you."

Chapter 19

One of Savannah's favorite pastimes for as long as she could remember was sitting in the swing on Granny Reid's front porch and watching as the setting sun gilded the cotton fields in soft patinas of copper and gold. The evening breeze would sweep across the green plants, stirring their delicate white and pink blossoms and wafting their sweet, fresh fragrance toward the house, like a gift from the angels.

And of all the times she had experienced that commonplace miracle, this night had to be the best ever.

Next to her sat her husband. He was holding her hand tightly, as he'd done almost constantly since they'd left the sheriff's station.

While Dirk's edges were a bit rough, and his idiosyncrasies somewhat difficult to ignore, Savannah never had to wonder if she was the center of his universe. He made that abundantly clear every day.

And there was nothing like the threat of losing a loved one to make a fond heart grow even fonder.

Nearby, Gran sat, rocking contentedly in her chair. The expression of profound peace on her face gave her an almost angelic look.

When Savannah thought of how Gran had placed her home on the line that very day to gain her freedom, Savannah knew that she had never loved her grandmother more than she did at that moment.

She also felt surprisingly close to her sister Marietta for the first time in many years. Savannah understood what Marietta's salon meant to her. She had worked hard for many years, cutting, curling, and coloring her town folks's hair, filing and polishing their nails, while listening to every detail of their personal lives—the good, the bad, and the downright ugly.

Savannah vowed that no matter how annoying her sister might prove to be in the coming years, she would always remind herself of this day and at least attempt to be more patient.

Sitting on a motley assortment of folding lawn chairs, Tammy, Waycross, and Alma were also enjoying the sunset and the celebratory mood resulting from Savannah's reprieve, temporary though it might be.

As always when members of the Moonlight Magnolia gang were assembled, a plate of warm-from-the-oven cookies was being passed around, and the general topic of conversation was whatever case they were working on at the moment. None had been so thoroughly discussed as this one, with so little progress.

"I don't know why," Granny said, "but I've just got a notion that this business with Jacob Barnsworth's half sister, it ain't gonna lead to nothin' in the end."

Dirk nodded. "Me too, Gran. But when it's the only lead you've got, you follow it to the end. Whether there's anything there or not."

"I know, grandson. I know."

Savannah felt a buzzing in her hip pocket, and a moment later the tune "I'm Too Sexy" began to play. She jumped up from the swing, saying, "That's Ryan, returning my call. Excuse me for a minute, y'all."

Tammy smiled brightly, as she always did at the mention of Ryan Stone. "Tell him hi from us," she said.

"We promise not to say anything important till you get back," Granny added.

"But if you take too long, we might eat all the cookies," Dirk said as Waycross passed him the plate of goodies.

"You better not!" Savannah shouted. "Somebody grab that plate and put it away somewhere safe till I'm done with this call."

As she hurried through the front door and into the living room, she answered her phone. "Ryan, thank you for getting right back to me. I know how busy you and John are with the restaurant and all."

"Don't be ridiculous," replied the deep, elegant, deliciously male voice that never failed to set her heart, and other parts of her, atwitter. "When our favorite damsel is in distress, we knights-errant come a-charging."

Savannah smiled at the imagery of Ryan and John atop white horses, suited in shining armor, lances in hand, riding to her rescue. Although, since they had become joint owners of a gourmet restaurant in San Carmelita, they were more likely to be wielding Sakai chef's knives than swords.

"And charging, you did," she said. "I so appreciate you scrambling to send those documents to Dirk right away."

"Anything we could do to get you out of that jail. John and

I were beside ourselves to think of you behind bars. Was it dreadful?"

"The gruel was moldy, and the water rancid, but I was starting to get the hang of rock busting."

He chuckled. "And your serial killer cell mate?"

"A far better conversationalist than you might imagine." She could hear a heavy door sliding open, then closing. "You're home, on your balcony," she said, picturing him in his white shorts and pale blue polo shirt, walking out onto his deck to enjoy his luxury condo's magnificent view of the Pacific.

"Yes, I am," he said, "and wishing you were here to share the sunshine and a glass of wine with me."

Ordinarily, if a man had said that to her, she would have considered it flirtatious. But Ryan and John had been a couple since long before she'd met them, so there had never been a chance she would be anything but the dearest of friends to either of them. And she had found that more than enough.

"I wish I was there, too, darlin'," she replied. "I've got myself in one helluva pickle here."

He cleared his throat. "Which reminds me, I spoke to that attorney that I mentioned to Dirk. He'll be happy to defend you if it comes to that. He's very good. Comes highly recommended."

"If he's a friend of yours, I'm sure he's excellent."

"I told Dirk, and I hope you know I mean it, that all you have to do is crook your little finger, and John and I will be on the next plane to Georgia."

"Of course I know. But you've done plenty already. How can I ever make it up to you?"

"Just come home to us, Savannah," was the heartfelt reply.

She could hear the love and concern so clearly in his voice that it made her ache to hug him and stand on tiptoe to plant a kiss on his cheek.

"Buy some good champagne," she told him. "I'll be there before you know it."

"I'm putting it on ice right now."

After she said good-bye, Savannah closed her eyes and pictured Ryan and John, drawing comfort from the mental images of their beloved faces that she had stored in her heart's treasure chest.

Ryan was exquisitely handsome with his black, wavy hair, darkly tanned skin, and pale green eyes. And John, several years older than Ryan, was the quintessential British gentleman, with thick silver hair and a lush mustache to match and a deliciously aristocratic accent.

How much you take for granted, she thought, *until your very freedom is threatened.*

She had always assumed that she would grow old with her loved ones on the porch and her dear friends in California around her. To be able to sit down and share a meal with them at will, to be able to pick up a telephone and call them just to chat for as long as she wished. Who would have thought such basic joys could be taken from her?

"No," she whispered. And because she liked the sound of it, she said it aloud. "No."

She recognized that tone of voice. It was the one she encouraged the women who attended her self-defense classes to use. "Shout it in your attacker's face!" she'd told her students over and over again. "Scream it at him! No! No! No! You will *not* be a victim! You refuse! You *will not*!"

She jumped up from Granny's sofa, punched her fist into the air, and shouted as loudly as she could, "No! No! No! No!"

She felt the power of her proclamation rise from her feet and flow upward through her, filling her mind, body, and spirit with resolve, courage, and confidence like she had never felt before.

For as long as she needed to, she stood there, her fist raised high, her backbone stiffer than it had been in a long time, her posture that of a defiant warrior.

Then she slowly lowered her arm and turned toward the door, where she saw her husband. He was standing, watching her, with a look of alarm on his face.

"Um. Are you all right?" he asked. "I heard you yell and, uh . . ."

She gave him a bright, cheerful smile. "Darlin', I'm way better than all right. This woman is *fine*!"

After her brief but effective self-administered pep talk, a good night's sleep, and one of Granny's fortifying breakfasts, Savannah felt like taking on the world. Or at least tracking down her one and only lead.

By eight thirty the next morning, she and Dirk were on their way in the rental car to the equally small neighboring town of Sulfur Springs and the nursing home where Mr. Jacob Barnsworth's final remaining blood relative resided.

They headed south, following the highway through acres of cotton fields, took a right at the Y, and continued on through more cotton fields. They found the nursing home on the edge of town, in the middle of a cotton field.

"You guys sure grow a lot of cotton around here," Dirk commented.

She shrugged. "Somebody's gotta do it, if you plan to keep wearing T-shirts, jeans, and cotton underdrawers."

"When you put it like that, guess I oughta be more grateful."

"You're darned right. Thank God for farmers. Ever put on a pair of wool boxer shorts?"

"Can't say I ever have. They'd probably be a bit scratchy."

"There ya go."

Savannah felt another butt buzz. "My rear end's sure getting a lot of action lately," she said.

"Excuse me?"

She held up her cell. "Phone."

Nodding solemnly, he said, "Thank you for clarifying that."

Her pulse quickened to see a number with an Atlanta area code. "This is the attorney that Ryan recommended," she told Dirk.

"Good luck."

Savannah answered the call, and for the remainder of the ride to Sulfur Springs, she discussed her situation with the lawyer. He was a good listener, and when it was his turn to talk, he had a soft, good old boy accent and a gentle manner that she found comforting. But his penetrating questions, astute observations, and sage advice assured her he was no lightweight. Her confidence in him was well placed.

By the time they arrived at the nursing home, Savannah had decided that she was in good hands, after all.

Once they had concluded their conversation, she turned to Dirk and said, "Well, I'd say, so far, so good."

But as always, Dirk wanted details. "Okay, fine, but what did he actually say?"

"In a nutshell, exercise my right to be silent, especially with Tom."

"Did you mention that's impossible for you? You know, being a Reid female and all?"

"Shut up. He did mention one other thing."

"What's that?"

"He said we'd better catch the person who really did it, or I'm going to be eating a lot of bologna and cheese sandwiches and sharing a cell with a gal named Toots."

Chapter 20

During her previous few visits to nursing homes, Savannah had developed a negative opinion of such establishments. So she was expecting something dark, drab, and depressing when she and Dirk entered the front door of the plain, utilitarian-looking building with its gray clapboard siding.

But the moment they were inside, she realized this was a place where she wouldn't mind spending her golden years. Perhaps she needed to reexamine her prejudices.

The receptionist sat at a delicate French desk, upon which was a small computer, a telephone, and a crystal bowl with one giant, floating peony. Beyond her lay a room that looked like a cozy reading area, with wingback chairs, plush ottomans, and elegant side tables, each chair lit with a Tiffany-style floor lamp.

A blaze glowed in the brick fireplace, which on closer inspection, she realized was fake. But considering it was the middle of a hot summer, she decided it was more practical than a burning log.

Bookshelves on either side of the mantel were well stocked, and Savannah recognized both classic titles, as well as current bestsellers. A large aquarium bubbled cheerfully against the opposite wall, its colorful residents swimming among the miniature coral reefs, seashells, and plants that had been artistically arranged.

"Hey," Dirk whispered in her ear, "this ain't half bad. Let's you and me move in here when we get old and gray."

She didn't bother to mention to him that without her six-week refresher of "midnight brunette" hair color, she was already halfway there.

Savannah walked up to the desk and addressed the pretty little blonde in a pale blue sheath dress, with a floral silk neck scarf tied jauntily to the side. Her name tag identified her as Margie.

"Good morning, Margie. My name is Savannah Reid." Savannah offered her hand. "And this is Dirk Coulter. We'd like to see Miss Imogene Barnsworth."

"Is Miss Barnsworth expecting you?"

"I don't believe so. But if you'd be so kind as to tell her that we're here, I'd be most obliged."

Margie reached for the desk phone, punched in a few numbers, and said, "Miss Imogene, this is Margie at the front desk. There are some folks here to see you. A Miss Reid and a Mr. Coulter."

Margie listened a moment, then said to them, "I'm sorry. But Miss Barnsworth is on her way to her morning dance class and can't see you right now."

Savannah smiled. At least the ends of her mouth curved upward, but there wasn't a lot of sparkle in her eyes when she said, "Tell her it's mighty important. We need to speak to her about her inheritance."

Margie conveyed her message, then hung up the phone. "Miss Barnsworth will receive you in the courtyard. It's right through those double doors over yonder."

Savannah laced her arm through Dirk's and headed in that direction. "I thought that might do it," she told him.

"I must admit, there are advantages to having a smart wife."

They found Imogene Barnsworth on her hands and knees in a bed of pansies and marigolds. Thinking the frail elderly lady had fallen, Savannah rushed to help her, only to find that Imogene was neither frail nor all that elderly. And apparently, she hadn't fallen, either. She was picking some weeds from among the flowers and placing them in a small, neat pile on the herringbone brick patio.

While Savannah was sure that Tammy had been correct in reporting Imogene's age, she hadn't met many women in their seventies who looked as youthful as this lady. Her shoulder-length hair was mostly silver but still held some strands of its original auburn hue. Her eyes were a strange shade of gold, like dried oak leaves in autumn.

When she saw Savannah and Dirk, she rose and brushed the dirt from the knees of her yellow yoga pants.

"Those gardeners," she said, "just never do a good job, no matter how many times you go after them. I guess I should be grateful. At least this time they didn't trample the flowers."

Imogene led them to a wrought-iron bench and invited them to have a seat. She started to drag a matching chair closer to the bench, but Dirk quickly took it from her.

"Here, ma'am, let me get that for you," he said.

She gave him a pretty, almost flirtatious smile. "You must've been brought up right. They say a man who treats a woman like a princess must've been raised by a queen."

Savannah winced. Dirk had not been raised by his biological mother. He had grown up in an orphanage. But how could this nice lady have known that?

To his credit, Dirk showed no sign of having been affected

by her comment. He simply said, "Thank you, ma'am. That's kind of you to say so."

They all three sat down, and Savannah wondered how to broach the topic of Jacob Barnsworth's death. But before she could even begin, Imogene jumped right into the deep end.

"I understand that with my worthless brother's death and with his snooty nuisance of a wife gone, too, I'm set to inherit a dump truck full of money."

Then and there, Savannah decided that she liked Imogene Barnsworth quite a lot. If for no other reason than that the lady had the courage to say whatever was on her mind. There was far too much dillydallying in the world these days to suit Savannah, but precious little of it was happening in the courtyard at that moment.

"Yes, ma'am, that's about the size of it," she told her. "It's come to our attention that you're the next one in line to inherit your brother's fortune."

"Or what's left of it, after that hussy spent far more than her share. I'd try to get all the stuff she bought as part of the deal, but who wants that much purple junk? Not me. I've always been more of a yellow kinda gal. Or green. Us redheads look good in green."

Savannah smiled. "I'm sure you do."

Imogene glanced from Savannah to Dirk, her sharp eyes missing nothing of their attire and demeanor. "I figured you two work for that attorney who called me yesterday. But you're not dressed like lawyers. And you don't act like them, either."

"I'll take that as a compliment," Savannah said. "At least the 'acting' part."

"Good. I meant it as one. But if you don't work for him, who are you?"

Usually, in a circumstance like this, Savannah thought up a lie. Experience had taught her that as a private investigator, it was seldom wise to lay all one's cards on the table at the outset.

But something about Imogene Barnsworth inspired her to be candid with the woman. Perhaps not completely candid, but more honest than usual. Something told her that this lady had an excellent internal lie detector. Savannah also had a feeling that once Imogene decided you were a liar, she'd have nothing more to do with you. You'd be out on your ear, figuratively, if not literally.

"We don't work for the lawyer. I'm a private investigator, and my husband here is a police detective. We're investigating the murder," Savannah said bluntly. "Trying to find out who did it."

She felt Dirk cringe slightly beside her. He was very much a cards-flat-against-the-vest sort of guy. She didn't expect him to approve.

"Investigating the murder?" Imogene asked. "Which murder?"

Savannah was surprised, but she quickly recovered and answered evenly, "Both."

Imogene sniffed and brushed one silver and copper strand of hair behind her ear. "I can't imagine why anybody would waste their time trying to figure out the first one. It's so obvious that purple piece of trash killed my brother. Everybody in the county knew that from the minute they heard he was dead. Some were even whispering at the wedding that it was bound to happen. Why else would a gal in her forties marry an old fart like Jacob? It sure wasn't for his sunny disposition or his good looks."

As Savannah listened to Imogene speak such critical words

about her brother, it occurred to her that maybe there were siblings in this world who got along even less well than she and Marietta.

"Actually," Savannah said, "we're concentrating more on the second murder, Jeanette's murder."

"I can't see why anybody would spend more than five minutes or so on that one, either," Imogene said. "She was a one-woman walking pestilence, that witch. I'll bet you there's not a soul on this earth who misses her. Whoever pushed her into that lake did the world a favor. And they sure as hell did *me* a favor." Imogene threw back her head and laughed uproariously. The eerie sound filled the courtyard and bounced off the surrounding walls of the building.

Savannah shivered inside. She had heard friendlier laughter coming from the monsters in horror films.

"Would you please tell us, Miss Barnsworth," Dirk said, "if you know anyone who might've had a motive to kill Jeanette Barnsworth?"

"She was a nasty, ornery woman who tormented every female who crossed her path, and tried to seduce every male within reach. She was a thief of the worst kind. She stole everything she could from everyone around her—their mates, their money, their time, their energy, their self-esteem. She would have taken their souls if she could have, just to satisfy one of her passing whims. Who *wouldn't* have a motive to kill a woman like that? That's the question you need to be asking yourselves. And good luck finding an answer."

With that, Imogene Barnsworth rose and said, "You two are going to have to excuse me now. I have a dance contest to attend. And if I don't go, that Sherry Hayes is bound to win it, and that won't do. After her nabbing first place in the beauty contest last week, her head will swell so big, there'll be no living with her."

She scurried away into the building, leaving Savannah and Dirk to sit on the bench in the courtyard and wonder.

"Well?" Dirk asked. "What do you think?"

"I like her."

"Me too. But do you think she might've done it?"

"I think she just might have done the world a favor, and herself one to boot. What do you think?"

"I think so, too."

"Shoot. I hate it when I like a suspect."

"Yeah. Takes all the fun out of it."

As they were leaving the nursing home, Savannah and Dirk stopped once again at the little French desk with the pretty blond receptionist.

"We have a couple of quick questions for you," Savannah said.

Margie's eyes widened with interest. Whether it was genuine or feigned, Savannah wasn't sure.

"I'd be happy to answer any questions you might have, if I can," she replied.

"When your residents come and go from your facility," Savannah said, "are their departures and arrivals noted anywhere?"

"Yes, we have an entry and exit log. It's necessary, you see, because"—Margie glanced around and lowered her voice—"some have degrees of dementia, and we have to keep a close eye on them. They need to be accounted for every moment of every day while they're in our care."

Savannah glanced at Dirk, and he took his cue. Stepping up to the desk, he took his badge from his pocket and flashed it ever so quickly under Margie's nose. "I'm Detective Sergeant

Dirk Coulter," he said. "And I'm going to need to see the log from this past Saturday night."

"Certainly, Detective." Margie quickly typed something into her computer. A moment later they heard a printer on a bookshelf behind them spring to action.

The receptionist jumped up from her seat, ran over to the bookshelf, and returned with a piece of paper, which she handed to Dirk. "We don't keep paper copies of the entry logs," she told him. "We scan them and save the files on the computer. I hope that'll be enough for you."

Savannah leaned over and peered at the paper as Dirk studied it. He ran his finger down the page and stopped over an entry that read:

> *Imogene Barnsworth – Departure – 8:00 p.m.*
> *Imogene Barnsworth – Return – 11:55 p.m.*

He tapped the entry with his finger, and Savannah nodded.

"Thank you," he told the receptionist. "Yes, this will be quite enough."

Savannah and Dirk turned to leave, but Savannah hesitated, then walked back to the desk for one more question.

"Do you have any idea where she might have gone Saturday night?"

"No. I wasn't here. I believe Gilda worked that shift. But I probably wouldn't know even if I'd been here. Miss Imogene's a very private lady. She doesn't have much to say about her comings and goings. A secretive person, if you know what I mean."

Savannah nodded solemnly. "I certainly hope I do."

Savannah and Dirk exited the nursing home, and as they strolled down the sidewalk toward the parking lot, they stopped in front of a large plate-glass window and observed the activity inside. A big, spacious room was filled with women and a few men, all dressed in comfortable workout attire.

Everyone was dancing. Moving with joyous and wild abandon, they were performing dances popular in every decade for the past fifty-plus years. And they were doing it with more enthusiasm, grace, and skill than could be found at any modern club populated by their children or grandchildren.

In the center of all the activity was a woman in a bright yellow yoga suit, doing a frenetic and highly energetic rendition of the Charleston.

Arms flying, knees knocking, Imogene Barnsworth was winning the contest hands down.

"Feeble?" Savannah said, more to herself than to Dirk.

But he replied, anyway. "Not so's you'd notice."

"And secretive."

"Yeah. Sweet."

Chapter 21

"Wouldn't you think that a place called Burger Igloo would at least have air-conditioning?" Dirk complained as he and Savannah slid into the red leatherette booth across from Tammy and Waycross.

Savannah promptly poked a few quarters into the table-side jukebox and selected some Elvis tunes. In spite of their interesting visit to the nursing home, the sleep-deprived Dirk had been somewhat cranky all morning. She figured a few tunes from "the King" might cheer him up.

He needed to perk up as soon as possible, because her own mood was pretty foul, and the last thing she needed right now was another assault and battery on her ever-growing criminal record.

Between the Jeanette smack down and then being accused of her murder, if Savannah accomplished one more violent felony, she'd probably earn her "career criminal" badge.

It was an honor she could do without.

Her wifely duty done, Savannah took a moment to look around the old café and reminisce.

As a teenager, she had spent every Saturday night within these walls, where the price of one milk shake could buy a poor kid an evening of entertainment.

No matter how hard the week had been, with schoolwork, the copious chores at home, and whatever part-time job she performed to bring home a bit of extra money to Gran, her grandmother had always made sure that Savannah's Saturday nights were free. And that she had the price of a chocolate malted in her purse.

Back then the bright red leatherette seats had been new and supple, not stiff and cracked, the way they were now. In those days, the chrome table edges and the jukeboxes had glistened like the freshly polished grille of a brand-new Ford Mustang. The framed vintage movie posters on the walls had been old even then, but Savannah didn't remember them being so yellow or dingy.

She was careful not to look at the booth in the back, where she and Tommy Stafford had sat for hours, exchanging kisses and contemplating the wisdom or foolishness of running away and getting married as soon as they turned eighteen.

Such memories, sweet as they might be, were best left in the past. Especially considering the present circumstances.

"I remember this place," Tammy said as she perused the plastic-encased menu. "The closest thing to a salad in here is some extra pickles on your burger."

Savannah looked indignant. "That simply isn't true. You can also order extra lettuce and tomatoes."

With a sigh, Tammy closed her menu and leaned her head on Waycross's shoulder. "Your fiancée and your child are starving for something alive to eat," she told him. "Something with a real nutrient in it. This constant diet of processed, high-sodium, fatty food just isn't cutting it."

He smoothed the top of her silky golden hair with gentle strokes and said, "Don't fret none, sugar. I'm on it. You'll have something nutritious to eat before the day's over. I promise. If nothing else, I'll raid Gran's garden."

Tammy looked down at her belly, patted it, and said, "Did you hear that, baby? Daddy's going to get us something yummy. Maybe some fresh carrots! Wouldn't that be good?"

Savannah turned to Dirk, a smirk on her face. "Are they just too sweet or what?"

"Way too sweet for my taste. Like Granny's iced tea. Can you imagine how sweet that kid's gonna be?"

Tammy laughed. "So sweet that Auntie Savannah and Uncle Dirk are gonna gobble it up. You wait and see."

"I have no doubt," Savannah said. "We can't wait to get our hands on that rug rat and spoil it rotten."

Once Savannah, Dirk, and Waycross had placed their orders—chocolate malteds and double chili cheeseburgers, with extra lettuce, tomatoes, and pickles for Tammy—the conversation turned far more serious.

Waycross's usually peaceful, cheerful expression was solemn as he asked, "How long's it gonna be before they do that arraignment thing, or whatever it's called when they make you go before the judge and say whether you're guilty or not?"

Savannah shrugged. "Haven't heard anything yet."

"The longer it takes, the better," Dirk added.

Tammy took a drink from her frosty water glass and popped some vitamins. "It gives us longer to solve the case and find the real murderer."

"I think," Savannah said, "Tommy might be dragging his feet a bit with the paperwork. That's good of him to help me out like that."

Dirk snorted. "He's a real pal, that guy, keeping you out of jail long enough for you to solve his case for him. Woo-hoo."

Note to self, Savannah thought. *Don't say anything positive about an ex-boyfriend in front of a cranky husband.*

She stuck another quarter in the jukebox and selected "Blue Suede Shoes."

"Either way," she said, "he's going to have to move forward sooner or later. I'm sure with the notoriety of this case, he's under pressure to wrap up his investigation."

"*Is* he investigating?" Waycross asked.

"Not exactly working up a sweat that I can see." Dirk scowled and wadded his paper napkin into a tight ball. "Looked to me like he was sitting there in his office, soaking up the air-conditioning, while Savannah's bacon sizzled in the skillet."

Savannah couldn't help snickering. "Bacon in a skillet? Boy, you've been hanging out south of the Mason-Dixon Line too long. You're starting to talk funny, Yankee boy."

"You know what I mean," he grumbled. "We've gotta get this thing solved now. Before an arraignment. Once court proceedings have started, it'll be a lot harder to turn things around."

"Sorta like getting an eastbound freight train to stop, turn around, and go west," Waycross said.

"Exactly." Dirk propped his elbows on the table and rested his head in his hands for a moment.

He looked dead tired, and Savannah felt guilty, as though she was somehow to blame for his current state. Then she reminded herself that she was . . . at least partly.

I hereby swear, Lord, she prayed, *if you help me get out of this mess, I will never, never strike another human being for the rest of my life. Not even a thump. Not even Marietta. Unless she flashes her hind end to my husband, and then I reckon you'd give me a pass.*

"Speaking of sisters . . . ," she said.

"We were?" Tammy asked.

"She probably was. In her head," Dirk told them. "She does that a lot now that she's going through the change."

Savannah raised her hand to smack him on the shoulder but quickly lowered it. You couldn't break a sacred vow. At least not ten seconds after you made it.

"As I was saying," she continued, "this Imogene Barnsworth is our strongest suspect."

"We have other suspects?" Tammy asked.

Dirk rolled his eyes, and Savannah braced herself for a "dingbat" or "fluff head" comment.

But Dirk seemed to think better of it. Probably because Waycross was sitting across the table from him and was in Protective Preggers Papa mode.

"No, we don't have any other suspects," Savannah admitted, "which puts her right up there in the number one spot. So, let's look at her close like."

Tammy pulled her ever-ready electronic tablet from her purse and scrolled through her notes. "Okay. Here's my latest. I found out that she's on the move. Literally. She's in the process of buying a luxury property about half an hour north of here. An equestrian estate with a beautiful old Tudor house, a lake, a creek, even its own waterfall."

"I know that place," Savannah said. "It's a far cry from the nursing home she's in now."

"And not only that," Tammy added, "but she's been working on the deal for the past three months."

Dirk perked up. "Three months? That was even before her brother died."

"Did she have money of her own three months ago?" Savannah wanted to know.

"Not unless she was stuffing her mattress with it there at the nursing home. There's none on record anywhere."

"Then she must have been pretty sure she was going to inherit her brother's estate," Savannah said.

The group fell silent as the waitress approached their table and served their burgers.

But the instant she was gone, Dirk said, "I got the idea that she was mad at Jeanette, thinking she might've murdered her brother. But what you just told me makes me wonder if Miss Imogene had something to do with both of them kicking the bucket."

"She didn't speak highly of Jacob, either," Savannah added. "Called him stupid and worthless, if I remember right."

Waycross giggled. "I call Jesup worse than that all the time. Not in front of Granny, of course."

"But if she had something to do with killing her brother," Tammy mused, "she'd have done so, knowing that his estate would go to his wife."

"And that'd require her doin' two killin's," Waycross said.

Savannah put a dab of mustard on her hamburger. And then, because the kitchen had been stingy with the chili, she poured on a generous dollop of ketchup. "Something tells me that Miss Imogene Barnsworth wouldn't be all that squeamish about committing two murders. Or, as she put it, 'doing the world a favor.' Maybe she decided to do the world *two* favors."

Dirk crammed a large portion of his sandwich into his face, shoved it into one cheek, and said, "What if Herb Jameson isn't a complete nitwit of a coroner, and the murder weapon really was a high heel?"

Tammy brightened. "It's a woman's weapon. And our number one, and only, suspect is female. Sounds pretty good to me."

"Except for one thing," Savannah said far less enthusiastically than Tammy. "A high heel is a weapon of opportunity. If she'd been planning these murders for a long time, surely she would've come up with something better than whacking a victim on the head with a shoe and drowning her."

They all sat in silence for quite a while, thinking, analyzing, and chewing.

Not surprisingly, Tammy finished her "lunch" before the rest of them.

"I was wondering," she said. "Do you suppose it might be worthwhile to sneak into the nursing home and check Miss Barnsworth's closet for a bloody high heel?"

Savannah dabbed her lips demurely with her paper napkin. "I reckon it is, darlin'," she said. "Yes. I reckon it is."

Chapter 22

The last place in the world Savannah wanted to go was back to the sheriff's station. But Tom Stafford's big patrol car was parked in front of the building, indicating to everyone passing by that the sheriff was in residence.

If they wanted to have a talk with him sooner than later, it had to be there.

"He's not going to tell us anything. You just wait and see," Dirk said as they strode up the sidewalk toward the front door.

"No, I don't suppose he will," Savannah replied. "But he's going to listen to what we've got to say. Even if you have to hog-tie him while I yell it in his ear."

"Gee, something to look forward to."

"And I'm going to read every single expression on his face. I've always known what that boy was thinking ten minutes before it crossed his mind."

"Unfortunately for us men, most females seem to have that ability." Dirk opened the door and ushered her inside.

The moment they entered, Tom looked up from his seat at

his desk. The first expression that Savannah had the opportunity to read was one of extreme annoyance.

He glanced up at the clock on the wall. "That's gotta be some sorta record. You stayed out of trouble and out of my hair for a whole four hours. Woo-hoo. Congratulations."

She gave him a big smile. "Now, Sheriff Stafford. Sarcasm does not become you."

"How's about you turn around and march out that door and stay away another four hours? That way, when you come back, I'll be home, watching the game and enjoying my evening beer."

"I wish I could catch a game and throw back a cold one," Dirk grumbled. "Seems like about a million years ago that I was able to do that. But then, I've got a murder to solve, so I don't have time to sit around on my fist, with my thumb up my ass, and swig beer."

"Oh, well," Tom said. "I'm plumb tore up with sympathy for you there, good buddy. Maybe if you were better at your job, you'd be able to close your cases faster. I, on the other hand, have got mine all sewn up."

Dirk took a couple of quick steps toward Tom's desk, and for a moment, Savannah thought she was going to have to separate a tangle of two very large, very angry men.

She hated doing that sort of thing. Especially with an extra-large chili cheeseburger and a chocolate malted in her stomach.

She quickly positioned herself between them and said, "Boys! Boys! Boys! Now ain't the time. If you two could stick your dickie-dos back in your breeches and stop this pissing contest, we might get something accomplished. And I, for one, would be most grateful."

She plopped herself onto the metal chair closest to Tom's desk, figuring that if she was seated, it would be a bit harder for him to throw her out the front door. Perhaps lying prone on the floor would be better still. But since the station house looked like it hadn't been swept for several months on end, she decided against it.

"We didn't drop by just to show our pretty faces, you know," she said. "And we certainly didn't come calling just to annoy you. I figure I had that covered this morning. No point in being redundant."

"You're right about that, gal." Tom leaned back in his chair and folded his hands behind his head. "What *did* you come by for? Spit it out and be done with it."

"We've got a good lead on that Jeanette gal's murder," Dirk said as he plopped himself on the chair next to Savannah's. "Thought we'd share it with you, for all the good it'll do."

"A lead? Goody." Donning his best fake surprised look, Tom rubbed his hands together gleefully and added, "This should be great! What is it? Did you bring me a witness who saw you do it? A high heel with some actual blood and brain tissue on it? By all means, lemme hear what you've got."

"What we've got," Savannah said, "is a real honest-to-goodness suspect. You know, the kind that you'd be looking for if I'd never smacked Jeanette."

Dirk chimed in. "Yeah, a suspect with a motive and an opportunity and all that good stuff they teach you in How to Be a Cop One-Oh-One. Or do you backwoods po-lice get your training from watching forensic shows on the television?"

Savannah poked Dirk in the side with her elbow and said softly, "Stop. You aren't helping."

"Listen to your woman there, Detective Sergeant Coulter," Tom told him with a sneer. "Once in a while she says something smart. It's a mite hard to pick it out from all the stuff that's flyin' outta her mouth, but—"

"And you stop, too, Tommy Stafford!" she shouted. "I've had it up to here with you both. My life's on the line, and if you care about me half as much as *you* used to tell me you did"—she pointed to Tom and then turned and stuck her finger in Dirk's face—"and as much as *you* say you do every night, you'll both put all this petty male jealousy and bickering aside and figure out who really killed Jeanette Barnsworth before I get convicted of a murder I didn't do!"

There was a long silence, and she was encouraged to see that both men looked a little ashamed of themselves. Neither appeared to be so overcome with guilt that they'd be hurling themselves off any cliffs, but the ill wind in the room did seem to have shifted a bit.

At least for the moment.

She figured she'd better take advantage of the lull in hostilities.

"As it turns out, Sheriff," she said, "we've uncovered someone who certainly had a motive. Somebody who disliked Jacob Barnsworth and hated Jeanette. A person who, as a result of these deaths, will be receiving millions of dollars."

Tom said nothing but just sat there, his hands behind his head, leaning back on the rear legs of his chair, looking at her.

"Miss Imogene Barnsworth of Sulfur Springs," she told him. "She's Mr. Barnsworth's half sister. She—"

"I know who she is."

"Then you've been investigating her, too?"

"I know everyone who's anybody in my county."

"You must know that with Jeanette gone, Imogene will inherit her brother's estate."

Dirk cleared his throat, and in a calmer voice than before, he added, "When we spoke to her a few hours ago, she told us how happy she is that they're dead."

"I imagine she is," Tom replied. "If I was gettin' all that money, I'd be kickin' up my heels at Whiskey Joe's instead of sitting here, chewin' the fat with you two. Doesn't mean I murdered him. Or Jeanette, either, for that matter."

"But it's a powerful motive," Savannah said. "And we found out that she's been in the process of buying that Tudor mansion up in Cedar Hollow for the past three months. Sounds to us like she was planning on a visit from Lady Luck before the lady even knocked on her door."

"Figured that out all by yourselves, didja?" he said with an unpleasant grin.

"Yes, we did." Savannah resisted the urge to take one of the pens out of the old, cracked coffee cup on his desk and shove it up his left nostril.

As she was fighting the inclination, she vowed to swear off making sacred vows. They certainly cramped one's style at a time like this.

"What's more . . ." Dirk fished around in his pocket and pulled out the sheet of paper that the receptionist at the nursing home had given him. "We've got this. Proof that she wasn't at her nursing home when the murder occurred." He held the paper out so that Tom could see it, but the sheriff hardly gave it a glance.

"I already know that Miss Barnsworth wasn't at her nursing home Saturday night," he said.

"You do?" Savannah was somewhat pleasantly surprised that he was still actually conducting an investigation. Maybe he wasn't as convinced of her guilt as he appeared.

"Yes. I do. I not only know the people in my jurisdiction— their names, their faces, where they live—but I also know their habits. And I know where Miss Imogene Barnsworth spends her Saturday evenings."

Savannah was almost afraid to ask, but she had to. "Where?"

"Playing poker. For money. In the back room of Arnold's Feed and Supply."

"Poker?" Savannah felt her mood slide down into the toes of her loafers.

"Yeah. And she's damn good at it. Been winnin' like all git out for the past six months. I'm not surprised she's been looking at buying a luxury property. She can afford it. Especially since her winnin's are all off the books."

"But, but did you at least check and *see* if she was playing poker *this* Saturday night?" Savannah felt like she was beating a dead horse with Tommy boy or, more like it, a lazy mule, but she had to try.

"Nope. I didn't have to. I know she was there."

"How?"

"She's a creature of habit. We all are, Savannah. That's what living in a small town is about, or have you forgotten all the Saturday evenin's you spent suckin' down chocolate malteds at the Burger Igloo?"

The twinkle in his green eyes told her he was thinking more about that corner booth than about chocolate malteds. She decided to steer the conversation back to less nostalgic topics.

"So Imogene Barnsworth is a degenerate gambler," she said, "and a good one at that. Just my luck. I can't believe, Tom Stafford, that you'd allow such a thing to go on here in your squeaky-clean community. And in the back of an innocent feed and grain store, too."

Tom grinned and held up both hands in surrender. "Hey, what's a lawman to do? I've got way too many jewel thieves and international spies and serial killers to deal with. Who's got time to break up a friendly little card game?"

*　*　*

A few moments later, as Savannah and Dirk left the station house and were walking down the sidewalk to their car, she said, "I don't know if you caught it or not, but when he was being a smart aleck, asking what evidence we'd brought him, he asked if we had a high heel that actually had blood and brain tissue on it.'"

"Yeah. So?"

"That means he's already tested the one he took from me there at the scene and knows it doesn't have any on it."

"We knew it wouldn't have any on it."

"But *he* didn't know. Now he knows. And if, God forbid, it comes to it, a jury will know."

"I doubt that's gonna help a lot, Van."

"It can't hurt."

"Yeah, well, whatever. But I caught something, too."

"What's that?"

"On his desk I saw both of Jameson's autopsy reports. The one he did on Jacob Barnsworth and Jeanette's, too."

"So?"

"So at least you know he's been looking at them. He's not just sitting around, watching games and sluggin' down beer, like he's letting on. He just said that to get under our skin. Mine anyway. You're right about it being a pissing contest between us guys."

"Okay, so he's looking at the autopsy reports. I don't know how much that's gonna help."

"Can't hurt."

"Whatever."

Chapter 23

"Yee-haw! It's been a long time since we've had this much fun," Granny proclaimed from the backseat of Savannah and Dirk's rental car.

Sitting next to her, Tammy laughed and said, "If by 'fun' you mean breaking and entering, burglary, robbery, and nefarious, covert activities, then yes, we're having a ball."

"Hold on back there," Savannah said, turning around in the front seat and staring at the ruffian miscreants in the rear of the car.

Granny, Tammy, and Waycross were grinning from ear to ear. They had been snickering all the way from McGill to Sulfur Springs like a bunch of teenagers on their way to toilet paper an unpopular teacher's house.

"There'll be no laws broken tonight," Dirk said, watching them in his rearview mirror as he drove through the ever-darkening countryside.

"What about the breaking and entering?" Gran wanted to know.

"Hopefully, you can enter without breaking anything," Savannah told her. "And for sure no robbing or burgling allowed."

"Not even if we find a bloody high heel right there in her closet?" Waycross asked.

"Definitely not," Savannah said. "You leave everything exactly where you found it. We just want to hear what you saw."

"I don't think it's fair that I can't climb in the window with Gran and Waycross," Tammy whined. "I'm not *that* pregnant, for heaven's sake. It's on the ground floor. I can see Miss Barnsworth's window right here in the picture on their Web site. It's in a nice, dark place and not high at all!"

"Tamitha, just stop." Savannah hoped her bossy big sister voice would work. It usually did the trick on Tammy. But lately, the girl had been a bit sassier and more difficult to handle. Pregnancy hormone fluctuations didn't exactly bring out the best in any disposition, even one as sunny as hers.

"We talked about this back at the house," Dirk said. "You did the research and found out which room was Imogene's and how to get to it. You're going to be the lookout while Waycross and Gran go in. That's enough for a woman in your, um, delicate condition."

"That's no big deal. And I'm not that delicate. You said you'd send me a text when you start talking to Miss Barnsworth and another one when she leaves your sight. How hard can it be to look out for a woman you know is on her way?"

"Someone else might try to come into the room," Gran said.

"Like who?"

"Maybe a gentleman caller. You wouldn't believe what goes on in these old folks' homes. A lot of hanky-panky. That's what."

Tammy groaned with frustration. "You guys aren't fooling me. Even if a whole troupe of exotic male dancers comes charging into that room for a wild night of senior citizen sex, they'd arrive by way of the hall, and I won't see them from where I'm standing under the window."

"She's got you there," Dirk told Savannah.

"Shhh."

"I'm afraid this is a harbinger of things to come," Tammy said with a sniff. "Just because I'm pregnant, I'm being downgraded to junior detective. Once I'm a mom, it'll be even worse."

"That isn't true," Dirk told her. "You'll be even more valuable than ever. We can stick surveillance equipment in the kid's diaper."

Savannah pointed to the lights of the nursing home, shining a bit farther down the road. "No more squabbling, y'all," she said. "We've gotta be serious. This is a dangerous mission we're on here. We must *not* get caught. But if, God forbid, you *are* captured, you know what you have to do. Bite your cyanide capsules and end it all. And don't get them mixed up with your Tic Tacs, the way you did last time."

Tammy giggled.

Waycross snickered.

Granny began to hum the theme song from *Mission: Impossible.*

This time when Savannah and Dirk entered the nursing home, they didn't find the pretty blond receptionist sitting at the French desk. Her replacement would have been attractive in a girl-next-door way, with her freshly scrubbed face and no-nonsense ponytail, except for the scowl on her face. She was frowning at her computer screen as they entered, and her disposition didn't seem to improve when she looked up and saw them approaching.

Savannah hoped this didn't bode ill for the visit overall. If there would be anything sweeter than clearing herself of a murder, it would be getting to rub Tommy Stafford's face in the proverbial cow pie in the process.

When the receptionist, whose name tag identified her as Gilda, didn't offer any sort of verbal greeting, Savannah said brightly, "Hi there. Nice to see you this evening."

Okay, that was over the top, she told herself when Gilda fixed her with a stare that was colder than twelve-hour-old coffee and just as appealing. *Dial it back a notch, girl, and don't look so desperate.*

Dirk stepped in to rescue the situation. Again, he performed a quick under-the-nose badge swipe and put on the grimmest version of his cop grimace. "I'm Detective Sergeant Coulter," he said, his voice half an octave lower than usual. "I need to ask you a couple of questions about a resident of yours."

"Got a warrant?" Gilda asked with an accent that sounded like she had been raised in the Bronx.

"No, I don't got a warrant," Dirk replied with equal charm. "And I don't need one just to ask you a couple of questions."

"I think you do," she said. "So I got nothing to say."

Dirk stepped to the back of the desk and peered at her computer screen. She quickly hit the OFF button, but not before he saw something that made him grin. "Does your boss know that you spend your time here at work looking at naked hunks on social media?" he asked.

She simply stared at him, but her jaw tightened, and her fingers clenched the back edge of the desk.

Savannah smiled. She had always gotten a kick out of watching her husband in action. Surgeons and attorneys might make more money, but she was convinced it was far more entertaining to have a cop for a hubby.

"So ask your questions," Gilda replied, crossing her arms over her ample bosom.

"That's better." Dirk walked back around to the front of the desk. "You were on duty this past Saturday night, correct?"

"Yes," was the curt reply.

"Then you must've seen Miss Imogene Barnsworth leave here about eight o'clock and return just before midnight."

"Yes."

"Do you know where she went?"

"No."

Savannah could see that Dirk was growing impatient with his interviewee.

"You're just a friggin' fount of information, aren't you there, Gilda?" he said.

"Nope."

Savannah decided to give it a whirl. "When Miss Barnsworth goes out for the evening like that, does she go with someone or does she drive herself?"

Gilda turned to Savannah and gave her a smile that was slightly less smirky. Apparently, she liked Savannah a bit more than Dirk. That was hardly a surprise. Most people did.

"Usually she drives herself," she said. "But last Saturday night someone picked her up."

"Do you know who?"

"Not his name."

"'His'? It was a guy?"

"Yeah, a really cute guy. Hot."

"How old?"

Gilda shrugged. "I don't know. About my age maybe."

"And how old are you?" Dirk asked.

"Thirty."

"Good thing you aren't thirty-one," he shot back. "That'd have required a two-syllable response."

"Yeah."

Savannah gave him a warning look and continued. "What did he look like?"

"Cool. He had a lot of ink and long black hair. Muscles. Dressed cool."

"And to you, dressing 'cool' would be . . . ?"

"All black. A big crucifix necklace. Biker boots. Leather vest. Big leather bracelets with silver studs."

"Ah, yes. Cool, indeed." Savannah smiled. "Did you happen to see what he was driving?"

"That was the best part. He had a General Lee."

"A General Lee? An old orange Dodge Charger?"

Gilda nodded. "With an oh-one on the door and a Confederate flag on the top."

"That's pretty memorable, all right."

"This guy," Dirk said, "he picked her up *and* dropped her off?"

"Yeah."

"Is there anything else you can tell us about that night? Anything that stands out in your memory?" Savannah asked.

"Just that she was dolled up a bit more than usual. Dressed all in red. Miss Barnsworth always looks nice, but it occurred to me that maybe she'd dressed up for him." Gilda made a face. "Kinda gross. An old lady like her and a guy my age."

"You say she was dressed up." Savannah's pulse rate increased a bit. "Do you recall what sort of shoes she was wearing?"

"Yeah, some cute red heels. Pretty high for an old woman like her. I'm telling you, she looked like she was going on a date or something. Yuck." Gilda glanced around, as though suddenly

239

aware she was being less than discreet. "You're not going to tell her I said that, are you?"

"Not at all. In fact, we won't tell her that we spoke to you about her at all. This will just be our little secret, okay?"

Gilda looked relieved.

Dirk glanced down at his watch. Savannah did the same and saw that it was 8:15 p.m.

The rest of the gang would be in position now. It was time.

"How's about you give Miss Barnsworth a buzz on your phone there," he said, "and let her know that we're here to see her?"

"Okay."

Dirk rolled his eyes. "Sheez. Two whole syllables. Hope you didn't strain yourself there."

"Nope."

Savannah and Dirk sat on the sofa next to the fireplace while waiting for Imogene Barnsworth to appear. They kept their voices low and tried not to sound too excited as they spoke to each other.

Why let the rather unpleasant Gilda know that she had made their evening? Doing so would, no doubt, ruin hers.

Dirk leaned close to Savannah and said, "This is gonna be a piece o' cake. How hard can it be to find a dude driving a General Lee and wearing a leather vest?"

"Well, the General Lee part . . . you might be surprised how many of those are running around these parts."

"But with a Confederate flag still on the top?"

"Again, in this part of the country, there are still strong feelings about the War of Northern Aggression."

"War of Northern . . . You mean the Civil War?"

"Shhh. Watch your language, boy. You're in Dixie now. But anyhow, this new information is certainly interesting."

"It's not really all that surprising that she might've had an accomplice," he said, dropping his volume another notch and looking around again. "After all, she may be spry, but she'd still have a hard time lifting Jeanette and getting her into that car all by herself. With a hole in her head, Jeanette must've been deadweight. No pun intended."

"Not just that," Savannah replied. "We should have realized right from the beginning that it had to be two people, not one. They dumped Jeanette and her car into the lake, and then they left in a second vehicle. It would have taken at least two people to drive Jeanette's Cadillac and the getaway car to the lake."

"Duh."

"Yeah, duh."

"Here she comes now. Text Tammy."

"Doing it right now."

Savannah fired off a message to Tammy that read **Go. Look for red heels.**

Almost immediately, Tammy fired back, **K.**

Savannah poked her phone into her back pocket just as Imogene Barnsworth came marching up. She was wearing a dark green velvet robe and house slippers with ostrich feather trim. With her makeup off and her face shining with moisturizer, she looked as though she'd been ready to retire for the evening.

She didn't seem all that happy to see them, either.

"You might have phoned," she said as she joined them near the fireplace, "and asked if this was a convenient time. At this time of the evening, I might have been entertaining someone more pleasant than the two of you."

G.A. McKevett

Feisty, Savannah thought. *There's nothing better than a feisty older woman. Why can't women learn to get feisty sooner?*

Imogene plopped herself on a nearby chair and ran her fingers through her copper-gray hair. "What is it?" she asked. "To what do I owe the honor of this ill-timed and unwelcome visit?"

"We just have a couple more questions," Savannah said. "We won't take long."

"You're right. You won't," Imogene snapped back. "Because now I know exactly who you are. I oughta be calling Sheriff Stafford right now and telling him that you're here, harassing me."

"Why, Miss Barnsworth, I—"

"*You* are the girl they arrested for killing my sister-in-law."

Savannah's eyes went a bit icy as she replied, "I am a woman, not a girl, and I didn't kill your sister-in-law."

"Why should I believe you?"

"Miss Barnsworth, if I'm taken to trial and wrongly convicted, I'll be going away to prison for the rest of my life. Unless I'm executed, that is. And if I thought these could be the final days of my freedom, I sure wouldn't waste them by running around, acting like I'm trying to find a killer. I'd be sitting in my granny's flower garden with my loved ones, eating all the chocolate I could lay my hands on, or making wild whoopee with my husband, or trying to sneak across the Canadian border."

Imogene took several moments to think that over. Then she nodded. "I suppose that's true."

"Thank you."

"And if you didn't do it, I'd hate to see you convicted of it."

"Then help us out here."

Imogene leaned back in the chair and rearranged the skirt of her robe in a more attractive pose. "I guess, since I'm going

242

to inherit my brother's money, I'm your number one suspect, right?"

"Yes, Miss Barnsworth," Dirk said. "You are. So, if it wasn't you who did it, help us eliminate you as soon as possible so we can go on to number two."

"You've got a number two?"

"We'll get one," Savannah told her. "Tell us where you were Saturday night."

"The same place I am every Saturday night. With friends."

"Doing what?" Savannah asked, anticipating the answer.

"Playing games."

"Playing poker's more like it," Dirk said. "And winning. A lot, so we've heard."

Imogene shrugged. "I play with a bunch of nitwit men who constantly tip their hands. Taking their money isn't hard, believe me."

"How did you get to this Saturday night's game?" Savannah asked.

Instantly, Imogene froze. Any trace of congeniality disappeared from her face. "Why?"

"Why would you mind telling us?" Savannah replied, lifting one eyebrow.

"I've been having a bit of trouble starting my car, and a friend was nice enough to give me a ride. The rest is none of your damned business."

"That doesn't sound so sinister," Dirk said. "Why are you afraid to tell us who it was?"

Imogene jumped to her feet, a dark scowl on her face. "Listen, mister. I've been to hell and back several times in my lifetime, and I'm not *afraid* of anybody or anything. But I make it a practice to keep my nose out of other people's business. And I expect them to honor my privacy, as I do theirs."

"We understand," Savannah began. "And we—"

"No you don't understand. But if you live long enough, you might. Not telling everybody all your business—that's wisdom that comes with age." Imogene smoothed the skirt of her robe, then her hair, and turned her back to them. As she walked away, she said, "Don't come by here again. You disturb my peace. And my privacy and my peace are the things I value most. That, too, is wisdom. Pay mind to it."

The instant she disappeared through the door, Savannah grabbed her phone and texted Tammy. **Get out.**

Knowing the way Miss Imogene Barnsworth felt about her privacy being violated, she sure didn't want the gang to get caught inside the lady's closet, their sticky fingers on her red party pumps.

Chapter 24

The next morning a relatively small group was seated around Granny's kitchen table. At least small by Reid standards.

Savannah, Dirk, Granny, and Alma had polished off a platter of pancakes and sausages, and now they were working on draining the pot of coffee.

"I've gotta tell you," Granny said, "if I had any cholesterol in my arteries this time yesterday, it's gone now, for sure. My heart was pumping like a locomotive engine when Tammy told us that gal was on her way back to her room. And we didn't have no time to spare, gettin' outta there, neither. Once Waycross pushed me out the window, he barely had time to dive out headfirst hisself and get that winder closed before she waltzed through the door."

"Sounds exciting," Savannah told her grandmother, smiling over the rim of her mug.

"It was! I think it does a body good, gettin' scared like that once ever' ten years or so. I reckon it tacked another decade onto the end of my life, for sure."

"You just let us know," Dirk said, "the next time you feel

like you need a tune-up. We'll do something wild and reckless, like go knock over an armored car or check out some books from the library that we have no intention of returning. I like the idea of you outliving us all."

Alma lifted her coffee cup. "Hear! Hear! To Gran living to be a hundred and sixty! At least!"

"I don't want you to think that your daring escapade was all in vain," Savannah told her grandmother. "Now we know that our primary suspect does, indeed, wear high heels. And she has a pair of bright red patent-leather ones right there in her closet. Probably the ones she wore Saturday night."

"I didn't see no blood on 'em, though," Granny said, looking somewhat disappointed. "Just a wee bit of mud, which ain't surprising, since it was raining like all git out that night."

"It's good that they still have a little dirt on them." Dirk nabbed the one remaining sausage link and put it on his plate. "That means she hasn't cleaned them. So they might have some blood evidence on them. Too small for you to see, but enough for a lab to find."

Gran shoveled a heaping teaspoon of sugar into her coffee and stirred it thoughtfully. "Something's been troublin' me, though. Kept me awake last night, puzzlin' over it. I have to ask myself, why would a woman intendin' to do murder that very night wear a pair of fancy high heels to the occasion? Seems like if there was ever a time for sensible footwear, that'd be it."

Dirk nodded and stuck half of the sausage link into his mouth. "It makes as much sense as a guy driving a tricked-out General Lee to and from a crime scene. Seems like he'd at least borrow his best friend's generic old pickup truck."

"Maybe the high heel was a weapon of opportunity. But not necessarily. There's no accounting for stupid," Savannah told them. "I once knew a guy who worked at a bowling alley, fumigating the shoes. When he decided he needed some extra cash, he ran next door to the convenience store on his lunch break and robbed it. He put a brown paper bag over his head, but he was still wearing his uniform with the alley's logo on the front. Needless to say, they arrested him ten minutes later."

Granny chuckled. "Yes, I reckon they did."

A light knock sounded on the back screen door, and they turned to see Tammy standing there, a bright, sunny grin on her face.

"Come on in, child," Gran said. "You don't ever have to knock on my door again. You're part of the family now. Just walk right in and set a spell."

Tammy hurried inside, and Waycross followed, along with Beauregard, Granny's bloodhound, who was sniffing the sausage-scented air.

The dog had no problem locating the remaining half link, which was just about to go into Dirk's mouth. Colonel Beauregard sat on his haunches at Dirk's feet and let out a soul-rending howl.

Laughing, Dirk tossed the tidbit to him. "Boy, you got it rough, don't cha? Eating Granny's leftovers three times a day. We should all be so lucky."

His treat consumed in one gulp, without chewing, the dog laid his head on Dirk's lap and gazed up at him with pleading eyes.

"Sorry, guy. That was it. I know how you feel," Dirk told him, stroking the silky ears. "Once the last bite's gone, life's hardly worth living. Until the next meal, anyway."

Tammy and Waycross sat down at the table, and Savannah jumped to get them something to drink before Gran could do it.

"You don't need to wait on me, sis," Waycross said when she handed him a steaming coffee mug. "We all know our way around this here kitchen."

"After what you did for me last night, I should be giving you a back rub *and* a foot massage, both at the same time," she answered.

"It's not his back or his feet that are hurting," Tammy said with a giggle. "Let's just say, it's a good thing we already have a family on the way. He did himself some mischief, climbing over that windowsill on the way into Miss Barnsworth's room."

Waycross's freckled face colored brightly. "And I smacked my noggin good on the way out. Maybe I wasn't cut out for this breaking-and-entering business."

"Well, I am." Tammy untwisted the cap from a bottle of mineral water that Savannah had pressed into her hand. "As soon as this baby's here, I'll be back to it."

"Just wait till she shows you what she's got," Waycross said, gazing at his fiancée with unadulterated adoration. "She was on that tablet of hers first thing this morning, searching this and posting that. She's a holy terror on that stuff."

"Of course she is." Savannah sat back down, her own mug refreshed. "Why do you think I pay her the big bucks?"

"You pay me big bucks?" Tammy asked, digging out her tablet.

Savannah reached over and pushed a strand of golden hair out of her eyes. "Not that big, darlin'. I could never pay you what you're worth."

"Let's see whatcha got, kid," Dirk said.

"What I have," Tammy said as she found the information she was searching for, "is the identity of Imogene's mysterious companion."

"Get out!" Savannah nearly jumped out of her chair. "Already?"

Tammy beamed. "Yes, indeedy."

"How did you do that?" Savannah asked.

Waycross answered, "When we were there in Miss Barnsworth's room, Tammy was watching us through the window. And she saw a picture of a guy on the lady's nightstand."

"I thought he was young and good looking, and I wondered who he was," Tammy explained. "So I passed my phone to Granny and told her to take a picture of the picture. Late last night, after we went back to our motel, I did a search on the picture itself, an image search, and there he was. Oh, Savannah, just FYI, you were right about the other guests there at the No-Tail Motel being restless. I never heard so much banging around in my life."

Waycross's coloring turned even ruddier as he stared into his coffee.

"Well? What's the name of the guy in the picture, and who is he?" Dirk asked.

"Rodney Ruskin," Tammy replied.

"Is he some sort of exotic gigolo?"

"No. He doesn't seem to have any form of income at all," Tammy said. "Hasn't for a long, long time. He lives in a shack there in Sulfur Springs, in the middle of a cotton patch, right next to the spring that reeks of sulfur. Seems that Charger is all he's got in the world."

"What's his connection to Miss Barnsworth?" Dirk asked.

"Must be something juicy," Savannah suggested, "considering how secretive she is about him."

Tammy looked a bit sad when she said, "Rodney Ruskin is Miss Imogene Barnsworth's grandson."

"Her grandson?"

"That's right. Her only grandchild. From her one and only child, an illegitimate daughter, who died several years ago."

"Wow. Didn't see that one coming," Savannah said, her mind spinning.

"You know what that means," Dirk added.

"Yes, I do." Savannah took a deep breath. "He's her heir."

"Her heir to that big fortune she'll get from her brother," Gran said. "That's a motive for murder if ever I heard one."

Savannah felt the phone buzz in her back pocket and heard "The Devil Went Down to Georgia" playing. "It's Butch," she said. "Sorry. Hold on."

She answered it and was greeted by her brother-in-law's nasal twang on the other end. "Vi says you wanted to ask me somethin'. Whuzzup?"

"I was going to see if you know anybody here 'bouts with a General Lee Charger. But I just found out the fella's name. It's Rodney Ruskin."

"Yessiree. Hot Rod. That's what the ladies call 'im. They say he fills out a pair of jeans good or some such nonsense. Funny you should mention him. I seen him just yesterday. Dropped by my garage here, he did."

"Really? What did he want?"

Savannah felt her world begin to turn in slow motion as she waited and waited for his reply.

"He bought a new brake light for his Lee. Seems his was burned out and . . ."

It took Savannah and Dirk the better part of the morning to figure out which cotton patch Rodney Ruskin lived in.

"These cotton fields are sorta pretty, but if you've seen one, you've pretty much seen them all," Dirk remarked after the first hour.

By the time they found Rodney's humble abode, Dirk was long past thinking there was anything pretty about farmland at all.

He was even ready to wear woolen briefs, if necessary.

And the smell of the area didn't help at all.

Sulfur Springs had been named for a natural hot spring that flowed downward from a crevasse in a rock on the hill above and through the small community. The water smelled like rotten eggs served in hell's dining room and did nothing to improve the ambiance of the little village.

As Savannah and Dirk reached the end of the dusty dirt road and found the rust-eaten house trailer, Savannah saw Mr. Hot Rod himself bending over, with his head stuck under the open hood of a Lincoln limousine. His General Lee, in all her glory, was parked in the shade of the property's one oak tree.

Savannah perused Hot Rod's shapely rear end, so well tucked into a pair of worn jeans that were molded to his every curve. But try as she might, she couldn't determine what all the women were swooning over.

That made her feel very old. Or very married. Or a bit of both.

Since when didn't she notice a tight pair of jeans on a nicely rounded male heinie?

Maybe there was something about having a fine domesticated rear within easy reach and readily available that made the exotic foreign brands less alluring.

Or maybe it was the menopause thing.

Either way, she didn't care if Hot Rod had hot buns, as long as he didn't try anything ugly with them out here in this lonely, isolated place.

She missed the comforting assurance of her Beretta. And she knew Dirk felt naked without his Smith & Wesson. Curse

Tommy Stafford for confiscating them like that. If she and her husband got killed because of that boy's foolishness, she would, well, she'd come back and haunt him, or whatever else she was allowed to do from the great beyond to make his life miserable.

"Watch out for this guy," Dirk said as he brought the car to a stop a few feet from the limo.

"I will. You too."

They got out of their vehicle and walked over to the limousine. Rodney came out from under the hood and squinted at them, his hand shielding his eyes from the sun.

"How do?" he said.

"Hi," Savannah replied. "You're Rodney Ruskin, right?"

"Guilty as charged." He pulled a greasy rag from his hip pocket and wiped his face. "And who might you be?"

"I'm Savannah. This is my husband, Dirk. We're acquaintances of your grandmother."

"My grandma?" He looked a bit surprised but quickly recovered. "She don't usually tell people about me. If she's gonna talk about me, she's gotta explain about my mom and why she never got married and all that."

Savannah gave him a sympathetic smile. "I guess things were different, you know, back then for single mothers. Not like it is now."

"No, I guess not. If she has to introduce me, she usually calls me her best friend's son or whatever. I don't mind. Whatever makes her happy." He turned to Dirk and gave him a wink. "You know, us guys have to do whatever it takes to keep our women happy. That goes for grandmas as much as for wives."

"I'm sure it does," Dirk replied. Pointing to the limousine, he said, "What's the deal with this? She's an old beauty. Are you fixing her up?"

Rodney's eyes glistened with something bordering on mania. "I sure am! I just got 'er, and she needs some work. But you just wait till I'm done with 'er. She's gonna be the finest machine in Georgia!"

"Yeah?" Savannah feigned great interest. "What are you going to do with her?"

"I've got so many plans, you wouldn't believe it! I'm gonna have the interior done all red, white, and blue."

"Very patriotic," Dirk mumbled.

"And I'll have a hot tub installed there in the very back. I hear they can do that. And then I'm gonna have 'er painted with red, white, and blue flames, going from the hood back and trailin' down her sides. And probably some stars and stripes thrown in to boot."

"Sounds amazing," Savannah said, wide eyed.

"It'll knock your eyeballs plumb out!"

"I have no doubt it will."

Dirk cleared his throat. "That'll set you back some major dough there, dude."

"Eh, I don't care. I'm comin' into some big bucks any day now. I'm gonna be gettin' more than I can spend in years. My grandma's buying a big house that's got a five-car garage. I'm gonna fill it up with all kinds of cool cars and maybe even get myself a monster truck or two."

He wiped his hands on the rag, then pitched it to the ground, where it lay among discarded beer cans, empty oil bottles, and old tires. "No more livin' out in a dang cotton patch for Hot Rod Ruskin. My ship's done come in, and she's a big 'un!"

"Which ship is that?" Dirk asked. "The USS *Barnsworth*?"

Rodney's broad smile lessened to half a grin. "Yeah. So?"

"Nothing. I just heard about your great-uncle's passing, and, well, sorry for your loss."

Dirk didn't sound that sorry, and Rodney seemed to notice.

"Him and my grandma weren't all that close. I didn't really know the man."

"And that would account for your lack of grief at his passing," Savannah supplied.

"Yeah. I reckon it eases the pain a bit that I never laid eyes on 'im."

"And how about his wife?" she asked. "Were you acquainted with her?"

Rodney's eyes were definitely guarded now. Savannah decided he might be a bit brighter than she'd thought at first glance.

"I think I saw her walking down the street a couple times," he said. "She was pretty hard to miss, struttin' around in purple all the time."

"Yes, Jeanette stood out in a crowd. That's for sure." Savannah took a deep breath. "It's pretty awful what happened to her. I guess you heard."

He thought it over for a moment, then said, "Yeah. I reckon it's bad, winding up in the lake like that. Figure she had too much to drink at that high school reunion or whatever."

"No. They're saying she was murdered," Savannah told him.

He didn't look at all surprised when he nodded and said, "I guess that was a stroke of luck for me and my grandma. Wasn't too lucky for Miss Jeanette, though."

"Reckon not." She searched his eyes for any compassion for his recently departed relatives and saw not a smidgen.

"Where were you Saturday night?" Dirk asked.

"Why don't you ask my grandma if you wanna know so bad?" he replied, suddenly looking confused and afraid.

"Because we'd rather hear it from you," Savannah said. "Where did you and your grandma go after you picked her up there at the nursing home?"

"I think that's not any of your business. And I think it's about time for the two of you to be making some tracks off my property," he said, walking away from them and heading toward the house trailer.

His stride was purposeful. And it occurred to her that he might be going to get a weapon.

Apparently, it occurred to Dirk, too, because he wasted no time in grabbing her by the arm and leading her back to their car. Once inside, he started it right up and sped away, kicking up an impressive dirt cloud behind them.

"Well, whatcha think?" he asked. "Time to go pay another visit to your old boyfriend?"

"Absolutely. And this time, if he doesn't listen, I'm gonna smack him upside the head."

"You be sure to do that, Van. Hit him twice, in fact. It worked out so well last time."

"Um, good point."

Chapter 25

Savannah and Dirk made record time driving to the station house, only to be told by Deputy Jesse that Sheriff Stafford was "out in the field." He was sitting behind the desk, his dirty boots propped on a stack of official-looking paperwork, sucking down a convenience store soda big enough for four people to take a Jacuzzi in.

"Where exactly 'in the field' is he?" Savannah asked, trying to hide her annoyance with the lackadaisical lawman, who had enough manure on the bottoms of his boots to fertilize Granny's garden. She'd always had contempt for those who worked "the job" with no intention other than to collect a paycheck and a pension.

Apparently, Jesse was irritating Dirk, too, because Dirk's face was an unhealthy shade of reddish purple when he asked, "Why can't you say? Is it because you're clueless? Or because you'd rather bust our chops than help us find the sheriff when we need him?"

"What do you need 'im for? Maybe I can help you out."

From the vacant, lazy look on Jesse's face, Savannah had the strong impression this man wouldn't fetch a garden hose if they were both on fire in a dynamite factory. So she wasn't hopeful.

"We need to talk to Tom directly," Dirk said. "We wouldn't say it's important if it wasn't."

"So, when we find him," she added, "and we will find him sooner or later, we'll tell him that his deputy was sitting at his desk, polishing off a gallon of soda pop, his filthy boots propped on what looks to be like some pretty important paperwork. But Deputy Jesse was too all-fired busy to even tell us where to find the sheriff."

That seemed to do the trick. Jesse shoved the beverage aside, set his feet on the floor, and adjusted his collar. "He went to see the undertaker."

"Mr. Jameson?" Savannah asked, a bit surprised.

The deputy nodded.

"Why?" Dirk wanted to know.

"He didn't say." With a sigh, he added, "Frankly, the sheriff ain't all that open about his business. Leastways, not with me, anyhow."

"Gee. Imagine that," Savannah replied evenly. "And you, so confidence inspiring and all."

Jesse smiled and nodded, obviously deeply touched. "Why, thank you, ma'am."

Savannah turned and headed back to the door. "Think nothing of it. I sure don't."

Rather than go into the funeral home and interrupt whatever might be passing between Tom Stafford and Herb Jameson, Savannah and Dirk parked behind a large billboard where the mortuary's driveway met the highway. They could see the sheriff's big cruiser in front of the building and knew he'd have to pass by them to exit.

"What do you suppose he's doing here?" Dirk asked as he took out a cinnamon stick to "smoke" as they waited.

"I don't know. But I take it as a good sign. At least he's doing some sort of investigation."

"But he's talking to Jameson. Jameson's the main one who's saying it was you who done it. Maybe the old guy's just convincing him all that much more."

She fixed him with an evil eye. "You know, I can think of depressing crap like that all by myself, without any help from you."

"Hey, I do what I can."

At the same moment, they both spotted Tom coming out of the funeral home.

"Thank goodness," Dirk said. "I was afraid we'd be sitting here for hours and I'd be starving to death. I need another of those Burger Igloo burgers. This time with extra cheese and chili."

"You're gonna die."

"With a full stomach and a song in my heart."

Tom got into his car and headed toward them.

"Fingers crossed," she said. "I want to do the talking."

"If you're doing the yakking, I'll cross both of 'em on both hands."

"And you be nice."

"I'm always nice."

"Be nicer than you always are."

They could see inside Tom's car well enough to know the moment when he spotted them. He frowned and shook his head. And kept going, driving right past them.

"Honk," Savannah said.

Dirk did. A long, long, long honk.

She groaned. "You don't even know how to honk nice."

"Honk *nice*? How the hell do you honk *nice*?"

"A pleasant little beep, maybe? Never mind. He's stopped. Let's go before he changes his mind and takes off again. You and your rude, nasty honks. Sheez."

They shot out of the car and scurried over to the cruiser, which was sitting on the side of the road. Savannah hurried around to the passenger's door and was happy to find it unlocked. She opened it and climbed in. Once inside, she could hear Dirk trying to open the back passenger's door—unsuccessfully.

Tom sat there, wearing his dark sunglasses, giving her an annoyingly smug look.

"For heaven's sake, Tommy. Let him in!" she said. "What are you? Five years old?"

He snickered, reached over, and flipped a switch. A moment later, Dirk was in the back, sitting in "the cage," staring unhappily through the wire security mesh that separated the front of the car from the rear.

"How's Mr. Jameson?" Savannah asked.

"He's fine," was the non-reply. "Peachy. Considering that he's dressing his girlfriend for her funeral tomorrow."

Savannah gulped. "That's tomorrow?"

"Yeah. Don't go. You won't be welcome."

"Well, yeah, I sorta figured that."

"Good." Tom took off his sunglasses and rubbed his eyes. "What do you knot heads want with me?"

It occurred to Savannah that Tom looked exhausted, like a man who was running on fumes and was badly in need of a restful night's sleep.

She knew the look all too well. It was the appearance of a

police officer who was working day and night on a difficult case. Was it possible that her ex-beau was expending far more energy on her behalf than he was willing to admit?

The thought warmed her toward him.

In spite of some ugly chapters, this story might have a happy ending, after all, she told herself.

"Tom, we need you to listen with an open mind when we tell you something, okay?"

"No way. You're down South, Savannah," Stafford said. "We figure if a person gets carried away with all that 'open-minded' stuff, like you California folks do, our brains might just up and fall outta our heads."

"Oo-kay. Then at least let us say our piece before you interrupt or tell us we're full of bull pucky."

"All right. Shoot."

She drew a deep breath and let it flow. "We're pretty sure we know who killed Jeanette."

"Who?"

"Imogene Barnsworth and her grandson, Rodney Ruskin. I know you said she plays poker every Saturday night. And maybe she does. But this last Saturday night was different. She dressed up fancy, red high heels and everything, and Rodney picked her up in that General Lee Charger of his. Then he didn't bring her back until just before midnight. And Butch just sold him a new brake light for his General Lee."

"That's right," Dirk said, chiming in from the backseat. "And if you question those two, even a little bit, you'll see that they're lying. Both of them. Try to nail 'em down on where they were that night and what happened, and they snap shut tighter than a clam's ass."

"A clam's ass? Really?" Tom gave Savannah a questioning look.

She shrugged. "He's been in Georgia too long. He's starting to say 'ain't' a lot, too. We need to get this case solved and high-tail it out of here before he starts whistling 'Dixie' and putting peanuts in his Coca-Cola."

"Lord forbid."

"Exactly."

"What do you think, Tom?" she asked in her most plaintive, wheedling voice. "Will you just go talk to them? Maybe check her closet and see if she's got a pair of red high heels with some sort of biological evidence on them. Maybe check the grandson's biker boots, too, while you're at it, and the trunk of that Charger."

Tom took off his hat, ran his fingers through his hair, and put the hat back on again. "I don't need to interview them or check their closets or cars, Savannah."

"Why not?"

"Because I know where they were."

"I remember what you said. 'Creatures of habit' and all that. But have you talked to them, just in case this Saturday was different? Did you question the regulars there at the card game?"

"Dadgummit, woman," he said, losing his patience. "I didn't need to question the regulars at that card game. I *am* one of the damned regulars. I was there Saturday night. I went over right after I left the reunion. I was there, looking right at both Imogene, in her red dress and red high heels, and her idiot grandson at the exact time when you say you heard that big splash in the lake."

"Oh." It was all Savannah could manage to say with a lump in her throat the size of a fist, and about as comfortable.

"Yeah, 'oh,'" he shot back. "She was dressed up because it was her birthday, and us boys had gone together and bought her a little cake and a bouquet of flowers. And that worthless grandson of hers hung around so he could get a piece of the cake."

Savannah heard Dirk mutter, "Damn," from the cage.

"Yeah," she replied. "No kidding."

Tom seemed to soften. To her surprise, he even reached over and briefly laid his hand on her forearm. "Look," he said, "if you really didn't kill that gal, and you really wanna help me prove it, forget about Imogene and her grandson and help me figure out if Jeanette murdered old Barnsworth."

Savannah's mind started whirring, but she felt like she was a gerbil on a wheel, getting nowhere. "Why?" she asked.

"Because I think the two deaths are tied. And you weren't even here when Barnsworth went toes up. So . . ."

"Gotcha."

Savannah's hopes rose to the level of her ankles. It wasn't enough to make her shout, "Hallelujah," but at least she wouldn't trip over them the next time she tried to walk.

"Thanks, Tom," she said. "I appreciate the help. A point in the right direction can make all the difference."

"Okay," he answered. "But try to not make things worse, all right? People've been accusing me of draggin' my feet and showing you preferential treatment. With elections comin' up soon, I don't need that."

"I understand. We'll tread lightly."

"Like a couple of rodeo bulls in a china shop."

"Ever so delicately. On our little tippy toes."

He laughed in spite of himself. "Yeah, yeah. Whatever. Get outta my car."

Chapter 26

With Savannah's blessing, Dirk remained at the Burger Igloo while Savannah took a stroll down Main Street to Lisa Riggs's florist shop.

The name on the sign over the door read MURLE'S FLOW-ERS. But Murle had been Lisa's aunt's name, and the business had been passed down from Aunt Murle to Lisa's mom, who then left it to Lisa. About ten years ago, when the video rental store next door had closed, Lisa had bought that space, as well, and had expanded her establishment. Now she had one of the nicest florist and gift shops in the county.

Savannah was overwhelmed with the sweet fragrance of flow-ers the moment she walked through the door, causing the silver bell above it to jingle merrily. The natural aroma of the blooms mixed with the more cloying artificial scents of the candles that were for sale on the left wall, creating an unsettling smell, which Savannah couldn't describe but didn't like.

On spotless glass shelves all over the store were frilly, girlie items that a guy like Dirk would have abhorred in his home. So she resisted the urge to buy a particularly sweet pink pillow covered with delicate lace and rhinestones and draped in strands of pearls.

He already slept on pink satin sheets when their regular ones were in the laundry, and you could expect only so much in the way of compromise from a manly man like Detective Sergeant Dirk Coulter without meeting some sort of resistance.

Savannah had several moments to herself to look around the store, at the handmade gifts, buckets and baskets of both real and silk arrangements, and home décor items, before Lisa emerged from the rear.

Savannah was glad to see her. The strong scent of the candles was starting to give her a headache.

But Lisa seemed far less happy to see Savannah. Her dark eyes blazed as the color mounted in her heart-shaped face. Her heavily frosted hair was mussed, and her dress rumpled, as though she had been working nonstop for the past twenty-four hours.

"How dare you set foot in my shop?" she told Savannah. "I'm surprised, cold-blooded killer that you are, that you'd have the gall to even show your face in this town."

Savannah was surprised . . . at herself for being surprised. She quickly reminded herself about her own theory about how people seldom changed.

Lisa had always been a mean mini-Jeanette. Quick of temper and unpleasant when she didn't get her way, she and Jeanette had been a natural pairing.

"You get outta here, Savannah Reid," Lisa said, waving a pair of stem cutters at her. "I'm working my tail off filling orders for Jeanette's funeral. And besides, I don't serve murderers!"

Normally, when encountering such hostility, Savannah would have entertained a few fantasies that might have included a swift kick to the booty and the offender flying out the door and landing facedown in a mud puddle.

But in spite of the anger in Lisa's words, Savannah could see a deep sadness in her eyes. She could tell that the woman had been crying, and she had the look of someone whose heart had been broken.

Instead of shouting back the sharp retorts that came readily to her lips, Savannah said softly, "I didn't kill your friend, Lisa. And I'm sorry someone did. Are you okay?"

"Okay? No! I'm not okay!" Lisa began to cry, and her dry, ugly sobs racked her body and contorted her face. "I'm back there making a big purple casket spray for the woman who was my very best friend for over thirty years. How the hell can I be okay?"

Savannah took a step toward her, but Lisa raised her hands, as though warding off an attack.

"No!" she shouted. "You get away from me, before I call Tom and tell him you're here, threatening me!"

"But I'm *not*. I just came here to ask you a couple of questions. I want to catch the person who really did kill Jeanette. You want that, too. Right, Lisa? Don't you want to know who really killed your friend? You wouldn't want her murder to go unsolved, would you?"

Lisa looked at her doubtfully. "I'm pretty sure you did it. The sheriff and Mr. Jameson say you did. But I'll hear what you've got to say."

Sensing that the sun might have emerged at least temporarily from behind the clouds, Savannah hurried on. "Lisa, you knew Jeanette better than anybody, being her best friend for so long. Please don't take this as an insult to her, but do you have any idea if she might, just might, have killed her husband? You know, for some very, very good, completely understandable reason."

"What?"

"I don't mean that in a bad way. Really, I don't. I'm just thinking that maybe, because you two were very close, she might have confided in you that he, oh, might have been awful to her, treated her badly. Maybe she was scared to death of him, and it might have just crossed her mind a wee bit to poison him or smother him in his sleep or whatever."

Lisa's dark eyes were growing larger by the moment. "You are *sick*! Sick, Savannah Reid! How dare you even suggest such a thing about a fine woman like Jeanette!"

"I didn't just make it up, Lisa. I'm suggesting it because I overheard you and Amy Jameson talking about it outside the school the night of the reunion."

Lisa stood there staring at her for a long time before she finally said, "What?"

"I heard you and Amy talking about how Jeanette killed her husband and got Amy's dad to go along with it to clear her of suspicion. Now, don't try to pretend you didn't say it, because I was standing not ten feet away, and I heard every word."

Lisa laughed, and the sound of it was creepy, maniacal, like that of a person with a fragile grip on reality. "You're not only a killer, Savannah Reid, but you're a liar. I never said any such thing. And neither did Amy. You're just talking crazy, and I don't have to listen to it. I told you to get out of here right now, or I'm calling Tommy."

"Why did she do it, Lisa? Why did Jeanette kill her husband?"

"Get out!"

"Was she afraid he was going to find out how in debt she was from all her extravagant spending?"

"I mean it! Now!"

"Was it so she could get her hands on all his money?"

Lisa reached into the pocket of her work apron, frowned, then marched across the room to a counter with a cash register and a phone on it. "That's it! I'm not going to listen to these lies about my poor dead friend. I'm calling the law on you."

"How did she do it, Lisa? Was it poison, or did she just give him an overdose of his own pharmaceutical drugs?"

Savannah felt her phone buzz in her pocket. Normally, she would have ignored it under such stressful circumstances. But she knew Tammy was spending the day trying to hack into the files of the laboratory that had processed the blood and tissue samples from Jacob Barnsworth's autopsy.

Perhaps this call would provide the answer to the question she had just asked.

She pulled the phone from her pocket and gave it a quick glance as she listened to Lisa calling the sheriff's office.

Tammy's text read **Lab report normal. No drugs. No poisons. Natural causes like Jameson's report.**

"Yes, she's right here right now," Savannah could hear Lisa saying into the phone. "She's raving like a crazy woman, asking me all these nutty questions. I think she's fixin' to do me serious harm. Get out here quick as you can."

Savannah decided it was time to leave.

The sickly sweet smell of those candles was almost more than she could stand.

When Savannah returned to the Burger Igloo, she found Dirk cramming the last bite of burger into his mouth. He gave her a semi-apologetic grin. "I waited for you."

"Sure you did. Like one pig waits for another one."

"Lemme order you a burger. I don't mind sitting here while you eat it."

Dirk didn't mind waiting? What was wrong with this picture? Usually, he wanted to run out the door before she'd even finished eating. If there was anything she hated, it was leaving a restaurant while still chewing.

Of course, she knew why he'd suddenly developed Gandhian patience. It was the first-degree murder charge hanging over her head.

No doubt, if she'd been arrested for littering, he'd be far crankier.

"I'll take a chocolate malted to go," she said. "I'm not all that hungry."

He scrutinized her face closely, like a parent checking out a kid who might be coming down with the bubonic plague. "Are you all right?"

"I'm fine. Actually, I'm very fine."

"You've got something!"

"I might." She motioned for the waitress. "I'm going to drop you off at Butch's again," she said.

His face brightened, but his happiness was soon followed by suspicion. "Why? Have you got something or not?"

"I don't know for sure. But I have a feeling."

"Wanna share?"

"Not yet. I need to have a girl-to-girl talk with an old friend. Then we'll see how much I do or don't have."

Chapter 27

Savannah walked up the broken sidewalk to the front door of her favorite building in McGill. Other than Granny Reid's home, of course.

When she was a child, Savannah had considered this wonderful old Victorian-style home a mansion. Even then it had been ancient and elegant, with classic architectural features, like a lovely round turret, gingerbread trim, stained-glass windows, and a door set with an oval of beveled lead glass that sparkled like the crystal chandelier hanging in the foyer.

Once this grand home had belonged to an eccentric lady named Mildred Hodge. When Mildred had died, having no heirs of her own but being an avid reader, she had donated her home to the town, with instructions that it be turned into a public library.

As a child without a television, a radio, or books of her own for entertainment, Savannah had thought she'd discovered heaven itself when she realized she could walk through that door and borrow all the adventures she could carry in two hands.

A loving, compassionate librarian by the name of Rose had introduced her to Nancy Drew, Trixie Belden, and the Hardy boys at an early age. And Savannah had never gotten over the thrill of solving a mystery, even all these years later. She blessed Rose every day for her love of books and her obsession with solving crimes.

The moment she opened the heavy door and stepped onto the foyer's terra-cotta tiles, Savannah drew a deep breath, filling her lungs with the intoxicating scent of books. And she felt right at home.

To her left was a graceful curving staircase; and beneath the steps, a cozy alcove furnished with an undersized child's chair, an accent table, and a stained-glass dragonfly reading lamp.

Anytime she'd found a rare hour to herself, Savannah had trotted over to this library, slid into that snug nook, and been transported to other places, times, and situations far more exciting and glamorous than her own.

She had loved books, libraries, and librarians ever since. Like policemen, doctors, nurses, teachers, and firefighters, she considered them heroes, and she couldn't imagine the world without them.

But as inviting and nostalgic as the house was that afternoon, her mission was far more important than a walk down memory lane. Sweet as that might be. She walked into what had once been the old house's fine parlor, where the current librarian's desk was located. She glanced around and found her former friend Amy Jameson filing books in the fiction section.

Amy heard Savannah's approaching footsteps and turned to greet her visitor with a smile. But when she saw the newcomer was Savannah, her smile quickly faded. She turned back to her cart and suddenly developed an intense interest in the books she had yet to replace.

"Hi, Amy," Savannah said brightly, as though she hadn't noticed the non-greeting.

"Oh, hi, Savannah," Amy replied, giving her the briefest nod.

"I'm sorry we didn't get a chance to talk there at the reunion," Savannah continued. "A lot's happened for both of us, I'm sure, in the past twenty-five years or so."

"Not that you'd notice," Amy said with an air of resignation. "Not for me, anyway. After graduation I went off to college. Came back here. Became town librarian after Rose passed away. That's pretty much it. You're now up to date on the exciting life story of Amy Jameson."

Savannah looked into her old friend's eyes and saw a bitterness born of disillusionment and unfulfilled dreams. She seemed to recall a time, decades ago, when Amy had said she wanted to be a fashion designer when she grew up someday. Or was it a ballerina?

She had forgotten.

She wondered if Amy Jameson had forgotten, too.

"Not all good lives are exciting, Amy," she told her. "What you do here is really important. Rose changed my life by introducing me to books and the love of reading. I'm sure you change lives for the better every day."

"But you didn't come here to talk about how important I am."

Amy shoved the last book from her cart into its proper place, and Savannah recognized it instantly. It was Jack London's *The Call of the Wild*. The very copy that she herself had checked out many times.

"You came here," Amy continued as she headed toward her desk, "to talk to me about Jeanette."

"Can't a friend drop by to say hi without . . . Okay. You're right. That's why I'm here."

Amy sat down in her desk chair and pretended to busy herself by stacking and restacking some piles of papers. Even though she didn't invite Savannah to have a seat, Savannah pulled a small side chair close to the desk and parked herself on it.

If Amy thought she could get rid of her with a frosty reception, she had another thought coming. It took way more than that to scare off a former cop. There was nothing quite like being shot at and critically wounded to reset the bar on how easily one got offended.

"What took you so long?" Amy asked. "I figured you'd be over here the minute you made bail."

What took so long? Savannah thought. *I had to go chase down some stupid leads that led absolutely nowhere. Just your usual homicide investigation. That's all.*

"I heard about the conversation you had with my father and his suspicions about you," Amy continued. "And I know you were standing there in the shadows when I was talking to Lisa about Jeanette."

"I hope you don't share your father's conclusions about me," Savannah said. "You knew me pretty well back when we were kids. I hope you know I wouldn't do something like that."

"People change, Savannah. And how well can any of us know anyone? People have secrets." Amy drew a shuddering breath. "Besides, my father's very good at what he does. If he says you killed Jeanette, that's good enough for me."

"Your dad's wrong about me, but as a general rule, he *is* good at what he does. In fact, that's one of the reasons I came by here today. I want to give you some information that might, well, set your mind at ease where he's concerned."

Amy looked genuinely puzzled. "Set my mind at ease? What are you talking about?"

"You saw me standing there in the shadows while you were talking to Lisa about Jeanette."

Amy's stared intensely into Savannah's eyes when she said, "Yes. And . . . ?"

"I heard what you said about your dad being, well, influenced by Jeanette to the point of maybe filing a false report and—"

"Whoa! Hold on! I never said anything like that."

"Actually, you did. You and Lisa talked about how persuasive she could be with men, and you admitted you never thought your father would give in to her so-called charms." Savannah stopped speaking because Amy was laughing.

But there was no mirth it in. It was a bitter, empty laugh that chilled the soul to hear.

"Some detective you are, Savannah Reid," she said when she'd finally recovered herself. "Here I thought you'd figure it all out right away, but you're clueless. You don't know half what you think you do."

Savannah plowed ahead, through the ridicule. "I have documentation that proves your dad is innocent of all wrongdoing. His autopsy report on Jacob Barnsworth was exactly as the lab reported. He doctored nothing for Jeanette. Mr. Barnsworth really did pass away from natural causes."

"I know that."

"But you didn't the night of the reunion. You were talking to Lisa about how Jeanette had manipulated him, got what she wanted out of him, how disappointed you were that—"

"Oh. I see." A light dawned in Amy's eyes. "I've got it now."

"You've got what?"

"Never mind."

"Come on, Amy. Help me out here. You and I used to play Barbie dolls together, for Pete's sake."

"You didn't have a Barbie doll."

"I know. But you had several, and you let me play with them. Even the prettiest ones. I remember it like it was yesterday. I never forgot your kindness toward me."

Amy glanced away. "I felt sorry for you," she said. "What with your parents the way they were. And there were so many of you. I knew you didn't have toys."

"I really appreciated your generosity back then. It was most welcome. Most needed." Savannah placed her hand on Amy's forearm. "Thank you, Amy."

Amy blinked rapidly a couple of times, and long wet lines streaked her cheeks. Finally, she composed herself and said softly, "Truly, I thought you'd figure it out on your own, Savannah. I didn't want to get involved. This is such a small town, and if people start thinking badly of you for some reason, any reason, they'll make you miserable about it for the rest of your life."

"I know. They do."

"I thought you'd be able to put it together yourself, considering what you heard that night there behind the school."

"I think I have," Savannah said, recalling her conversation in the florist shop with Lisa.

She remembered the look on Lisa's face. The expression that was supposed to be grief but wasn't.

It was fear and anger, mixed with guilt.

It was a look that Savannah, a former police officer, had become all too familiar with.

"That night, after the reunion, behind the school," Savannah said, "the man you were talking about with Lisa, the man who gave in to Lisa and did what she wanted, I thought it was your father. But it wasn't, was it?"

Amy shook her head slowly. "No."

"It was Lisa's husband, Frank, right? Jeanette seduced Frank."

Savannah's heart pounded so hard, she could feel the blood throbbing in her temples as she waited for Amy's reply.

After what seemed like an eon, Amy nodded. "Jeanette didn't know the meaning of the word *loyalty*. Lisa thought she was so special to Jeanette. Best friends forever and all that. Year after year, she watched Jeanette hurt other people. She even *helped* her hurt them. But Lisa thought she was immune."

"Jeanette might sleep with every other woman's husband but would never do that to her," Savannah said.

"Right. But, of course, it doesn't work like that. None of us are special or immune. If somebody's hurting others, it's just a matter of time until they do the same to us."

"If they do it with you, they'll do it to you. That's a lesson hard learned."

"For Lisa, it sure was."

"Thank you, Amy, for helping me," Savannah said. "Is there anything else you know that you could tell me? I'll take anything."

Amy wiped her eyes and nose on a tissue, then said, "She didn't leave the school right away that night. After I left you and Lisa, I got halfway to my car and realized I'd forgotten some books I was supposed to bring back here. I returned to get them, and I saw all the ruckus with you and Jeanette. Saw you slug her and her hit the ground."

"Not my shining hour, for sure."

"Actually, I thought you did pretty well. Most of the people standing around watching were rooting for you, no doubt."

"That's good to know."

"And Lisa was watching. She hadn't left yet. She was watching from over there in that dark area by the fence, where she was parked. I saw her."

"That's interesting."

"And later, when I pulled out of the lot, she was still standing there, watching you talk to Jeanette and Tommy and your husband."

"Okay. Again interesting."

Amy gave her a loaded look. Savannah prepared herself to hear something of importance.

Amy said, "Lisa was parked right next to Jeanette's purple convertible."

"There in that dark area."

"By the fence. It's not well lit over there, but I could see well enough to make out that ugly hot pink satin outfit Lisa was wearing. I'm absolutely positive it was her."

"Okay. That's all good to know. Thank you," Savannah said. "Did you see Lisa leave? Or Jeanette?"

"No. When I drove away, Jeanette was back on her feet, complaining like a scalded skunk to the sheriff. You were talking to your husband."

"And Lisa?"

"Still standing there beside the cars. In the dark. Watching. It was creepy."

"Thank you, Amy. This is all such an enormous help."

Savannah stood and took one more long tender look around the room. "I envy you, working here like you do. The peace and quiet. The gentleness of it all."

The defensive look returned to Amy's face. "Sure you do. You wouldn't trade your life for my boring one. Not for anything."

"No. I wouldn't. Because I love my life. The craziness of it, the ups and downs. But you wouldn't like everything about mine, either. I guarantee you."

Amy shot Savannah an angry glance that cut deep into her and confused her.

"What is it, Amy?" she asked her. "Why are you so mad at me? What have I done?"

It took the librarian a long time to reply. And when she finally did, she sounded ashamed. "You got out," she said, almost in a whisper.

"I got *out*?"

"You had a dream and you followed it. All the way to California."

"Aw, Amy. Dreams can be followed and fulfilled anywhere. Good lives can be lived in any corner of the world. You don't need a sunny beach to follow your destiny."

"You did. You needed a sunny beach."

Savannah thought only a moment before agreeing. "Yes. I did."

Savannah's memory returned to Amy's pretty pink bedroom, the frilly bedspread and matching curtains, the soft white carpet covered with Barbie dolls and miscellaneous fashion doll paraphernalia. She recalled how Amy could take two strips of shiny fabric, twist them this way and that, and create a beautiful evening gown on the spot.

No doubt about it. Amy Jameson's Barbies had been the best dressed in town.

Searching her childhood friend's sad eyes, she said, "Yes, I did need a change of scenery. It's true. And maybe you do, too. Fortunately, it's never too late to chase a dream. Never."

She reached into her pocket and pulled out one of her cards. "If you ever want to 'get out,' as you call it, give me a call. I know people who know people in the Los Angeles fashion industry. We'll see what we can do."

Laying the card on the desk, she added, "But don't discount the value of being a librarian in McGill, Georgia. Because to my way of thinking . . . what you do here . . . it's a darned near sacred calling."

Chapter 28

Half an hour after Savannah left the library, the eager members of the Moonlight Magnolia Detective Agency, working and honorary alike, were assembled in the parking lot of the McGill High School.

Near the fence.

In the area that, once the sun went down, was destined to be the darkest.

"Listen up, everybody. We've got a lot to do and only a few more hours of daylight to do it in," Savannah told Tammy, Waycross, Granny, and Alma. She had already briefed Dirk on the drive to the school. "This may or may not be the actual crime scene," she told them. "But it's the last place where someone saw our victim in close proximity to our main suspect."

"There wasn't a lot of time between when they were last seen here," Dirk added, "and when Savannah heard that splash at the lake. Less than an hour. So there might have been time for them to meet up again somewhere else. But it's not likely. It might have happened right here."

"At least where she got bonked with the high heel," Gran said. "And Lord knows, at a high school reunion, there's an abundance of those around."

"Among other things, we're looking for one high heel in particular," Savannah told them. "If it's here, it shouldn't be too hard to spot. It's hot pink, with rhinestones and sequins on it."

"But we're not just looking for the weapon," Tammy said. "We're looking for anything at all that seems out of the ordinary."

"Like what?" Alma asked, all excited to be included in the search.

"You won't know till you see it," Dirk told her. "Let's get looking."

It took only twelve minutes for them to make their first find.

"Over here!" Alma called out as she dropped to her hands and knees and stared at something on the pavement.

They all ran over to inspect her discovery.

Savannah knelt on one knee beside her younger sister and saw something glittering among the rocks and dirt on the asphalt. More than one something. Sequins. Two hot pink ones and four purple ones lay close together. They were muddied and somewhat faded, but there was no mistaking what they were.

"That's important, isn't it?" Alma asked. "I mean, sequins fall off of dresses all the time. But you wouldn't think they'd fall off together, from two different dresses at the same time."

"You sure wouldn't," Savannah said. "Not unless there was some sort of tussle going on." She patted Alma on the back. "Good work, girlie! You earned an extra scoop of ice cream on your cone for sure!"

Tammy appeared with a bright blue index card folded in

half, forming a small tent. "This is the closest thing I could find to evidence markers there at Granny's," she said, placing it beside the sequins. "Hopefully, the wind won't blow it away."

They continued to examine the immediate area surrounding the sequins, and it was Waycross who made the next find.

"More pink," he said, pointing to the pavement, where tiny bits of fabric appeared to be ground into the rough surface.

"We've seen this sort of thing before," Savannah told Dirk. "Remember when we processed that awful motorcycle accident? That guy went flying off his bike and skidded on the road. There were little bits of his denim jacket embedded in the rocks like that. There was a lot more of it, mind you, but it looked like that."

Dirk nodded thoughtfully. "I remember. And it looks like somebody skidded along here, too."

"Maybe somebody's shoe?" Tammy said. "Like if Lisa fell down and the side of her shoe slid along the asphalt."

"Or maybe she was pushed down," Waycross suggested, "or the two women got to wrestlin' around after they hit the ground? That would account for the sparkly things coming off both of their dresses."

Tammy placed another marker by the tiny fabric bits.

Savannah stood for a moment, looking at the school, looking over the lot, trying to imagine what it had been like for Lisa, standing there, watching the action at the school.

But Lisa had been in the lot several minutes before the altercation. Why hadn't she left?

What was she doing all that time out here by herself?

"Tammy!" Savannah said. "Get me Lisa Riggs's phone number."

"Why, Van?" Dirk asked. "What's up?"

"If you were Lisa, why wouldn't you just drive away, like

you'd told others you were going to do?" she asked. "What would you be doing out here all by yourself in the dark?"

All three of the youngest members of the search team answered in unison, "I'd be checking my phone."

"That's right. That's what everybody does these days when they've got a spare minute. Even if they don't make a call, they check their messages. What if she was about to get in her car, checked her phone, and had a chat or sent a text or two. Then she heard my, um, lively discussion with Jeanette and watched that for a while."

"That sounds likely, sugar," Gran said, "but what's that got to do with anything?"

"When I talked to Lisa there in her florist shop, she got mad at me and called Tom to come arrest me. She was wearing an apron with big pockets on it to work on her flowers there in the back. When she went to call him, she reached into her pocket, like it was an automatic action. But then, to make the call, she walked all the way to the other side of the store and used a landline phone on the counter."

"She's lost her phone!" Tammy shouted. "Otherwise, she'd have used it!"

"Most likely, she was reaching for it there in her apron, like she always did," Waycross said, "but she'd forgot it wasn't there."

Savannah grinned. "Bingo. So, Tammy, get me her cell phone number, would you?"

Tammy's tablet appeared, screens were scrolled, and a moment later, the number was given.

The group stood, silent and breathless, as Savannah made the call.

At first, the call didn't seem to go through. So she tried again. And once more.

Then they heard a faint chiming coming from somewhere in the weeds around the base of the fence. En masse, they rushed toward the sound.

Savannah saw it first. A smartphone well hidden in the under-brush. "Don't touch it!" she said as she reached into her pocket and pulled out a pair of surgical gloves. "Anybody got a pen?" she asked.

As she was putting on the gloves, Dirk produced a ball-point.

"Take a picture of that," she told Tammy, pointing to the phone.

Tammy did so, her pretty face flushed from the joy only a forensic photographer who had read too many Nancy Drew books could know.

Then Savannah carefully laid Dirk's pen alongside the phone, marking its exact position.

"Okay," she said, carefully lifting the cell from the weeds. "What I'm doing now is an absolutely no-no."

"Not as bad as breaking and entering a nursing home winder in the dead o' night," Gran said with an evil snicker.

"No, definitely not as bad as that. So what you're witness-ing right now didn't happen. Even if they beat you with tele-phone books to get you to confess, it did *not* happen." Savannah quickly accessed the phone's call log and said, "There are the three calls I made. Half a dozen calls in a row Sunday morning from Frank Riggs's cell."

"They were probably out here looking for it themselves," Dirk said. "Good thing they didn't find it."

"Very good thing," Savannah said. "We've got some extremely interesting text messages here, sent back and forth between Lisa and Frank right after she walked away from us and headed back here."

"Let us see!" Dirk peered over her shoulder, trying to read the small print.

Gran added, "Yeah, we wanna read 'em, too!"

"Come on! We helped you find the phone!" Tammy complained.

"Okay, okay," Savannah said. "But as soon as you read them, we have to call Tom and tell him we found something for him in the weeds. Whatever you do, don't spill the beans that you know what's on it."

"Of course not!" Tammy said. "We're highly trained agents who never, *ever* spill our secrets!"

"And ole Tom won't finagle it out of us, either," Waycross said proudly. "'Cause if all else fails, and he ties us to the rack, there's always—"

In unison, they shouted, "Cyanide capsules!"

In the course of their careers, Savannah, Dirk, and the Moonlight Magnolia entourage had endured their share of Dumpster dives in the never-ending quest for evidence. They had sifted through garbage from private homes, grocery stores, restaurants, medical facilities, paint shops, and Savannah's personal favorite—pet stores.

But they had never enjoyed a search as much as the one conducted late that afternoon, after Sheriff Stafford had studied their evidence at the parking lot, and once they had watched him and his deputies search for the offending hot pink, rhinestone-enhanced high heel—aka the murder weapon—in the Riggs's residential garbage.

Having come up high and dry at the home, they, the sheriff, and his deputies had decided to search the waste bin behind Frank Riggs's workplace, a butcher shop called Fancy Meating You.

As at the residential search, the gang didn't need to lift a finger. In fact, they had been expressly forbidden to do so. While Tom, Jesse, and Martin crawled among discarded entrails, slabs of fat, bones, gristle, and other unidentifiable gore, Savannah and her friends sat on a nearby curb, watched, offered bits of unsolicited advice, and drank Dr Peppers.

"I hate seeing you boys slave away like that," Savannah called over to Tom as he rose from the heap to catch a breath of slightly less foul air and then sank into the pit once again.

She had no doubt that he had begun the day as a handsome man. But he was now in desperate need of a shower and all new clothing.

Not just clean clothing, she told herself, sniffling a giggle, *but an entire new uniform*. She was pretty sure he was well greased in pork fat all the way to his underdrawers.

In years past, she had seen Tom in a far better mood, though not as good as the one Dirk was in at the moment.

"Don't give up now, Sheriff Tom," Dirk hollered. "You've almost reached the bottom. You know the rule. The evidence is always in the last place you look."

Tom popped up and fixed him with a deadly glare over the top edge of the Dumpster. "We had better find a pink high heel in here with blood on it. *Human* blood and some brain tissue, too," he said, tossing out something that looked like a massive congealed pork liver. "Or that wife of yours is gonna be in more trouble than she knows what to do with."

"I offered to help you," Savannah said most sympathetically. "We all offered to help, but *no*. You boys wanted to do it all by yourselves, so—"

"Shut up," Tom snapped, bobbing down for more. "And, Jesse, if you toss one more handful of that crap over here on my boots, I swear I'll draw my weapon, shoot ya dead, and tell God ya died."

"Yes, sir. I mean, no, sir," Jesse replied, wiping his forehead with his bloody hand.

Savannah had seen less gruesome faces in slice-and-dice horror movies. They looked like escapees from a zombie flick.

Another twenty minutes passed, and even Savannah was starting to worry a bit. What if she *was* wrong, after all? What if her instincts about Lisa's reactions were off? What if there was an innocent explanation for everything they'd found at the parking lot, including the seemingly incriminating text messages on Lisa's lost phone?

If Tom wallowed in gore for an hour in the hot summer sun, only to come up empty-handed, there would be hell to pay.

She wasn't sure what price hell was going for these days, but she was pretty sure she couldn't afford it.

To her dismay, Tom crawled out of the Dumpster and wiped his hands on his ruined khaki slacks. "There's nothing in there, gal," he said. "I'm starting to think you and your buddies here have enjoyed watchin' us look for that nothin' *way* too much."

Savannah switched into defense mode. "Now, don't go gettin' all huffy with me, Thomas Stafford. When you saw that stuff on the pavement and read those texts, you were just as excited as we were."

"Yeah, but what am I supposed to do with any of it if I don't have a murder weapon that can be traced back to her? *Nothin'.* That's what it's worth. Not a piddlin'—"

"Sheriff!" Jesse yelled. "Lookie! Lookie what I found!"

The deputy held the hot pink, rhinestone-studded pump aloft with all the gruesome aplomb of Attila the Hun lifting the head of a decapitated foe.

The Moonlight Magnolia crew sprang to their feet and danced a jig, and no one more energetically than Granny.

Savannah walked over to the bin to look at the shoe. She had no doubt whatsoever that it was the one worn by Lisa Riggs the night of the reunion.

"We've got to send that off to a lab right away and get it tested," she said. "As soon as the results are back . . ."

"That might be how y'all do it in California," Tom said. "But we got our own way of handlin' things around here." He turned to Martin and Jesse. "I'm fixin' to go home and grab a shower. You two fetch the Riggses and drag their asses to the station."

Jesse and Martin looked down at their own soiled uniforms.

"But . . . but . . . ," Martin said.

"I mean now! Make tracks!"

"Yes, sir!" Martin jerked to attention.

Jesse gave a curt nod. "Right away, Sheriff,"

As the three policemen headed for their respective vehicles, Tom carrying the high heel in a brown paper evidence bag, Dirk turned to the Magnolians. "I hope you're all taking notes, because in the future, that's how I expect you all to address me."

A moment later, he was sprayed with spit from his five comrades, their tongues fully extended in noisy, enthusiastic raspberries.

"All right! All right! It was just a thought."

Chapter 29

Before Lisa and Frank Riggs were brought into the sheriff's station, the Moonlight Magnolia team was sent home. Except for Savannah and Dirk. And they were allowed to observe the interrogation only after they swore an oath to, in Tom's words, "not even so much as twitch, let alone utter a word, upon pain of death."

"I think he meant it, too," Savannah whispered to Dirk from their seats right beside the air conditioner and well apart from the desk and the chairs set directly in front of it, where the suspects would be seated.

"I figure he did mean it," Dirk replied as they watched Tom take his seat behind his desk. "I remember most clearly the moment he lost his sense of humor. It was when he slipped on that liver and went down, headfirst, in the muck."

Tom shot them a look and cleared his throat.

They both shut up instantly. They didn't want to miss a moment of the upcoming proceedings.

Savannah only hoped that Tommy was half as good at "sweating" suspects as Dirk was. Without laying a hand on them, Dirk could have perps begging to be moved from the interrogation room to a jail cell in twenty-eight minutes.

She glanced up at the clock on the wall and made a mental note of the time to see who between the two would hold the record when all was said and done.

Tom ran his fingers through his hair, which was still wet from his shower, and told Martin, who was loitering near the bottom of the stairs, "Okay, haul 'em down here."

A couple of minutes later, a miserable-looking Lisa and her equally dismal husband were brought down the stairs, Jesse leading them and Martin close behind.

The deputies herded them toward the chairs in front of the desk and directed them to sit down.

Savannah barely recognized Frank Riggs. The last time she'd seen him, he was a robust high school football player brimming with health. But now he looked pale, gaunt, and exhausted. He moved like he was made of brittle glass and could shatter into slivers at any moment.

Then Savannah reminded herself that the act of murder often destroyed the person who did the killing almost as effectively as it did their victim. Guilt and fear of that magnitude were heavy burdens for any human spirit to bear.

Once they were seated, Tom gave them both long evaluating looks. Then, with his poker face securely in place, he said, "Did y'all know that the left brake light on your pickup's out?"

Lisa and Frank looked at each other, astonished. Expressions of enormous relief flooded their faces.

"That's why you had brought us in, Sheriff?" Frank asked. "A busted brake light?"

"That's one of the reasons. I have others," Tom said with a grim smile. He turned to Lisa as she sat stiffly on the chair across from him. "I'm not sure if my deputies read you two your rights yet or not, so here they are. Listen up."

Tom carefully recited the Miranda warning and informed them they were under arrest for the murder of Jeanette Barnsworth. Then he asked Lisa if, knowing her rights, she was willing to talk to him.

"No!" she stated most emphatically, with an angry look in Savannah's direction. "You've already got one person under arrest for killing Jeanette. I can't imagine why you'd bring me and my husband in, too. And that's all I've got to say to you. I want an attorney."

In a voice as cool as the air-conditioning, which was about to blow Savannah and Dirk into the next county, Tom said, "No problem. Jesse, please take Mrs. Riggs back upstairs and return her to her cell."

Tom glanced over at Savannah, and she could swear she saw a bit of mischief in his eye. "On second thought," he said, "put her in the cell directly across from Yukon Bill. It's been recently fumigated."

As Jesse led Lisa back upstairs, Savannah whispered a silent prayer that Yukon would take a strong liking to Lisa. Lust at first sight and all that.

It was hardly a Granny-approved prayer, but the woman had been willing to let her take a murder rap for her, so Savannah wasn't exactly overwrought with guilt.

Once Lisa was taken from the room, Tom took a long, hard look at his second prisoner. "How about you, Frank?" he asked gently. "Are you willin' to talk to me?"

Frank nodded.

"I'm sorry. I need a spoken reply," Tom told him.

"Yes. I'll talk." With his head bent as he stared down at his hands, which were folded in his lap, and his shoulders stooped,

Frank Riggs looked like a man who was utterly defeated, scarcely able to bear the crushing weight of his own soul.

"Good," Tom said. "You'll feel a lot better if you do. I assure you."

Tom reached into a drawer and pulled out a miniature tape recorder. After setting it on the desk between them, he switched it on. The sheriff identified himself and Frank Riggs for the tape and stated the time and place. Then, before he could even begin to question Frank, the suspect started to talk.

"I just want you to know, Sheriff—I want everybody to know—that this was one hundred percent my fault, not my wife's. I take full responsibility for it."

Savannah reached over and slid her hand into Dirk's. He gave it a squeeze.

Nothing beat a confession in court. Absolutely nothing. And there it was.

"That's mighty honorable of you, Frank," Tom said. "Why do you figure it was all your fault? Did you kill Jeanette Barnsworth?"

"No. Not directly. She died, accidental like, by my wife's hand. But I caused that to happen. And what happened afterward, that was also me. All me."

Tom leaned forward in his chair and propped his elbows on his desk. "Just start from the beginning, Frank. We need to hear it all."

Frank shivered, as though he had just stepped, naked, into a snowstorm. Then he began, "I'd have to say it started when Miss Jeanette bought those ribs from me last Fourth of July. I talked to her a long time about how to cook them up nice and tender, and by the time we was done talkin', we were friends."

"*Good* friends?" Tom asked.

"Not yet. We got to be *real* good friends on Labor Day week-end. Lisa went to see her folks in Mississippi, and Jeanette dropped by my house that night to make sure I wasn't too lonely."

"Were you? Lonely, that is?"

Frank gave a shy, awkward smile. "Not after she got there."

"And what happened then?"

"We got together off and on. After a time or two, I started feeling guilty about it, and I told her I'd rather not do it no more. But she was a bossy gal. Hard to turn down."

"Yes, she certainly was the determined sort. Did your wife find out about it?"

"Not for the longest. Jeanette threatened to tell her a time or two, if I didn't wanna, you know, with her. And I couldn't have that happen, so I did what she wanted. Whenever she wanted it. And she had a big appetite, that gal."

"Did anyone else know?"

"A couple of folks had suspicions. Word got around, like it does in a small town. But Lisa said she didn't believe it. She didn't know for sure until the night of the reunion. I guess during the party she overhead some people talking about it. And she got to thinkin' maybe it was true. Then she said in front of Jeanette that her and me had romantic plans for after the party. I felt guilty for not taking her to the reunion, but I had to work late getting some ribs on to smoke."

He paused a moment to catch a breath, then continued. "Anyway, Jeanette was mad that I was doing something nice for Lisa. And she'd had a big fight with her boyfriend, so she wanted me to lie to Lisa and tell her I had to go back to work again."

"That's a lot of overtime for a butcher shop," Tom observed.

"Yeah. Lisa mentioned that in a text she wrote me when I told her our 'date' was off."

"I know."

"You read our texts?" Savannah watched Frank turn, unbelievably, whiter still.

"Yes, sir. We found your wife's phone by the parking lot and read 'em all. There's some incriminating stuff there."

"I know. We tried to find the phone Sunday morning, but we couldn't."

"How did it happen, Frank? The actual killing, that is."

"Lisa, she'd just had enough. There in the parking lot, she outright asked Jeanette if she was steppin' out with her husband. Jeanette laughed at her, and the two of them got in a scuffle. Lisa told me that Jeanette pushed her down on the ground and then kicked her. So Lisa pulled her down with her. And the two of them had a free-for-all."

Savannah leaned over and whispered to Dirk, "That's one I would have paid big bucks to see."

Frank crossed his arms over his chest. "Lisa said Jeanette was getting the best of her, and she was scared. So she grabbed the first thing she could get her hands on to defend herself and swung it at Jeanette's head. Turns out it was Lisa's own high heel, which came off her foot when she fell. She said she hit Jeanette with it—one good lick—and the gal just laid right down and died."

Tommy sighed and sat back in his chair. "But she didn't die, Frank. Not then."

Frank started to cry, his shoulders heaving with his sobs. "I know that now. Mr. Jameson says she drowned. But I swear to you on my momma's grave and the Holy Bible itself, we both thought that gal was dead when we put her in the car and pushed it off that cliff. She never moved a muscle or said a word. We weren't trying to kill her. We just wanted to make it look like she had a car wreck. That was my idea. All my idea. Lisa sent me that text saying to get over to the school right away. I did, and she was all tore up over what happened. She wanted to call you, but I was afraid you wouldn't believe her. So I told her how we'd handle it."

"I wish you'd let her call me, Frank. As it is, I gotta arrest you both."

"I know. But I swear, I did the dirty stuff myself. I drove her car up to Lookout Point, with Lisa following along behind in ours. I put Jeanette in the car. I rolled it off the cliff. All my wife did was defend herself with her shoe. You can't blame a woman for that, Sheriff."

Tom sighed and looked over at Savannah. They exchanged a moment of sadness, both feeling for the man who sat, broken, before them. His life ruined by a set of terrible decisions, all made at a time of high stress.

Savannah looked up at the clock.

Sixteen minutes from the start of the interview to the end of the confession.

Tom had broken Dirk's record. But then she reminded herself, records were made to be broken. And she would still choose Dirk over Tom all day long and twice on Sunday.

Meanwhile, Frank had covered his face with his hands and was continuing to cry. "The worst thing is, I started it all by going for that silly piece of purple fluff, Jeanette. I've never been especially good lookin'. I've never had two nickels to rub together. Other than Lisa, no woman had ever given me a second look. Then that Jeanette starts wagglin' it under my nose, telling me how cute I am and how much I turn her on."

"I understand," Tom said, with another quick glance at Savannah. "You're not the first man that traded the heart of a good woman for a cheap piece o' tail. You're not the only guy to do something stupid that he regretted for the rest of his life."

"But I'd never been unfaithful to my wife before," Frank said. "Not in twenty years of marriage. But then I was, and look where it led. To hellfire and damnation."

Tom handed him a wad of tissues and said, "I'm sure it doesn't make you feel any better, buddy, but you've got a lot of company there in purgatory. We'll all have to scooch over to make room for ya."

Chapter 30

The first time Savannah had visited the old cemetery on a hill outside McGill, she had thought it was a pretty good place for its residents to sleep away eternity. The peach and pecan trees that surrounded the little graveyard, the view of the farmland below, and the soft breeze that always seemed to blow, causing the grass and the trees to dance, lent the place a gentle charm.

Other than the seasonal workers who picked the nuts and peaches, and the caretaker who mowed once a week in the spring and summer months, nobody came up Randall Hill except to be buried, to lay someone to rest, or to visit somebody interred there.

Today, as Savannah parked the rental car and got out, carrying a handful of peonies cut from Gran's garden that morning, she was doing the latter. She had come to pay her final respects to Jeanette Barnsworth.

Or maybe she just needed to make sure that her old tormentor was truly dead and gone.

She hoped it was the first, but she knew herself a bit too well, and she figured her motivation was closer to the second.

The dirt was piled atop the grave, along with a plethora of purple flower arrangements, left after that morning's private service. Apparently, it had been very private. Word around town was that only the local minister, his wife, and Herb Jameson had attended.

Savannah wondered who in their little town thought so highly of Jeanette that they had forked over big bucks for those oversized bouquets and sprays decorating the grave. Then she started reading the notes on each one and found that nearly all of them were from organizations Jeanette had chaired or founded or both.

The largest was from the Park Beautification Committee. Jeanette had created the group to plant flowers in a tiny, seldom used park directly across the street from her house, clearly viewed from her living room window.

With city money, of course.

Meanwhile, the children's swings, slide, and teeter-totter in the main park were in ruin due to lack of town funds to fix them.

Most of the other organizations Jeanette had formed in her lifetime were equally self-serving. But then, Savannah decided, what else could you expect?

Standing at the grave, looking down on the flowers and the mound of dirt beneath them, Savannah tried to grasp the fact that her tormentor was gone forever.

But she couldn't.

Death was such a mystery. The complete disappearance of something as complex and miraculous as a living, breathing human being had always been beyond her comprehension.

She had never been able to accept the idea that people, like machines, could simply turn off. Leave their physical vessel and go elsewhere? Yes. She had held dying people in her arms and had felt their spirits leave their ruined bodies, which could no longer sustain life. But just quit? No.

Savannah wasn't sure where Jeanette was or if she could hear her, but she felt obliged to say something. Anything. If for no other reason than that she sensed that a uniquely important chapter of her own life was closing. And she felt her words would somehow mark and honor that transition.

"I'm sorry I hit you," she began, speaking to the ornate gravestone, where cherubs held a banner bearing Jeanette's name in their chubby baby hands. "You may or may not have asked for it. But I shouldn't have done it. If it makes you feel any better, I paid for it. Big-time."

Savannah paused, feeling the breeze stir her hair. It sent a slight chill down her neck and into her spine.

"I'm sorry for something else, too. I regret that I didn't do it sooner. Not smack you, but stand up to you. If I'd set you straight on the first day of kindergarten, who knows how different our lives would have been? Well, mine anyway.

"Also, I want you to know that I forgive you," she said. "And by that, I don't mean that what you did was okay or that you couldn't help how cruel you were. I mean, I'm cutting you loose, Jeanette, from my mind and my heart. As far as I'm concerned, you don't owe me anything. Not anymore. I used to want your acceptance, your understanding. I used to hope that you'd realize how much you were hurting me and apologize. I thought I'd feel a lot better if you did."

She paused a moment and steeled herself for the hardest part of her declaration. She wanted her words to sink all the way down into the soil at her feet and reach the soul of the woman buried there.

"But I stopped hoping for your compassion, Jeanette. I stopped needing that apology. I finally came to understand that you *did* realize how much you were hurting me. You intended to hurt me. You wanted to cause me pain. But that was about you. Who you were. What was inside you. It was never about me."

Savannah was silent for a while as she tried to think of something good to say about Jeanette before leaving. Surely, everyone deserved to have some kind words spoken over their grave.

Finally, she came up with something. "As I recall, you were pretty good at geography. And you won that spelling bee that time."

There. That was enough.

Savannah knelt to place the peonies on the grave. Then she thought better of it, stood, and dusted the dirt from her knees. "You wouldn't like them, anyway," she said as she walked away. "They're pink."

She passed grave after grave until she came to her grandfather's. "Hello again, Pa. It's me, Savannah," she whispered as she laid the flowers lovingly at the base of his headstone. "Since I was here last, I got married. My husband's a good man. A *really* good man. But you're still the best one I ever knew."

She readjusted the flowers a few times until she had them just right. "We all still miss you," she continued. "And we're looking forward to being with you again in heaven one of these days. Oh, and Gran sends her love."

She kissed the tips of her fingers, then pressed them to the top of his stone. Then she stood up straight and turned to walk back to her car.

That was when she saw him.

Tom Stafford was leaning against the passenger door of her rental, watching her, his burly arms crossed over his chest, a half grin on his handsome face.

The sight of him annoyed her and set her pulse to racing at the same time. What a lot of nerve he had, intruding on her privacy with his good looks and his easy smile. If she'd wanted company on this trip, she'd have brought her husband.

Warily, she approached the car, trying to round the back of it and avoid him as much as possible.

"Saying your good-byes?" he said when she reached the driver's door.

"Well, yeah. You think? Reckon you're a better detective than I gave you credit for."

"That should be my line." He gave her a look of sincere respect and affection that went straight to her heart and gave her a warm feeling all over.

She didn't like it.

Tom Stafford had given her a lot of warm feelings like that in the past. And with those and a quarter, she still couldn't buy a candy bar.

What was it worth?

It had taken her a lot of living to realize that flattery from a great-looking hunk was an overrated commodity.

"I gotta go, Tom," she said. "We're having Gran's birthday party today, and tomorrow we're heading back to California. I'd say it's been nice seeing you, but . . ."

"I understand."

"Don't get all sweet and easy to get along with now, boy," she said, digging the car keys out of her purse. "Just don't bother. It won't work anymore."

He looked genuinely distressed at her words. "Are you sore

at me for arresting you? For locking you up? For putting you across from Yukon?"

"No. You were just doing your duty. I'd have done the same."

"Then what's the matter? Is it still what I did . . . back then? You gonna hold that against me forever?"

She thought for a while, trying to come up with the most honest answer she could give him.

"No, Tom. I don't hold anything against you. I forgive you. Back then, you did, well, what you did, and our lives took a different turn. We took separate paths. I can't wish it hadn't happened, because that's the path that led me to where I am today."

"Do you like where you are today?"

"I sure do."

"Are you happily married, Savannah?" He blurted the question out, as though the words had been ready to erupt from inside him for some time.

"Yes. Very."

He gulped and looked down. "Are you happier with him than you would've been with me, you think?"

Savannah considered being kind but quickly decided to be honest. The truth seemed to be the best choice today, all the way around.

"Definitely."

"Why? What's he got that I . . ."

"He's loyal."

"Loyalty?" He looked disappointed and a bit confused. "That's it? That's all?"

"That's everything."

Tom wiped his hand across his face and took a deep breath. "When I came up here today, I was going to tell you that I'm really, really sorry for hurtin' you, for being the reason we broke up. I wanted you to know that I miss you somethin' fierce ever' single day. And I hate it that I lost you. I wanted to tell you that I've never loved any gal like I loved you and never will. I wanted to make sure you know that if you ever decide that guy ain't all he's cracked up to be, and you wanna move back home, I'll be waitin' here for you with open arms."

He stopped to catch his breath. "But from what you just said, I reckon you don't wanna hear any of that."

"No, Tommy," she said softly. "I don't. I'm glad you didn't mention it."

He sighed. "Me too."

"I wouldn't want you to embarrass yourself."

"Yeah. Thanks."

"I'd better run along back to Gran's. They're waiting on me to get back before they start the party."

"Tell her I said, 'Happy birthday.'"

Savannah paused. "I think I'll just let you tell her yourself the next time you run into her. I'm gonna keep this little conversation we had, and the fact that we ran into each other up here, all to myself."

He nodded and walked around the car to where she stood. "That'd probably be best."

After opening her door for her, he looked down into her eyes and held her gaze for a long time. Then he said with a husky voice, "You be well, darlin'. Be happy."

To her own surprise, she stood on tiptoe and gave him a quick peck on the cheek. "You too, Tommy," she told him.

Then she got into the car and drove away, leaving two of the heaviest burdens of her life behind.

"Happy birthday to you! Happy birthday to you! Happy birthday, dear Granny! Happy birthday toooo yooouuu!"

Savannah and her family were in full chorus as they belted out the celebratory little tune in honor of their grandmother, who had patiently waited for this joyful, unencumbered day to arrive.

No more thoughts of murder, arrests, or false accusations interfered with this jubilant affair, and Gran and her clan rejoiced in proper Reid style.

Rather than remain in the stuffy, little kitchen after their feast, they had decided to go out into Granny's flower garden to enjoy the birthday cake.

Sitting at the makeshift picnic table, her loved ones surrounding her, Gran blew out all eight of the candles on her birthday cake with no problem or hesitation whatsoever.

They had decided that adorning the cake with the accurate number of candles would, at the very least, cause the cream cheese frosting to melt, if not start a bonfire that might set the entire county ablaze.

"Bring out the ice cream, boys!" Butch called to Marietta's sons, who had just finished cranking the old-fashioned churn on the back porch.

Their faces were red from the exertion but glowing with smiles as they carted the heavy wooden machine over to the picnic table, slopping salty ice water all over their bare feet and legs in the process. Savannah rescued the churn from their clumsy hands, removed the inner cylinder, and transferred it to the table, where she began to scoop the precious contents into serving bowls.

She smiled at the large chunks of pineapple and strawberries among the creamy goodness. Granny hadn't been able to decide between her two favorite flavors, so they had combined both.

Nothing was too good for Gran.

Neither the ice cream nor the cake was long for the world. Both disappeared in record time.

As soon as the plates were cleared away, a stack of gifts was placed in front of Granny, and in moments, she was knee-deep in such treasures as handprints enshrined in clay, compliments of Vidalia's youngest twins; a wall hanging with beans and macaroni glued on in the shape of a sunflower from the older set; and a collection of chandelier earrings; a rose-spangled nightgown; a bottle of cologne; and a pretty dress of sea foam–green lace from Savannah and Dirk.

While Gran was examining her new goodies, Savannah pulled a white garbage bag out from under her chair and discreetly handed it to Marietta. "Here," she said. "I would say this is to thank you for putting your shop on the line to bail me out of jail. But truth is, I owed it to you, anyway."

Marietta opened the bag and pulled out the pink paper bag with the NAUGHTY LADY'S NOOK logo on it.

"Hey, don't let Gran and the kids see that!" Savannah grabbed the garbage bag and half covered the paper bag.

Tittering like a teenager, Marietta reached inside and pulled out a shoe box. Her eyes lit up like the sky on the Fourth of July. "You got me shoes?" she said. "From a sex shop! Ooh! Cool!"

"Shh. Just open it and tell me if you like them."

She tore into the box and yanked out a pair of hooker heels. Tammy had chosen well. They were the perfect Marietta shoes—leopard-print uppers with snakeskin on the two-inch platform soles and the six-inch heels, accented with silver studs and chains.

Marietta let out an orgasmic squeal and an accompanying groan, the kind that Savannah had heard only in porn films. "Ohhh!" she shrieked, making such a scene that everyone, including Gran, turned to see what was going on.

Tammy laughed and said, "I see she likes her shoes."

"A job well done, sugar," Savannah told her.

Granny sniffed. "I'd say they're perfect for our Miss Mari, considering her leaning toward all things floozy. But if I see those monstrosities at any social functions in this town, I'm disowning you for sure."

Dirk leaned over and said to Savannah, "She'll never be able to walk on those things."

Savannah whispered back, "She won't have to. With shoes like that, she'll be on her back, heels pointed toward the ceiling."

Gran stood and announced in a loud, authoritative voice, "Y'all gather round. I've got something to say, and I want everybody to listen up."

All chattering stopped, and those who had walked away from the table returned to their matriarch's side.

"As y'all know," Gran continued, "on my birthday, I make some sort of a daring change. This started on my eightieth, when I got my ears pierced. On my eighty-first, I bought myself a bright red swimsuit. Last year I took up wearing those big, shoulder-duster earrings."

She pointed to the flashy sparklers that dangled from her earlobes to her collar, and everyone cheered.

"But this year," she said, "I'm gonna top 'em all. And I'm happy that you're with me here today for my big announcement."

Savannah watched her grandmother, her bright blue eyes shimmering with the pure joy of living.

When I get to be that age, let me be like her . . . so positive, happy, and excited about life, she silently prayed. Then she laughed at herself. *What the heck. Let me be like her at* my *age.*

"About twenty years ago," Gran was saying, "my oldest granddaughter left this place and traveled all the way to the other side of this great country of ours, in search of a better life for herself. She was, and still is, the bravest, strongest woman I've ever been blessed to know."

Instantly, Savannah felt tears welling up in her eyes, a constriction in her throat, and a lightness in her soul as it took wing.

Dirk reached over, grasped her hand, and squeezed it.

"And by doing so, she set a fine example for us all. So . . ." Gran paused and looked at her loved ones, each in turn. "After giving it much thought and prayer, I'm going to do the same thing. Tomorrow morning I'm turning my house here over to Alma, and I'm packing my bags and moving to California. In a world where there's beaches, life's too short not to live on one of 'em."

The West Coast crowd erupted in a joyous roar. The Georgia group sat in stunned silence.

"I'll miss every one of you that I leave behind," Gran said. "But with me out there in sunny California, you'll have another reason to pay a visit. Come out and we'll go see the Mouse together."

She turned to Tammy, who was hugging Savannah. Both women were crying. "And you, young lady," Gran said, "are gonna need a good, reliable babysitter. 'Cause after that little ankle biter of yours arrives, you're gonna want to get back to your sleuthin', and it ain't always convenient to have a youngun with you when you're breakin' into houses and such."

She turned to Savannah and Dirk. "I won't ask you to share your roof with me. Wouldn't want it myself, bein' independent like I am. But as soon as Waycross and Tammy tie the knot and he moves into her house, I'd be happy to buy your house trailer off you, Dirk."

Dirk started shaking his head. "Oh, Gran, it's not fit for a lady. It's all rusty and—"

"Don't say another word, grandson. By the time I get done with it, you won't recognize it. It'll have a red- and yellow-striped awning, for one thing, and flower boxes hangin' off every winder. Though if you don't mind, I'd like to move it to a fancy senior citizens' park on the beach."

Savannah sat speechless with joy as she listened to her husband and her grandmother discuss the ways and means of fulfilling Granny's dreams. And she wondered at the strangeness of this journey back to her roots.

Before, when she left Georgia, she had carried a number of heart-heavy burdens with her and had left behind her grandmother, the one thing in the world she loved best.

Now, all these years later, she was once again walking out of her past, her feet rooted in the present, her face to the future.

This time she would leave those sorrows and hindrances behind and take Gran with her into the sunlight.

And what could be better than that?